just happy to be here

just happy to be here

NAOMI KANAKIA

HARPER TEEN
An imprint of HarperCollinsPublishers

HarperTeen is an imprint of HarperCollins Publishers.

Library of Congress Control Number: 2023936880
ISBN 978-0-06-321657-0

Typography by Catherine Lee
23 24 25 26 27 LBC 5 4 3 2 1

First Edition

For every teacher and librarian
who bought this book anyway

1

OBVIOUSLY WHEN I INVITED TWO friends over, I was hoping we'd have some classic teen-girl-trio drama, but I didn't expect the crying to start so quickly.

Hannah was locked in the bathroom. Whitney was outside talking to her. I was standing in the doorway, feeling terrible.

"I'm sorry," I said. "I didn't say the right thing."

Whitney ignored me. She was tall (though nowhere near so tall as me) and put-together in that perfect Ainsley Academy way, in a pale cardigan and pink scarf and jeans. "Hey," she said. "Are you all right?"

"Sorry, sorry." The door opened, and there was a moment where Hannah stood in the doorway. She was shorter, with brunette hair, a tiny nose, and teeth that were brilliant and white like a row of Tic Tacs. She gave us a weak smile. "Sorry, I am so sorry. I am so embarrassed."

"But I'm the sorry one," I said. "I did the bad thing. You were just being polite. You expected me to disagree with you."

"No," Hannah said. "What I said was so racist and, just, awful."

"Oh." I squinted. "It was?"

"I'm sorry," she said again. "I just can't believe that came out of my mouth."

Within a few minutes, Whitney had gathered us together, and even though we were in *my* house, she took control, brought us to my room, pulled some pillows onto the ground, sat Hannah down, adjusted the lighting so it was a bit dim. Hannah had her phone out—that was the weird thing about Ainsley girls (maybe all girls, I wasn't sure); if you were quiet for a second, their phones suddenly appeared.

Hannah looked up, her eyes glowing in the dim light. She put down her phone. "Hey," she said. "I'm really, really sorry. We should start over."

"But you were . . ." *Right.*

I stopped myself from saying that last word. I could see how she had been racist or transphobic or whatever, but I'd agreed with Hannah when she said, "Whitney is a legacy, and you're trans, so there's no chance they'll pick a boring white girl like me."

We were three friends who all wanted to be Sibyls, but they could only pick two. Whitney's big sister was a Sibyl, so she'd get in, and I was literally the only trans girl who'd ever gone to

Ainsley in history, and I was a dark-skinned person—if they believed in diversity at all they would want to take me. So I'd said, "Yeah, that makes sense that you won't get it, and I'm sorry; that's not fair."

"No, the thing is, *I'm* the one who won't get it," Whitney said, sitting cross-legged. Her voice was deep and hoarse, like a movie star's, and she sometimes ended words in a little growl. The videos I'd watched called that *vocal fry*. I'd tried it myself, but I just sounded like a boy with a cold—maybe it only worked if you were skinny and pretty and didn't read as a guy.

"But, Whitney, you won the Greek *and* Latin prizes last year," Hannah said.

"That's cool," I said. I hadn't known that! Whitney never, ever spoke up in class, unless she was called on. "Did you have to do a translation to win that or something? I've never won any kind of prize. Sometimes I think that I ought to play sports and lose horribly, just to show trans girls don't have an advantage in everything."

"No, but Antigone is already a legacy, and with my sister in the Sibyls, they're not gonna want a second legacy. So don't worry, it'll be the two of you."

"I mean, sure," I said. "But technically isn't it all about the classical civilization stuff? If you do the best job and clearly care the most about ancient stuff, then they can't really turn you down."

Until last year, everyone thought the Sibyls were just this

quirky club where you wore badges and blazers and took on the names of the women of ancient Rome and Greece. But then one of the newer girls let slip that being selected came with a serious amount of money, and people got pissed, so this year they were making the application more transparent. It would be decided by an intense interview, right before the Christmas break, with the current Sibyls and with the funder of the scholarship, Evangeline "Angel" Beaumont. The rumor was that you were supposed to talk about a Greek or Roman woman who best represented ideals that modern girls could learn from.

"I don't think they care about that," Whitney said. "Ancient Rome and Greece—that's not important anymore. They're looking for someone who can do the best for the world."

"But if they didn't care about that, couldn't they have done a general scholarship? I dunno—I like the Latin stuff. I'm not great at it like you, but I think that's cool. I've been thinking about my person for months. Do you guys know what classical woman you'll pick?"

They looked at each other again, not saying anything. "N-no, not really," Hannah said. "We don't even know for sure that's the interview question."

"Sure," I said. "But if it is, we should be prepared, right? Want to think about it together? I've been googling and googling ancient Roman and Greek women, but there's not many who I identify with. I was thinking Tiresias, since he spent seven years as a woman, but maybe that's cheating since he's mostly a man."

"No," Whitney said. "That could be too on the nose."

"Or there was one of the Furies, Alecto? I might go with her."

"Hmm," Whitney said. "Okay, but . . ." She and Hannah looked at each other. "Just be careful. Strife was the one who outed the scholarship last year, so this year they might not want anyone who seems angry."

"Oh, I hadn't thought of that," I said. "Anyway, I think it'll be you two. My Latin grades are so bad. It'd be an insult to the scholarship if I got it."

We were having the classic Ainsley conversation, where girls talked about how terrible they were and how they didn't deserve to have nice things. I was starting to realize it was a way of passing the time, like maybe girls at some other school would've discussed guys they liked or dieting (those are stereotypes, I know, but how am I supposed to know what girls at other schools talk about?).

The strange thing was, at my last school—an all-boys school, St. George's—usually the guys *were* angry; they were like, *Ugh, yeah, we're so oppressed, people discriminate against us because we're white!* But at Ainsley, the whole tone of the conversation was different.

"No, but you've shown the most courage out of anyone," Whitney said. "We're all just regular white people. You've gone through so much."

"I *would* like to meet Angel," I said. "And wear the laurel crown. And make speeches. And go to salons up in the mansion. That all sounds kind of amazing. You know her, right, Whitney?"

"No," Whitney said. "Where did you hear that?"

"I just meant—through your sister—"

"Angel is so busy," Whitney said. "We're lucky she makes time even for the Sibyls. My sister says she's started taking on death penalty cases too. Like last week, they literally stopped someone from being executed."

"Cool," I said. "Did they lobby the Governor?"

Whitney gave me a blank look. I crept a little farther away on the blanket, feeling hot and sticky even though the air-conditioning was flowing over me.

"I just meant . . ." I clutched at the crocheted blanket, my fingers slipping through the holes. "What did she do? How did she do it? Was there a trial? I really am into speeches, and Clarence Darrow has a famous one about Leopold and Loeb—they were the worst; they killed someone for fun."

The words of his defense speech went through my mind: *You may hang these boys; you may hang them by the neck until they are dead. But in doing it you will turn your face toward the past.*

I was thinking whether it'd be weird to quote the speech, but Whitney said, "A lot of her clients are innocent."

"Sure, but even if they weren't. If you're really against the death penalty, then you'd defend guilty people too! That's what Clarence Darrow did anyway."

Another blank look. Whitney reached out to Hannah. "You feeling okay?"

"Sorry," Hannah said. "I still feel so bad about what I said."

"It's Ainsley," Whitney said. "It puts *so* much stress on us. . . ."

That's *definitely* what Ainsley girls liked to say. And it seemed true. They all spent hours studying and worrying every night. But I didn't exactly see the point: they were mostly rich, like Whitney, so why be stressed out? They'd go to college and do fine. Meanwhile, I was *not* rich, and my mom kept saying I'd need to really pull up my grades to get into an out-of-state school with good financial aid. Otherwise, all we could afford was one of the state schools in Virginia, where we lived. I really didn't want that, given our Governor had gotten elected on the "trans kids are sick" platform, but I still had fun and enjoyed myself and didn't go crying because I might not win an award.

"Angel's great," Whitney said. "My sister says she's so normal—"

"Does she do her own shopping?" I said.

I guess I was making fun of Whitney, but also—what does normal even mean when you're talking about someone really rich and beautiful and famous? It was impossible to imagine Angel cooking or cleaning or shopping.

Both of them had blank looks. Somehow they'd scooched closer together in the pile of pillows and blankets, and I crept toward them, feeling sweaty and underdressed. I was wearing a denim skirt and tank top, and I realized the style was all wrong—not preppy at all—and my armpits and face and back were covered in sweat too. The two of them shifted slightly as I got closer, and some weird tension hummed between us all.

"I don't know . . ." Whitney said.

"So how's she normal?" I said.

"Just . . . really generous. Asks about your life? My sister goes to *all* her visiting hours, and you never know who'll be there. One time it was—" Whitney then mentioned the name of basically the most famous Democratic senator. "And my sister just chatted with the two of them."

"About what?"

"I don't remember."

"What I like about Angel," I said, "is have you read her closing arguments? They're pretty incredible. I have a book of them. Wait a second . . ." I got up, brushed off my skirt, made sure it hadn't crept down to show my underwear, then went to my bookshelves. I could hear my parents talking in Hindi downstairs, but it was too indistinct for me to make out the words.

I came back with the book, which was dog-eared to some of my favorites. "She's basically the only lawyer who still delivers these kinds of closings. Look here: 'You can choose to disbelieve my client. That she didn't fear for her life every single day she was on this job. That she has weathered thirteen years of litigation simply in the hopes of a payout.' That's her best thing, she really reduces each case to a simple question, and then she goes logically through the implications of choosing each side. Each case becomes a big moral question about who to trust and who to believe."

"Oh! That's really cool!" Whitney said. She glanced through the book. Hannah leaned in a little bit.

"This is great," Hannah said.

"It's okay," I said. "You've looked enough to be polite."

"No, no," Whitney said. "Can I borrow this?"

"Sure, I guess," I said. "Sure."

"That's so cool," Hannah said.

We were quiet for a second, and I couldn't help thinking, *Is it my imagination, or is this really awkward? Literally everything I say falls flat.* I chewed on my lip.

Whitney laughed, and she leaned over, showing Hannah something a friend had posted online. I leaned in too, not really listening to the explanation.

"Umm," I said. "Yeah. Angel is great. She's also really pretty."

"Oh yeah, totally," Hannah said.

I asked if people wanted to go to bed, but Hannah looked at her phone, and she said her mom was still nearby and maybe it'd be easier to head back tonight (Hannah lived two hours away, in Howard County).

And Whitney said, "Hey, can I get a ride too? Oh hey, and thanks for loaning me the book, Tara."

I got some very long hugs, and they made me promise to tell them if I needed anything, ever. I thought of saying: *Wait, what happened here? What did I do?* But instead I walked them to the door and left them on our porch.

My parents appeared in the kitchen, and my mom put water to boil for tea. While we waited, she said, "I looked up Whitney's father online—they donated to *Him*." She was talking about the anti-trans Governor we hated.

"Well, yeah," I said. "Her dad is some property developer guy."

"Are you sad that your friends left early?"

"I guess not?" I said. "It was getting really awkward. We had nothing to talk about. And Hannah got upset early on." I explained the fight to my mom.

She snorted. "What an absurd idea," she said. "That you would have any advantage. After years of wrangling with these people, I can say it isn't so. This is why you need better grades! And some outside interests! If you're seen as just 'the trans girl,' then you will always lose!"

"Sure," I said. "Oh, they did seem interested in my book of Angel's speeches! Whitney took it with her."

My parents would've been surprised about how *much* people at Ainsley cared about race and gender stuff. To Mom and Dad those things didn't matter at all. They were very practical people.

"Ahh, my beautiful girl," she said. "Perhaps these two weren't exactly right. You'll find your true friends yet."

"I wonder if . . . you know, maybe . . . because I look basically like a boy, if they didn't want to sleep in my room."

"Hmm," my mom said. "That seems possible. You know . . . it's very possible. What have you told them about the hormones?"

I wasn't on hormones yet. My parents were afraid of the Governor, who'd said he was going to make child welfare agencies investigate any parents who allowed their kids to take them. I should be old enough soon for estrogen, in any normal state, but instead I wasn't even on puberty blockers. My skin, hips, shoulders, and face had zero idea that they belonged to a girl; they were like, *Welp, let's turn this kid into a* man.

"Nothing. But they had to know we'd all be sleeping in the same room."

"Perhaps they thought we had a guest room."

"But then what would be the point of coming over? If we were in different rooms?"

"I don't know," she said. "We cannot control other people. But if that was the problem, simply give them time."

She kissed me on the head, and I went back to my room to be depressed. It was never a good idea to tell my mom gender stuff. Her answers were usually a polite version of *Yes, you are a freak of nature, so it wouldn't be a surprise if someone feared you.* Whereas a good answer from her in that situation would've been *No, they didn't think that.* Or *If they thought that, they were transphobic idiots.* I reached up and tried to feel my brow bone. Face stuff was the major thing hormones couldn't correct. If my brow was really heavy, I'd never pass. I had posted online a few times and gotten different responses, some said mine was probably fine, others said I'd probably need surgery (which our insurance didn't cover and I couldn't afford). But everyone said to get on hormone replacement therapy right away! A few people had even offered to mail me estrogen and spiro illegally.

Sometimes, when I was all alone, I let myself get mad at my parents. Like, obviously it wasn't fair. The first time I came out to them was after we all watched a newscast during dinner about the plague of gender diversity sweeping the nation. I'd been like, *Oh, hey, what would you say if I told you that I too was this trans thing.* And *right* at that moment, they should've been like *We've gotta get you out of that all-boys school and definitely fix you up with a therapist and get you on puberty blockers so your body doesn't change irreversibly.* And after the Governor was elected, they should've said, *Screw the Governor; we'll move to California, or at the very least to Washington, DC, which is literally right next door and very trans-friendly.* For that matter, there shouldn't have been a transphobic governor. And we shouldn't need to worry about finding a clinic that would take me on my dad's health care. But why stop there? My dad should've been born in America, so he didn't need to work at the same job for twenty years while his green card came through (it can take

Indians literally forty to fifty years to float to the top of the pile, since so many of us want to stay here, and there are limits to the number of Indians who can get green cards each year). Or, even better, I should've just been cisgender. But no, that's offensive. I'm not supposed to want to be cis. Not supposed to think "cis" is normal. My friend Liam would totally call me out for that. Instead, I'm supposed to wish for a world where being trans wasn't stigmatized. But even in that world, I'd have needed to feel weird and not right for twelve or thirteen years before the thought even occurred to me. *Hey, maybe I'm a girl.* So, no—I would kill a bat and drink its blood in a satanic ritual if it could make me a cisgender girl.

I sat in my desk chair and pulled out the book I'd gotten for my birthday: *A Compendium of Great Speeches*. Because I'm a nerd, I had little metal book darts to mark my favorites. And my finger found this one right away: Sojourner Truth. What a great name. I should've gone with something like Sojourner.

Anyway, she stood up at this 1840s conference of white feminists, who were all like, *Blah blah, we can't work, and we can't own property, and it's just so hard.* And Sojourner said:

> *I want to say a few words about this matter. I am a woman's rights. I have as much muscle as any man, and can do as much work as any man. I have plowed and reaped and husked and chopped and mowed, and can any man do more than that? I have heard much about the*

sexes being equal. I can carry as much as any man, and can eat as much too, if I can get it. I am as strong as any man.

I said the words under my breath, while tears gathered in the corners of my eyes. But the part I liked better was the next paragraph.

Whenever I thought, *Oh, you know, there's something wrong with me; I look like a monster; I'm not a real girl*, I'd think of this paragraph:

> *As for intellect, all I can say is, if woman have a pint and man a quart—why can't she have her little pint full? You need not be afraid to give us our rights for fear we will take too much—for we can't take more than our pint'll hold. The poor men seems to be all in confusion, and don't know what to do. Why children, if you have woman's rights, give it to her and you will feel better. You will have your own rights, and they won't be so much trouble. I can't read, but I can hear. I have heard the Bible and have learned that Eve caused man to sin. Well, if woman upset the world, do give her a chance to set it right side up again.*

Okay, maybe I didn't look like a girl (yet), and maybe I wasn't on hormones, and maybe I didn't know the first thing about how to be or act like a girl, and maybe my sad, pathetic attempt at having a sleepover had failed, and maybe I had no idea what it even meant to say "I am a girl," but so what? My pint of girlhood still deserved to be respected.

Whitney and Hannah should burn in hell.

The thought came suddenly, and I couldn't stop the tears falling. Which was *absurd* and stupid. They were allowed to be friends with whomever they wanted.

But how dare they talk about racism or transphobia or how much I'd suffered or what I deserved, and then leave my house early like that.

I hadn't wanted them to say the right things. I didn't care if Hannah *had* said something transphobic. What I'd wanted was to have fun with a pair of friends! And if they were too stupid or too heartless to understand that, then they were the people with the problem, not me.

2

MRS. GIMBEL HAD US IN a circle—we sat in big circles at Ainsley, because it was nonhierarchical—and she raised a finger. Jeannette pointed at her.

"Thank you, Jeannette, for relinquishing the floor."

"That's no problem, Sara," Jeannette said, using Mrs. Gimbel's first name, which was something I still couldn't get used to. At my last school, St. George's, we called all teachers by their last names, and I still used last names even in my head.

Unlike at St. George's, most students at Ainsley didn't take any ancient languages, which meant Latin III was an elective, with a mix of seniors, juniors, and even sophomores like me who'd tested in.

You know how even though most classes don't have assigned seating, people sit in the same place day after day anyway? Well, my unassigned place was right next to Mrs. Gimbel, who even though she was a great teacher was still a teacher, and all through class I could hear her breathing and shifting next to me, and I had to crane my neck to look at her.

But right across from me—and I mean directly across, so I could look at her naturally, without seeming weird—was a junior, Felicity Beaumont, who was one of the two Sibyls for her year. Her Sibyl name was Antigone, which was what Whitney had called her the other night.

She hardly ever wore the badges of her office, but that day she had a laurel wreath pinned into her brown hair, and she was wearing a tan blazer (Sibyls could wear blazers with their uniform) and a brown-and-white scarf. She was dressed up because it was the one and only day when the Sibyls opened their secret sanctum and allowed girls to sign up to join.

Last year when I took a tour of Ainsley, the tour had ended at the mansion, up on the hill, where Angel lived and ran her legal practice. Angel was a descendant of the Coatesworths, who'd donated the land to create the school, and most of the house was a museum to her legacy.

On the tour, we'd actually *seen* her and Felicity sitting upstairs, in a broad, sunny room with flapping curtains. Angel was in a white minidress, and Felicity was in a woolen dress with a Peter Pan collar, and they were sitting and eating cakes and chatting about something.

"Oh, hello," Angel had said to the tour group. "Don't worry about bothering me. It's one of the hazards of living in a historic building. Just take your time."

But Felicity had gotten up and cocked her head. "You're the trans girl," she said to me.

My face had gone a deep, deep red, and she'd laughed.

"Hey," she said. "Why would you ever leave St. George's? It's a much better school."

She'd haunted me through the tour, asking questions about St. George's, until I'd had to leave. We hadn't talked much since then, but on my first day at Ainsley, she'd said, "Welcome to hell, nice to have you here."

She had high cheekbones and hollow spaces under her eyes, and small, sharp pupils that darted around whatever room she was in. She sat with her back straight up and one hand on a notepad, and she wrote with a fancy Japanese pen that made little tiny scratching marks on the paper.

I was terrified that someday she'd meet my eyes and be like, *Why are you staring at me? Please stop staring at me.*

"Now, as you know, the Sibyls are open for membership today," Mrs. Gimbel said. "And because of certain complaints last year, we've democratized the process somewhat. I've already privately discussed this opportunity with those who I think are the best candidates, but I've been asked to say that all of you, by virtue of your Latin attainments, are eligible to sign up to be interviewed for inclusion in the group. I'd ask you, however, to remember the group's illustrious history and its mission, which is to highlight the importance of classical principles even for the modern-day woman. It is *not* simply a checkmark for your CV."

Felicity snorted. Everyone hated Felicity, because she was Angel's niece, and people said her being a Sibyl meant someone else couldn't get the scholarship. People also said that the kids and relatives of Sibyls got extra coaching on how to pass the interview, even though the process was supposed to be secret.

I raised my hand. "Do you know what questions will be in the interview? I think that I heard . . . you know . . . that it would be less secret."

"Hmm," she said. "Can I ask how many of you are interested in joining?"

My hand went up, and Hannah and Whitney put theirs up too. We weren't the only class with eligible people. Teachers were probably asking in the ancient Greek and biblical Hebrew classes too.

Hannah's eyes met mine for a second, and I looked away. My ears instantly went red. Neither Whitney nor Hannah had said a word to me since our sleepover.

"I was told . . ." Mrs. Gimbel spoke slowly, "that I should offer you the ability to run a practice exercise. As you know, the Sibyls model ourselves"—oh, yeah, Mrs. Gimbel had been a Sibyl when she was at Ainsley—"on the women of classical times, whether real or mythological. The core of the interview will be your explication of a classical woman and your analysis of how her example allows you to make a greater impact on the world."

Felicity snorted again.

"I don't know why you're laughing," Mrs. Gimbel said. "Your talk last year on Antigone was quite moving."

"Sure," Felicity said. "But she's one of the only women who ancient Romans and Greeks actually liked. Most of their women were troublemakers. Like, they'd hate for us to use Cleopatra as an example."

"That isn't true. Many praiseworthy women existed," Mrs. Gimbel responded.

"Who?" Felicity said.

"Athena. The Muses. Ariadne—"

"Helen. Medea. Cleopatra. Julia Domna. Juno. Clytemnestra. Livia. Agrippina. Messalina. Aphrodite . . ."

"Electra," I said.

"Tara!" Mrs. Gimbel said. "You do *not* have the floor. That's two demerits."

Felicity smiled. "People liked her. But they wouldn't want her daughters to *be* like her."

"Alecto," I said.

The smile got wider. "You know," Felicity said. "That's not a bad one. It's kind of perfect, actually. She represented justice, but she was justice for women—she ignored the other gods and pursued Orestes even though Apollo protected him."

"Right?" I said. "And she wasn't beautiful. Nobody's wife or daughter. And she represented sisterhood."

"I guess you could say that," Felicity said. "We've never had an Alecto. How did you think of that? It's kind of obscure. . . ."

"Umm," I said. *She was a boss in a video game I played over the summer* didn't seem like a great answer.

"Tara!" Mrs. Gimbel said. "Again you've spoken out of turn! That's two more demerits! Remember I'm an adviser to the Sibyls, and my opinion matters quite a bit. Now, if the class truly wishes, I've been told I ought to allow you some time to discuss your chosen ideal."

"Right now?" Hannah said. "But . . . I thought we'd have longer to pick. The interview isn't until December."

"You cannot study for this," Mrs. Gimbel said. "This is about character and worldview. I personally did not agree with this change of direction. Normally we asked the question in the interview, and you were given mere moments to prepare. This is a compromise."

My stomach thumped. I pulled on the edges of my skirt—I hadn't worn tights today.

Should I choose Alecto? Whitney and Hannah had said the Sibyls wouldn't want someone who represented anger, but Alecto seemed so right for me. . . .

The Furies had snakes for hair and bat wings. They were from an old pantheon, before the Titans and before Saturn and before Jupiter or any of the more modern gods. They represented an archaic justice, punishing the crimes of powerful men against weak people, especially women. They'd pursued Orestes, driving him mad, when he'd killed his mother, Clytemnestra.

Also, I just liked the sound of the word. I'd considered so many other ancient women but none of them had *sounded* right. I wanted to be someone powerful, but I didn't want to be someone beautiful or womanly—that would make me feel fake. I wanted to be someone terrifying but not evil. Alecto seemed perfect to me, and it had to be a good sign that Felicity knew who she was!

"Another part of the interview is that you'll often be paired with another candidate, so you can discuss the differences and similarities between your two chosen figures. This was an extremely *common* activity in Roman times, when it was held that only by discussing and analyzing the great figures of history could a person learn true virtue."

"Hey, Mrs. Gimbel, who did you choose when you were a Sibyl?" I said.

"Two more demerits, Tara!"

"I think you were . . ." Felicity frowned. "Weren't you Cassandra?"

I squinted. That didn't seem right somehow. Cassandra was the priestess who was cursed to foretell the future but never be believed. I'd always loved that myth—loved the idea of being right but ignored.

"I was," Mrs. Gimbel said. "A very powerful tale. Now, quickly, we've only half of class left, can any of you name a classical woman who'd be a good model?"

Whitney raised her hand. "Penelope," she said.

"Excellent choice! And it's been a long time since she's been represented."

That had come really quick. Two nights ago she said that she didn't have anyone! I squinted at Whitney. She looked down, marked something in her notebook with a pen.

Hannah asked to be skipped. She was still thinking. I chose Alecto. Since it was just us three going for the Sibyls in this class, my heart hammered, wondering if I'd get paired with Whitney. Alecto wasn't a great match for either Penelope *or* Antigone, though she was maybe a tiny bit closer to Antigone, since both represented justice and respect for elders.

My stomach churned.

Mrs. Gimbel said, "Since it's only you three, I'll pair one of you with Felicity so you can practice a bit. Penelope, perhaps you can go with Alecto? Hannah, what have you decided?"

Shoot. I closed my eyes, thought with all my heart. Prayed for Hannah to think of another famous wife, one who could go well with Penelope. Right at this moment I *needed* to be paired with Felicity.

"Clytemnestra!" I suggested.

Hannah blinked.

"Tara, that's two more demerits!" Mrs. Gimbel said. "How many is that now? With your grades, you cannot afford to be taking these risks!"

"Not sure," I said.

"Eight," Felicity said.

"You are supposed to be keeping track so you can report them to the office, Tara," Mrs. Gimbel said.

"Why? Don't you report them?"

"It's in our honor code!"

"Well I'm not technically an Ainsley student—nobody ever gave me a copy of the honor code."

"I don't know who Clytemnestra is," Hannah said.

"Agamemnon's wife," I said. "She avenged her daughter, executing her husband. Like, he sacrificed her daughter to get favorable winds. Kind of like Stannis did on *Game of Thrones*."

"Oh," she said.

"You'd be reclaiming her," I said.

"We haven't had a Clytemnestra in fifty years," Felicity said.

"This is ten demerits for you, Tara," Mrs. Gimbel said. "And I'd like to see you after class. And, Hannah, this has become absurd. You must pick someone."

"Okay, her," Hannah said. "Clytemnestra."

Mrs. Gimbel sighed. "Very well. Go practice with Penelope. As for you, Tara, I've been extremely disappointed with your behavior today. You've interrupted and undercut all of your classmates and introduced numerous irrelevancies into our discussion."

I was smiling stupidly, looking at Felicity, who rolled her eyes. I don't know whether it's okay to say this, but Felicity was beautiful. Like, not glamorous, I guess, but beautiful in that Ainsley way—really preppy and sporty, with her hair in a constant ponytail, and a sort of slouchiness—she never straightened up even when she was raising her hand, asking questions in class. I loved looking at her face, at her eyes, at how alive they were, how they took in everything and judged everyone.

"Okay," I said.

Hannah raised a finger. "What if I want to change my person?"

"You don't really have to make a final choice until the interview in December," Felicity said.

"And—and what if I don't want to pick a woman?" Hannah said. "I mean, no offense, I don't even know Clytemnestra."

"The assignment is to pick a woman," Mrs. Gimbel said.

"B-but what if I'm not a woman? What if I'm genderqueer? What if a woman doesn't really represent me?"

This was the kind of silly, random stuff girls said at Ainsley. It was like none of them noticed that I was literally genderqueer (albeit *very* binary) and never complained about any of Ainsley's gendered language. Like . . . I didn't want anything at Ainsley to change just because I happened to be a student there.

Mrs. Gimbel frowned. "I have to say, I am appalled that so many girls feel compelled to reject very straightforward assignments like these. For years, girls *fought* to see themselves in ancient history. They fought for the wisdom and knowledge their husbands and brothers were given. And now you simply want to throw it away, as if all that struggle had no meaning."

"But what if we're not girls?" Hannah said.

Mrs. Gimbel glanced at me, then back at her. "I won't even dignify that with a response."

"It's just not inclusive. Someone could be genderqueer and not even know it, and you're talking as if we're all girls in this room. Like, they could feel compelled to pick. And that has consequences, you know, like they might think, *Oh, I don't fit this certain ideal and—*"

"None of this bothers *me*," I said. "Happy to be one of the girls. I like it."

"Two more demerits, Tara!" Mrs. Gimbel said. "No interrupting! And as for you, Hannah, this is the most inclusive school I've ever taught at, and we are in the most inclusive time in American history, and if that's still not good enough, I have nothing more to say, but I will *not* shortchange you or anyone else who has to go through life as a girl and as a woman. I will *not* deny you the role models and the wisdom you will need in this male-dominated world. And *that* is something you can count upon."

I clapped for her, giving a little holler. She glared at me, and I wanted to be like, *No, I'm not joking. That was a great speech. Reminds me a little of Socrates, speaking to the court that was considering sentencing him to death, when he was like, "I cannot keep quiet . . . to talk every day about virtue and to examine myself and others is the greatest good to man, and the unexamined life is not worth living."*

"Now if we are done with these political digressions," Mrs. Gimbel said, "perhaps the prospective Sibyls can move to the nook and stop dominating our class time?"

Felicity winked at me. The two of us sometimes joked around in Latin class, and sometimes I was like, *Wait, are the two of us flirting? Is this a flirt?* But whenever we met outside class, Felicity barely talked to me. People said she was rude and selfish, and Liam (who was her cousin) said she was a secret transphobe, which I guess was possible, but I didn't believe it.

Sometimes I wondered if Liam understood transphobia wasn't something a person could turn off or on. It was something deep inside their eyes—deep in the way they looked at you—like there was Magic Marker scrawled all over your face. And I just didn't get that vibe from Felicity. She might be rude, but she treated me exactly the way she treated everyone else.

Felicity stood up from her desk, walked over, and tapped Mrs. Gimbel on the shoulder. "Sara," she said. "Can I sit with my partner?"

She dragged over a desk from the corner, and I dragged my desk into the corner, and then we were together.

After sitting, she raised her clasped arms behind her back and she let out a long yawn as she stretched.

"Alecto was good," Felicity said. "But you've got to know that Gimbel hates it."

"Does it matter?"

"She's on the interview committee this year."

"Can't I change her mind? I thought the point is make a convincing case that your person is good."

"Maybe," Felicity said. "But I don't know. If all you want is to win, then you should pick someone safe. Like Clytemnestra is actually really good. She's one of these people you can twist around and make all feminist and modern. Alecto is just . . . angry and vengeful and ugly."

"Okay, but . . ." I took a breath. "I don't know, I've been kicking people around for a while. I thought about Medea, Clytemnestra, Artemisia . . . and nothing really worked. Alecto is the only fit. She's the only person who's ugly, angry, and *right*. Do you really think I have no chance?"

"Uhhh," Felicity said. "If you make a good case, you could still win. I'd vote for you probably."

"And Angel won't care?" I said. "I know the Sibyls hate Strife, because she told everyone about the scholarship, but Alecto isn't about mindless conflict. She's about justice."

"No . . . no, no, totally," Felicity said. "Totally. I think . . . if that's who you really like, you can't go with anyone else."

"Right?"

"And you wouldn't *want* to get in and be called some strange name you didn't believe in."

"Yes!" I said. "Like . . . if people called me Cleopatra for three years, it'd feel fake."

"I get it," Felicity said. "As long as that's what you feel, you should go with Alecto. That's how I felt about Antigone. I think

28

a real Sibyl always feels that way about her person. And, you know, getting picked or not picked, that's not what makes you a real Sibyl, especially not now."

"Still," I said. "It seems good to get picked."

"Oh, it's incredible," Felicity said. "It was the best thing that ever happened to me."

She said that without a trace of a smile. I leaned forward, letting myself look into her eyes, thinking of the words from *The Iliad* about *gray-eyed Athena*. *The Iliad* was full of little phrases like that: *the wine-dark sea*; or *Hector, breaker of horses*; or *white-armed Helen*. Felicity's eyes weren't gray, they were brown, but they made me think of someone with cool, all-seeing vision.

"Why was it the best?"

"The people," Felicity said. "Hecuba and Strife are the two best people I've ever known. And last year, Andromache and Thetis were . . . interesting. I didn't get as much of a chance to know them, but I really liked them."

"So you don't like Calliope?"

The normal Ainsley thing would be to say, *Oh, what? No, I just don't know her very well*. But Felicity said, "She was a mistake. But she mostly hangs out with my aunt. I should mention: you can either hang out with my aunt and Calliope or with me and Hecuba and Strife. You can't have both."

I frowned. I did actually want to see Angel. I'd seen her car pull up sometimes to the circle on the hill above the campus, had surreptitiously scoped her out with my cell phone at maximum zoom. She always looked so elegant and ethereal. Sometimes as the evening fell, lots of cars would pull up, and people would come out in tuxedoes and evening gowns, and the whole house would be lit with paper lanterns, and everyone would stand on the balconies or veranda or in the garden and talk to each other. The Sibyls had a standing invite to her parties and her visiting hours.

"Why not?"

"My aunt hates Strife and never invites her to the house, so me and Hecuba are boycotting it too."

"Okay," I said. "I . . . I could do that."

"You'd probably love my aunt. Everyone does. Even Hecuba. I'm the only person who doesn't. But that's fine. Choose her if you want. I don't care."

"Okay . . ." I said. "I probably won't get picked anyway."

"No, you will," Felicity said. "Or you could. If you convince my aunt. She's awful, but not completely stupid. Don't be such an Ainsley girl!"

"Oh my god," I said. "I know! Ainsley girls always talk about how they won't get things! It's really funny."

"It's pathetic."

She bit off the last syllable, saying it so loud I thought the room would fall silent. Mrs. Gimbel was leading the rest of the class in a translation exercise, and Hannah and Whitney were leaning together, going over something on the room's computer, in the far corner, underneath a big poster of a Roman emperor. Hannah caught my eye and looked away.

"Even if you don't become a Sibyl it's no big deal. The Sibyls are basically dead now. I love Strife, but she killed us—made the school angry and gave them a reason to tame us. They're trying to make us like the rest of Ainsley. We're like the Furies after they get turned into the Eumenides."

"Huh?" I said.

She laughed. "Oh my god," she said. "You haven't read the play. How did you think of Alecto?"

"Err, have you ever played this game called *Hades*?"

"You know . . . the fact that you admitted that makes me like you even more," Felicity said. "You are *so* unique. You must know that, but you are *so* unique for Ainsley."

"Well, yeah, I'm the only trans girl here. . . ."

"Oh, not because of that." She waved a hand. "Everyone's queer now. I'm probably queer too, if I bothered to think about it. No . . . because you're . . ." She shrugged.

"What?"

"Honest."

"Thanks," I said. "I really, really like that."

For the first time I saw her give a smile that was more than a cynical grin. Her whole face transformed—eyes got big and she sat up straight for once. "You're not offended," she said. "My cousin Liam is always offended by me."

"No. I mean, my mom says I'm *too* honest."

"I bet she loves that about you though."

I thought of how my mom always made me wear a big coat when I went out so nobody would see my skirt and uniform polo.

"Anyway, so don't worry if you don't get in," Felicity said.

A normal thing at this point would've been for Felicity to say, *But we can be friends anyway!* She did not say this. Her smile just got dimmer and more sad. I was tempted to take out my phone, just to avoid her eyes.

And then, thank god, the bell rang.

"Thank you, Sara."

"Thank you."

"Thanks, Sara."

"Thanks."

That was something people did at Ainsley that nobody did at St. George's. It was tradition at Ainsley to thank your teacher after every class, which I thought was super weird. It felt wrong for thanking to be compulsory like that, so I didn't do it.

And I noticed that Felicity didn't either. We looked at each other, and she gave me a wink, then pulled out her phone and was tap-tapping on it.

I didn't think she disliked me. Obviously, she liked me a lot! But somehow I felt like my existence wasn't real to her yet. Not a part of her life. Something about her suddenly ignoring me felt weirdly . . . normal. As if I was being dismissed in a totally different way than anyone else bothered to dismiss me.

"One moment please," Mrs. Gimbel said. "I just want to congratulate everyone who is offering themselves up to become a Sibyl. You are the best and the brightest that Ainsley has to offer. It's a venerable institution, built on trust, sisterhood, consensus, and the love of wisdom, and regardless of who is ultimately chosen, you should be proud to be a part of this process."

Everybody left, but I sat there for a few moments, until finally I said, "Umm, hey? Weren't we supposed to talk?"

Mrs. Gimbel said, "Now's not a good time. Please report those demerits and ask the office to assign you a detention with me. We can speak then."

I said okay and raced out of there.

3

"OKAY, NO MORE FELICITY!" LIAM said. "You've used up your three Felicity facts for the week. Pretty bold to use them all on a Monday, but there you go."

"But she said I'm unique!" I said. "And not because I'm trans. She sees the world *exactly* the way I do."

"When will you believe that there is absolutely nothing you can tell me about Felicity that I don't already know? Bad enough my whole family is obsessed with her, now she's all you talk about too! It's just not okay. It's an abuse of my human rights."

Liam wasn't the *only* transmasc kid at Ainsley, but he was certainly the *most* masculine—the one who belonged here the least. He'd transitioned freshman year, and his parents had let him take blockers on the condition that he not leave Ainsley, because the education was *so* good. Liam also thought I was obsessed with his cousin, which I don't *think* was true. It's just that Felicity and I had Latin right before lunch, so she was usually on my mind when Liam and I ate.

Anyway, I didn't have a crush on Felicity. I just thought she was the greatest human being who had ever lived and that she was wise and beautiful and friendly and could probably talk to birds, and I'd definitely kiss her if she wanted to. I thought Liam would understand that this wasn't a crush—that when you're trans, you don't *crush*, you idolize.

"Can I say one thing though?" I said.

"No."

"Just that she *really* understood the person I'm picking: Alecto. One of the Furies, and when I admitted I got her from a video game, she thought it was great."

"Tara," Liam said. "You're not really gonna join the Sibyls, are you?"

"Well, they probably won't want me. But sure. I've always wanted to join."

"They'd *love* having you around to brown- and pink-wash their racist patriarchal mess," Liam said. "Last year we got within an inch of getting them banned, and now you're gonna give them a win? Why are you doing this?"

"Err . . . because they're everything I love? And Felicity is one of them? And I could hang out with your aunt?"

"My aunt is a TERF."

That was a trans-exclusive radical feminist: someone who called themselves a feminist but was anti-trans and thought we were just men trying to sneak into women's spaces to hurt them.

"She's never said a single TERFy thing online. I've checked."

"My aunt *always* asks me if I'm really serious about top surgery. If I don't think I'll regret it. If I'm not just a butch lesbian. Every single week."

"So?" I said. "My parents ask me that stuff all the time. And I don't hate them. It makes sense. Surgery is a big deal."

"Only because they *make* it a big deal. People can join the military and go off and *die* at eighteen. But you ask for top surgery, and it's some kind of biiiiig decision. Abortion gets banned, and they're still worrying about top surgery? To them we're just machines for making kids—that's why they care about breasts so much."

"Ooookay," I said. "Your aunt is not antiabortion."

Liam shook his head, which he did a lot around me. Liam was completely dialed into trans stuff. He was on blockers and passed pretty well: he looked like a teenage boy, although maybe more like a thirteen-year-old than a fifteen-year-old. If I could pass, I would *never* mention being trans—but he mentioned it all the time!

We were at a table at the edge of the Ainsley cafeteria, which was filled with chattering girls. Over Liam's shoulder, Felicity and her friends were sitting at a table, arguing about something. Felicity was excited, waving her right arm. Andie leaned back in her chair, and Naia was nodding along. Whitney's sister, who went by Calliope, was there too, looking at her phone. All four of them wore the blazers and scarves and badges of the Sibyls.

"All right, now what happened over the weekend?" Liam said. "It seemed really problematic. Whitney and Hannah said you're gonna be a Sibyl because you're trans?"

"No, I don't know. They left really quickly. And I wondered, was it because they were uncomfortable we were gonna sleep in the same room? And my parents were like, *Yep, that's definitely why.*"

"If they felt uncomfortable, you're better off. You do not want to be their friend."

"Except here's the thing . . . I *am* essentially a boy."

"But you're not."

"No . . . but I sort of am. Like I'm not even on hormones. They really would be alone in a room with a male-type person, with male-type parts, and . . . you know . . . maybe they were right to be uncomfortable."

"But they'd sleep over with a girl. Even a queer girl. Whitney is bi."

"Sssssssure," I said. "But . . . I'm different."

"If they treat you differently from cis girls, they're transphobes. That's the definition of transphobia."

"I dunno," I said. "Yeah . . . I really have no idea what's going on with me. Sure, okay. I'm a girl. I've got it. That's the party line. That's how I'm allowed to be here, and I definitely appreciate that. In the olden days, they'd be like, *No no no, you've gotta snip off your balls to get through these gates.* So I *definitely* appreciate the party line. I *love* the party line. I'm physically indistinguishable from a boy under these clothes, but I'm actually a girl. Totally. That works for me."

"You are so frustrating," Liam said.

Liam was always calling me out, even when I was talking about myself! Which was fine. I guess I needed him for that, but still, it'd be nice if he didn't always just repeat the typical trans kid party line: *Yes, you're 100 percent [insert gender here], and anyone who doubts that is a transphobe.*

"Let's look at the facts," I said. "I have gone to an all-boys school since the sixth grade. I'm friends with no girls. I don't even have a sister. Like, if there's any facet of girlhood that's not given to me by birth, there's no way I have that thing. And that's a fact. I just don't know anything about being a girl. And I *definitely* don't look like one."

"Yes, you do, because you are one. So what you look like is what a girl—"

"Liam," I said. "Are you not understanding me on purpose? Whatever it is in people's minds that they associate with being a girl, it's not me."

"But that's *their* problem," he said.

I shook my head. Liam and I had been getting into terrible fights lately, where I was like, *You don't get it, our lives are totally different.* Except then Liam would get mad and be like, *You don't know what I've gone through.* And, yeah, his life was hard: his parents wouldn't let him switch schools, and he was always like, *I'd kill for parents who were as supportive as yours are.* But the thing was . . . I didn't *care* what Liam had gone through. We were talking about me, not about him. His experiences didn't matter there. Mine did.

From my perspective, if my parents were gonna risk fighting the government—were gonna risk losing their visas or whatever else the Governor might do to them—then I had to be absolutely, positively certain that going on hormones was the right thing for me, and that meant being totally sure that I really *was* trans. And I was certain that I wanted whatever physical changes hormones would give me. And I hoped that those changes would make me feel more like a girl, since I wanted to be a girl. But people kept being like, *No, you're already a girl,* and somehow that idea didn't seem right to me. Sometimes I felt as if I was forcing it.

"Okay, look," I said. "The other day, my mom said, 'But if you are a girl right now, and you have the male hormones, then why do you need to add the female hormones? Either you are a girl already or you are not a girl and need some girl qualities added. What you are saying—that you are a girl but need medical help to make you a girl—does not make sense.' What am I supposed to say to that?"

"Are you serious?" he said. "I thought they were on board with you transitioning!"

"N-no, they are, but—what do I say to that?"

"You're a girl, and you need gender-affirming medical care. It's that simple."

"But how am I a girl? Most people are like, *It's your biology that makes you a girl,* and don't say all that stuff about how biological sex is a fuzzy spectrum. I know that stuff. I am so tired of you guys treating me like I am stupid."

Whenever transphobes came out with stuff about how girls have holes and boys have poles, people on our side would be like, *Aha, but what about all these cases of people born with such and such intersex conditions, so they have genitalia or hormones or chromosomes that don't quite match up with what you'd expect a girl to have?* And yeah, I could technically claim to be one of those people. My brain had some kind of intrinsic girlness to it, so I'd never feel right in a boy body. But then my mom said, "I personally have never felt my brain was inimitably female. I have always felt my femaleness was a function of how I am seen. And you, until recently, were not seen as female at all." And also, if it was just about the biology of it, if it was about having a girl's *body,* then why did socially transitioning make

40

me so happy? Like, all I'd done was put on a skirt and some lipstick and change my name, and it'd made me ten thousand times happier! Did my inborn biology somehow care if I wore lipstick? Or what mouth noises a person made when referring to me in the third person?

"This stuff matters, Liam," I said. "It's not a word game. It's not like, *Oh, the definition of* girl *and* boy *evolves over time.* Or it's not like, *Gotcha, you don't understand biology.* It matters. I mean, look at this school, the whole school exists because boys are bad to girls. That's real."

"Single-gender education shouldn't exist," Liam said. "That's a fact. In the future, people are gonna look at it and be like, *That's exactly the same as segregated schools*, and it's exactly because—"

"Liam," I said. "I *like* Ainsley. I like how nerdy the girls are here. I like how they don't care what boys think, don't talk about them, aren't worried about them. I like that *we* are the center of attention here. I like how nice and close and interested in each other everybody is. I even like how intense and driven the teachers are. None of that would *ever* be true in a coed school. I *like* this. I *hated* St. George's."

"But I love St. George's," he said. "Because I'm a boy, and you're a girl."

I shrugged.

Whenever he could, Liam took classes at St. George's,

but he still didn't understand the core of the place, because to be honest, the boys over there treated him like he was a girl, whereas they treated me like I was a freak.

He thought St. George's was all fun and pranks and laughing at crude jokes. But it wasn't—it was barely concealed violence, always, all the time. It was never feeling safe, never feeling close with anyone, never being able to trust a person with your secrets. St. George's was the equivalent of getting a knife in your ribs on the first day of school and being forced to scramble to find medical care without being late for class.

But maybe he felt the same way about me and Ainsley—that I could never know it the way he did. After all, he'd been the butch girl all through middle school, and Ainsley had a side that was super feminine. Like, this was the kind of school where debutantes and socialites came from. And he was still at Ainsley, while I almost never had to go to St. George's.

My eyes went to the four Sibyls, who were still sitting just past us. Felicity glanced up and caught my eye. I quickly looked away, focusing on the red door tucked between two bookshelves, with the Greek words written above them that I'd had to translate myself—they said something like "Wisdom is the highest virtue, and wisdom is speaking and acting the truth, paying heed to all things." The word for "wisdom" they used was *Sophrosyne*, a minor goddess who all women were meant to emulate—she represented restraint, patience, knowing when to act. When I'd told Liam what it said, he was like, *That is so misogynistic, to assume the main problem at a girls' school is people being all flighty and acting too hastily.* And he wasn't wrong, but I still liked the quote.

Watching the Sibyls argue, I couldn't help thinking, *They would understand what I'm saying.*

"I'm gonna sign up," I said. "Wish me luck?"

Liam rolled his eyes, and he tried to give me one of the handshakes he'd learned at St. George's. From the way he did it I instantly knew he'd learned it from Brandon, and that it'd been taught to Liam as a joke—it was a made-up secret handshake Brandon used to make fun of the lower-form boys who idolized him. But I did it anyway, and then I stood up, hovering by our table.

The four girls got up, holding their trays, and they handed them over the counter. Felicity moved so gracefully. Anyone else would've had trouble juggling their backpack and the tall drink on their tray—she held the tray wedged next to her body, and she talked with one hand. Andie rolled her eyes. The trays were taken away, and Felicity gave a smile to the lunch lady and waved two fingers, and then the Sibyls opened that red door. Beyond it, I saw wood paneling and tall shelves of books.

But, for once, the door didn't slam shut. Felicity nudged the doorstop with her toe. Immediately, some girls swarmed the door—all of them sophomore girls I recognized from my advanced classes. Hannah, Whitney, Robin.

They went in, but I didn't. Instead, I just hovered, staring

43

out of the corner of my eye. Liam was already on his phone.

The annoying thing about Liam was that he would've been a gorgeous girl. He had fine auburn hair with a slight wave and beautiful green eyes. He'd been on blockers for a year, and he was still small, kind of androgynous, but with his mouth twisted up and to the side, and in his very trim sport coat and perfectly knotted tie, he made a very pretty boy.

Meanwhile, the sound of the lunchroom was sucking at my ears. The door would only be open for a few minutes. People waited all year for this. Waited for their whole Ainsley careers, in fact.

The girls started to troop out, talking to each other. Andie came to the door, saluted them as they left, and then she looked around. She was about to bend down and pull out the doorstop when a sound came out of my throat.

She looked up without smiling. The lunchroom had emptied out—just a few girls here and there rushing to finish up their homework. My saddle shoes clip-clopped over the tile, and I smoothed out the hem of my skirt, which was way too short even though it was the longest the uniform store had.

Andie narrowed her eyes. One of the leaves of her wreath had strayed down onto her forehead. She was red-haired and freckled, and she always seemed a little sad. Her blazer was a solid purple.

"Hey," Andie said.

My voice was hoarse. "Hey," I said.

"So you're Antigone's girl," Andie said. "I didn't think you'd come."

Then Felicity was at the door. "Hecuba!" she said. "What's happening? Who— Oh, Tara! Here, here, come in." And then her hand was on my shoulder, pulling me into a different world.

4

WHERE THE LUNCHROOM WAS LONG and painted white and gray, this room had dark hardwood floors, covered by plush rugs. The intersession bell rang, and the door slammed shut behind me.

There was a piece of cream-colored paper on the coffee table, next to an inkpot that had a quill pen lying in it. Three names were written on the piece of paper, all of them executed perfectly. Hannah's had a little swirl done underneath it.

"You have to write your new name without a blot," Naia said. She was on the couch, huddled forward, with an old book in her lap. "For good luck."

"Shhh," Felicity said. "You guys are terrible. You're being so off-putting. Stop it. Don't worry about them."

"Don't mind me, I'm the diversity," Naia said. She was

Black, probably one of five Black kids at Ainsley. When they'd tried to revoke her Sibyl scholarship last year, the whole school had rallied around her, but she wasn't really in with the activist kids, and some of them called her an Oreo.

Calliope (Whitney's sister) was in the corner, as far as possible as she could be from the other three. Her phone was in her hand. "Don't I know you?"

"I'm friends with your sister," I said.

"Oh," she said. "Not to be a dick, but aren't you still technically enrolled at St. George's?"

"Boo," Felicity said. She pulled out a piece of paper from the pad, crumpled it up, and shot it toward Calliope, who rolled her eyes. Naia bent down, scrabbled for the paper, then tossed it over too. Both of them had missed her.

"Boo," Naia said. "What are we booing?"

Calliope rolled her eyes again. "You can put down your name, but we'll need to talk to Angel and to Mrs. Gimbel about this."

"Uh, sure," I said.

Felicity took a seat in the middle of the couch, and Andie sat next to her. I knelt by the coffee table, and I picked up the pen, and Andie said, "Wait . . . first let's talk."

"Uh, okay," I said, glancing nervously at Calliope in the corner. I liked how school uniforms made us all look the same and how our uniform shirts were kind of baggy and an ugly color, but Calliope still looked radiant—she looked like an adult, to be honest, with clear skin and long straight hair. She was tall and long-limbed and controlled. She'd put down her phone and was staring at me.

I got up, smoothing my skirt down nervously over my legs, and I sat in the other chair. The room had a few tablets in the corner, chained to a desk, and was lined with books—some of them old and some of them looking nearly new. The shelves were tall, and there was a little ladder you could wheel around, but piles of books crowded the floor. There was a skylight above us that filled the room with light, and there were some hanging plants crowding around the ceiling, which made the place feel like some atrium or secret-garden type of place.

"Do you know why you're doing this?" Andie said.

"Of course she does," Felicity said. "It's because of me."

"Antigone," Andie said. "You are breaking one of our rules—you're trying to speak for someone else."

"You're right, Hecuba," Felicity said.

"I don't know. I like the whole environment. The fake names. Everything. It's exactly what I always hoped school would be like. And Felicity said it was the best thing that ever happened to her."

Andie turned and pursed her lips, her eyes going soft. "Aww," she said. "Really?" She brushed at Felicity's hair a little, and the other girl shook her off, like a startled horse.

"Do you have a name?" Naia said.

"I think so," I said.

"So you're really going with that name?" Felicity said. "The one we talked about?"

Suddenly I felt a weird out-of-body experience. I imagined being crowned with the laurel wreath during the next Founder's Day, the big event in March where Sibyls got officially celebrated.

I'd be surrounded by all the Sibyls from past years. And I imagined them speaking the name *Alecto, Alecto, Alecto*, and then for some reason I imagined them all raising their swords and clanging them together. I'm not sure why everyone had swords in this vision, but I liked it.

"Yeah," I said. "Alecto."

"Oooh," Naia said. "That's good."

"Who?" Calliope said.

"Yeah you'll need to fill me in too," said Andie.

"She, umm, she's one of the Furies."

"Unceasing anger," Felicity said. "Why her and not Megaera or Tisiphone?"

"Just liked the sound of Alecto better."

"That's a really weird one," Andie said. "Like, really strange. Did you put her up to this, Antigone? I can tell you Mrs. Gimbel really won't like that."

"I told her that too," Felicity said.

"So just take a second," Andie said. "Come up with some-one else. It doesn't have to be a big deal. I just googled famous Greek ladies to get mine."

"Stop it," Felicity said. "You're such a Hecuba." That was the name of King Priam's wife in *The Iliad*. She was the mother of Hector and Paris, and she wept when Hector died.

"I don't think the *name* is that important," Calliope said. "You can keep it if you want. We look at a bunch of other things."

"Should you even be here, Calliope?" Felicity said. "Isn't this a conflict of interest? Your sister was just here."

"Yeah," Naia said. "You should really go."

Calliope blinked a few times. She looked at Andie, who shrugged. "I need to get to class," Calliope said. She picked up her bag and walked slowly out the door. "Good luck, Tara."

After she was gone, everyone let out a breath. The door slowly, creakily shut.

"Don't worry about her," Felicity said. "She's almost always at the mansion in her free time."

"Oh," I said. "She, uh, does seem kind of . . . like . . ."

"She's okay," Andie said. "But she's a senior and not as into Sibyl stuff anymore."

"Yes . . ." Naia winked. "That's what we're telling you, and since we're saying it, you have to believe it. The answer isn't just that she hates me and Antigone."

"Shh," Andie said. "She won't want to join if you guys act like jerks."

They bickered like I wasn't there. But then I realized the bickering was actually *for* me. They liked having an audience. The moment Calliope had left, everything had gotten a lot more relaxed.

"Umm, yeah," I said. "Alecto. I genuinely couldn't think of anyone better."

"And our Alecto knows everything and everyone in the ancient world," Felicity said. "So you know it's true."

"Oh, okay, so the nerd contingent grows," Andie said. "Fine . . . fine. I guess it needs all kinds."

The whole vibe was absurd. But what made it great was that the school *knew* we were there. That this ritual was absurdly old. That it was something that mattered. And that all these girls had gotten there by valuing knowledge.

"So . . ." Andie said, making her voice low and booming. "Let's get back to the Sibylline *mysteries*. Do you know what this is?"

"It's the Sibyls," I said. "You're a . . . club? Society? This is the membership period?"

I took a breath. They were beautiful, the three of them on the couch, in their laurel wreaths, with the hanging vines coming down around them, drifting across the many bookcases.

"And why should we pick you?"

"Ummm," I said. "Because you'll have fun hanging out with me? Err . . . probably?"

Naia cocked her head. "Wait . . . you're the trans girl."

The other two looked at her and then at each other, and I laughed. The whole scene was just absurd.

"Yeah," I said. "Didn't you know?"

"I mean . . . just checking," Naia said. "I'm Strife, by the way."

"Eris?" I said. "Or Discordia?" Those were the Greek and Roman goddesses for Strife. Eris/Discordia had started the Trojan War by creating conflict between the goddesses over who was the most beautiful.

"Don't start this," Andie said.

"I prefer Strife," Strife said. "Just Strife."

"And I'm Hecuba," Andie said. "It's my job to keep the peace and be *normal* and not be a dick all the time. I seriously worry about what'll happen when these two are in charge. That's our main criteria this year: pick someone who'll keep these two from killing each other."

"Well, write your name," Felicity said, pointing to the pen.

"No, wait," Hecuba said. "Are you joining for the money?"

"I mean, no . . . ?" I said. "I'm on reduced tuition, so we only pay like seven thousand a year for Ainsley. But if we could pay even less, that would be great, I guess."

"Mmm-hmmm," Hecuba said. "Okay. Well, she's definitely not here just for the money, then."

"What's happening?" I said.

"Just that Strife here completely changed the rules of the game," Hecuba said. "Normally you wouldn't even *know* there

52

was any money until after you'd become a Sibyl. But last year Strife got all upset and said it wasn't fair to keep it a secret and—"

"Posted it online," Strife said. "Yeah. I'm terrible. It's a well-known fact about me."

"And posted it online," Hecuba said. "Making us look like what we are, which is a bunch of elitist white people."

"Hey," Felicity said. "No we're not."

"Oh, come on," Strife said. "Antigone. Let's be real."

"We aren't. The money isn't a core part of being a Sibyl. That's my aunt who changed things. The money only came along like ten years ago. And we kept it secret so people wouldn't join *just* for that. It's my aunt you want to blame, not us. Without her, we wouldn't even *have* people like Calliope."

"Sorry for them," Strife said. "They don't get that they're outliers because they're not intolerable. Most Sibyls are the worst."

"I . . . I see why you have your name."

"Anyway, what they were trying to figure out is whether you knew the Sibyl scholarship also includes an extra fifty thousand for college too," Strife said.

"Strife!" Hecuba said.

"What? She should know . . . everyone else already does! Calliope's sister definitely knows. Why shouldn't Alecto?"

"Uh, uh," I said. "Ummm. What?"

"Yep, courtesy of *her* aunt," Strife said.

"Err . . ." I said, opening my mouth, stretching my jaw, try-ing not to look shocked. That would be . . . that would be . . . that would be really good. Like, life-changingly good. I could go anywhere. I wouldn't need to stay in Virginia for college, no matter what. I could go anywhere. Or if I wanted, I could stay in Virginia, use the money to pay for college, and use my par-ents' saved money to get whatever I needed done so that I could fully pass and wouldn't need to worry about getting murdered in the streets of Charlottesville or Blacksburg or Williamsburg (our state's top colleges were all in conservative rural towns).

"So now think, do you *really* want to go with Alecto?" Strife said.

"I . . ."

"Knowing that Angel and Gimbel will probably hate it?"

Felicity looked up, squinting. "They won't—"

"Yeah, they will, Antigone," Strife said. "Come on, let's be honest. They hated Strife last year, but you picked me anyway, and I was their worst nightmare. Now you've got another angry dark-skinned goddess of anger, and she's an angry trans girl too? They're gonna be so terrified of picking someone who'll call them out."

"But they'll also be scared *not to*—it's not a good look to turn down the first-ever trans girl . . ." Felicity said.

"Your Latin grades suck, don't they?" Strife said.

"I, umm, I love Latin, but you guys use different textbooks and— Wait—how do you know about that?"

"They must, if Gimbel never mentioned you to us," Strife said. "Okay, so she's got bad grades, and if they want a reason to reject her they'll be like, *Oh we really* wish *we could pick her, but her grades aren't good enough.* Even though lots of Sibyls have been so ignorant. Lots of them never picked up a book, and it didn't matter. You know there's only like five Sibyls in history who didn't go to the Ivy League? That's the *real* reason this club exists: it's so old DC families can hang a wreath on their daughters' heads and get them into school. You know. Come on, you all know it even if you don't want to admit it. To get in she needs to be perfect. Aside from her grades, everything needs to be perfect."

Hecuba nodded. "Yeah," she said. "They might not like Alecto. You really do want someone Angel likes. . . ."

"No," Felicity said. "No. She *is* Alecto. That's who she is. It's not even worth being a Sibyl if you can't be the person you are."

"Antigone," Strife said, "you are literally the only person who thinks that. Of course it's worth being a Sibyl and having money and going to Harvard, even if you have to be Dido or some other dumb person."

"I . . ."

Felicity looked at the ground. I was still standing by the door, in the middle of this weirdly airy room, with its skylight and its hanging vines.

"I'm not sure," I said.

Hecuba sighed. "So just put down your real name; you can figure out your Sibyl name later."

I nodded, not sure what to say. I knelt, taking up the pen. Ink welled on its tip, and already there were dark smudges on the edges of my thumb.

"Just wipe off the extra ink before you start," Felicity said.

"Stop it," Hecuba said. "Don't be anxious. It's not a secret ritual. It's just a sign-up sheet."

Wiping three or four times along the side of the inkpot, I took the quill and started to write my name. Began with a big cursive *T* but realized I'd forgotten all my cursive and switched to print. The ink was fading halfway through my last name, and I dipped the pen again, finishing just as a drop of sweat fell from my forehead.

Strife looked over me. "Good job. Sweat doesn't count."

"Shh, that's not a real rule, about the ink blots," Felicity said.

"It could be!" Strife said.

Felicity stood up, and so did I, holding my bag. Naia swooped forward, caught the quill, put it back into the inkpot, and wiped up the ink with a little handkerchief that'd appeared from nowhere.

"Let me walk you out," Felicity said.

Then she opened the other door, the one leading into the back hall, and we were plunged into the noise and warmth of the lunchtime corridor.

* * *

"Sorry Hecuba was so intense. I think she's worried about me and Strife," Felicity said.

"Err . . . why?"

"Why is she worried?" Felicity squinted. "Well, Hecuba is, like, a normal Ainsley girl. She's got a boyfriend. She wins fancy science competitions. She's good at talking to people and being friendly and stuff. But me and Strife are, umm . . . well, we're normal in a different way."

"What does that mean?"

"Just that we're not easy to be around," Felicity said. "I hate most people. Strife doesn't, but she loves to cause trouble. You'll get to know her soon. And Calliope seriously hates both of us. Like, deep down to the very marrow of her soul. She thinks we ruined the Sibyls and stole her best friend, Andie. Which is kind of true, from her point of view."

"Calliope was intense. . . . It was really different after she left."

"She's like my aunt: completely fake."

"It's cool that An—Hecuba cares so much about you," I said. "And, like, whether you'll still be okay after she leaves."

"Yeah," Felicity said. "It's great. It's amazing."

I stopped. "Wait . . . did you say it was great?"

"What?" she said. "Why?"

My ears were burning.

"No reason," I said. "I just always think of you as cynical.

57

But today you've smiled twice talking about your friends."

"Hmm," she said. "I'm not cynical about them! Those two are my life."

"So . . . am I gonna be your life too?"

"No," Felicity said. "I don't know. Maybe. I hope."

We were walking aimlessly. My next class was actually right down the hall, but we passed it and walked on. Felicity talked about her joining, about how Hecuba had teased her for being so rich.

"I'm sorry," I said. "I let you down. By not committing to Alecto. . . ."

"Don't be sorry. My aunt and Mrs. Gimbel, they don't understand anything, Tara. They have zero idea about what's important and what's not. Mrs. Gimbel's just funny, but my aunt actually scares me. It's terrifying that she's so important and that everyone loves her so much."

"But it sounds like she decides who becomes a Sibyl."

"I . . . yeah," Felicity said. "She didn't want Strife last year, but the Sibyls picked her anyway, and then Strife posted that stuff about how there's a scholarship. So now my aunt's allowed to veto anyone we want."

"I'll pick Athena. Or—or . . . I don't know. Someone else. Someone she'll like."

"Okay . . ." Felicity said. "Sure. That makes sense. She ruined the whole thing anyway, you know. It's just sad because, look, they all laugh about it, but their names are really the core of who they like. Do you know Hecuba?"

"Priam's wife," I said. I'd read a translation of *The Iliad* last year. It was boring in parts, but I remembered Hecuba's powerful cries, her worries over the safety of her sons.

"Yeah," Felicity said. "That's Andie's core. The leader, the voice of reason."

"I don't know," I said. "Tara is a name I picked. I used to be Tanay. I just picked Tara because it's an Indian name that white people can pronounce. I thought of picking Kali, but it would've been too . . . I don't know . . ."

"Too revealing," Felicity said. "You can't use a real name in public. Can't let other people know you that way. It's totally fine. I just want to say— Hey, why are we outside?"

She frowned. The bell had rung, and we were all alone in the cold, at the edge of the parking lot. The sky above was a stone gray, and the wind swept across the grass. Ainsley was white and cheerful, low on the hill, with lots of glass and little picnic tables around it. But on top of the hill St. George's squatted like a great stone toad, with its scarred brick and its ivy and its stained glass.

"Just walking," I said.

"It's cold."

"Mm-hmm," I said. "Yep, it's almost winter I guess. . . ."

Cars went by on the other side of the fence, and I put out a hand to grab a wrought iron bar.

"You're tall," she said.

"Mm-hmm," I said. "More than six feet."

We stood across from each other, and I could feel the static in the air, from the cold and the humidity, from the rain gathering in the gray clouds. Wind whipped the edges of her blazer, and my arms were drenched in sweat. I reached out and touched the leaves of her wreath, trying to pat it down a bit.

"It's escaping."

"Oh god." She put up a hand, holding down the wreath. "It's such a pain to weave these things."

"You do it yourself?"

"Mm-hmm, until this year Andromache used to do it; she thought it was relaxing. But she graduated, obviously."

"So . . . yay," I said. "I'm here, I'm gonna do it! And if I don't get in, then at least we'll get to hang out at the mansion for a day or two, right?"

The mansion was tucked way back on the property, over near the creek, and the Sibyls and the prospective Sibyls used it during the solstice season as part of their interviews and their initiation ceremonies.

"Yeah, you don't have Christmas plans, do you?"

I smiled. I knew it hadn't even occurred to her—the way it would've occurred to Liam—that I might not celebrate Christmas because I wasn't Christian. "No. I mean, we have a tree."

My hand went out, and I rubbed her arm, and I smiled, not believing what my body was doing. Like, this was a different person acting through me. Maybe my real self—my real name.

"Hey, anyway," she said. "You should go to class. I'll see you during the interviews, I guess."

"Uh, yeah," I said. "Unless . . ."

We looked at each other.

"Yeah?" she asked.

"We don't *need* to be Sibyls to hang out, right?"

Felicity's brow furrowed, and for a second she looked confused. I was having an out-of-body experience. My hand went up, touched the open air. "I, umm, like, I could text you sometime? Just to talk about ancient stuff?"

"Y-yeah," Felicity said. "Sure. Yeah. I'll give you my number. Yeah."

She put her number in my phone, and then she hit call, and her own phone rang.

I muttered something to her, gave a quick wave, and walked off, wondering who I could tell about this—wondering who could possibly understand.

After my mom picked me up, she asked, "Did anything happen today?"

"Nothing much." I crammed my backpack into the space at my feet.

"I got a call from someone at your school," she said. "They left a message, I couldn't understand . . . ? Something about this Sibyls club? They wanted your St. George's transcripts mailed over."

"Mom," I said. "You have to do it. This is really, really important."

"Okay, okay."

I held my phone, looking down at the list of famous Greek women, not sure if I should tell her about the scholarship part. My mom spent her days taking care of other peoples' kids illegally, ever since she'd lost her work permit. She would get way too excited if I told her there was a chance at a fifty-thousand-dollar scholarship.

"Make any new friends?" she said. "You're not too depressed about those two girls?"

"Whitney and Hannah? They're dead to me," I said.

"Do not be so hard on them," she said. "They felt awkward, perhaps. But they've still been nice to you."

"I guess," I said. "But being a friend isn't just being nice. Like, you can't just *want* to help someone. You have to actually *do* it, at least some of the time."

"Acha, acha . . ." She trailed off, and we drove for a while, through the bumpy cobbled roads, where we were surrounded by little townhomes that were probably two hundred years old.

"And in this case, helping is . . . ?" she said.

"Listening to me," I said. "Understanding. Being there for me. I spent a week looking forward to them coming over, and they just left, even though they knew it was weird and awkward and I'd feel terrible."

"It is hard though," she said. "This is a new thing, being

trans. We've had to work very hard at it too. And these girls have known you for less long."

"No, it's their attitude," I said. "Like, you guys suck and are terrible, obviously." I put out my fingers, wondering if I'd gone too far, and I touched the top of her hand. "Just kidding. What I mean is, even when you don't get it, you do. I don't exactly know what I'm saying, but . . . uhh . . ."

"So *think*," my mom said. "Think hard and put your thoughts together clearly."

I shook my head. That was just like her. And to someone like Whitney and Hannah, obviously it'd sound like a harsh way to talk to me. But the other side was, my mom really *tried* to understand. It was that invisible thing that was missing from most people: their heads ought to be churning, trying to figure out where you were coming from, but most of the time, they were just trapped in their own point of view. So even if they were nice and good and never said mean stuff, like Hannah and Whitney, it was no good, because deep inside, they weren't really trying to understand.

"Okay," I said. "You have *ideas* about my gender stuff. Like, you think I'm just super gay and am ashamed of it and that I'd prefer to be a girl because that seems more normal."

"I wouldn't put it like that. My thinking has evolved," my mom said.

"Sure, sure," I said. "But you're willing to listen to me, when I'm like, *No, it's not about sex and romantic stuff, it's about wanting to be a girl*—whatever that means."

"Yes, I understand that it's more focused on your self-image."

"And my place in the world," I said. "But other people, they don't ever let go of their own ideas. Like, their ideas might be nice and liberal—they might be programmed to just accept *Oh, Tara is allowed to be whatever she wants to be*, but they don't know how to accept a new idea. So I tried to explain to them, *Hey, you know, maybe you're right. Maybe I shouldn't be a Sibyl. After all, compared to you guys, I don't get good grades. I don't win prizes. I only do debate, and I'm terrible at it. Does being trans really make me special enough that I should be guaranteed to get into Harvard? I just want to talk to you about it, as friends.* But instead they repeated robotically, *We're sorry, we never meant to offend you. I think you're so wonderful, and you've suffered so much.*"

"Acha," she said. "I understand. Well I am of two minds about what you've said. The first is, what is the point of this expensive school if you've no open-minded, thoughtful people in it?"

"There are some! Today I—"

"And the second is, my baby boy—" When she was feeling sad, she usually slipped back into calling me stuff she had when I was a boy.

I murmured *baby girl* under my breath, but not too loud.

"I'm sorry, baby girl. The second point is that there aren't many thoughtful people in the world. Most are too busy and too self-involved. That is what makes you special. Not being trans. Being trans is simply an outgrowth—you are wise, so you figured out early what takes other girls years and years, perhaps their whole lives, what to do. You are special because you know what is right, and then you do it. And that's a rare enough quality that if you demand it of your friends too, you'll likely be disappointed."

"No, but these Sibyls are cool," I said. "They get it, I think. That's what's so exciting. Like, they're the *real* Ainsley."

"Tell me more."

So I told her a whole bunch of stuff, stream of consciousness, about Felicity and Naia and Andie, and how they were committed to total rigorous honesty and to the concept of Sophrosyne—wisdom—but, like, a feminine sort of wisdom—the kind of wisdom that was mixed with prudence and restraint.

"Acha," she said. "You are the model of restraint, I know. You *neeeeever* speak out of turn."

"Shh," I said. "Anyway, they also have a secret room, and they get special privileges: they can wear a crown and a blazer, and they've got a network of famous alumnae. . . ."

My mom didn't believe me at first about how important the group was, but when we got home, she must've looked it up, because she yelled at me from her room, and I rushed in and we both read the group's Wikipedia page. And then she called my dad, and he came home excited, and we ordered a special meal, and they made an offering to the statue of Krishna in the corner of our kitchen, to pray that I would do well in my coming trial. Even our dog got to celebrate—when he started nosing around under the table, instead of shooing him away, my mom went to the closet and found a rawhide. She said when the master of the house succeeds, nobody is left out of the feast!

5

EVERYONE WHO HEARD I DID speech and debate said something like, "You must be so good at that!"

Unfortunately, they were wrong. I had a terrible record as a debater, losing way more matches than I won. The thing about debate is you have to think quickly on your feet, responding to their arguments with only a few minutes to think about it, and the pressure always got to me. I choked, overthinking things or overemphasizing one argument and not hitting all of them. Debate operated by very specific rules about what made for a good argument and what didn't, and those rules were the complete opposite of what I valued in a speech. I didn't want to rebut each of the other team's points, one by one. I wanted to cut to the heart of whatever was the great big flaming thing that made this issue so complicated.

I also hated that our speech and debate team was mixed: both Ainsley and St. George's participated, so every Tuesday and Thursday I had to walk up to St. George's and face the guys.

This year, Mr. Danyon had offered to switch me over into solo speaking, where you just talk in front of an audience, which seemed better to me, and closer to what an ancient Roman orator would've done when they were speaking on the Forum in favor of or against some policy. But he said all the solo speakers needed to start with impromptu speech, which meant I was in a corner of the room, sitting at the back left of two rows of chairs.

"Miss Rituveni," he said. "I believe it's your turn."

"Umm, yeah."

I got up, hunched over, wiping my hands against my skirt. Just being at St. George's made me feel more boyish. I'd waved to Henry and Brandon and a few guys I knew from last year, and they'd waved back at me. But they were all parliamentary debaters.

The speech guys were older, juniors and seniors, who joked around with each other, jerked on each other's ties, and laughed and hooted at each other's speeches. I tried not to look, in particular, at Drew Handy, who had bullied me last year. I mean, he bullied me for years, even before I came out as trans. But afterward, it was intense.

He wasn't in speech, but he had come over to our side of

the room and was standing, smirking, leaning against a post. With his acne-ridden face and dark, heavy brows, he looked like some pox-scarred veteran of an ancient war. Girls thought he was really handsome—or at least he always had some Ainsley girlfriend—but I didn't get the appeal.

"Okay, Miss Rituveni," Mr. Danyon said. "Let's start you off easily. Why don't you give me a four-minute persuasive speech about universal health care. Remember, we want to incorporate ethos, logos, *and* pathos." Those were ancient Roman terms for the different modes of persuasion: appealing to authority, appealing to logic, and appealing to the emotions.

"Ummm," I said. "Okay . . ."

Handy parroted, "Umm . . . okay . . ."

"Mr. Handy!" Mr. Danyon yelled. "Quiet, please."

I licked my lips, felt my voice drop, and tried to tug it upward again. "Well . . . universal health care is when the government pays for all the health care, right? Hmm . . . okay. Shoot. Let me start over." I searched through my brain for famous speeches. *"Blood, toil, tears, and sweat." "The bomber will always get through." "The Nazi's aim is slavery. . . ."*

"I guess what we're discussing is profit," I said. "Whether health care is better or worse if large corporations can make a profit on it. And there's good reason to think it might be better. After all, lots of things are better when there's competition. You wouldn't want the government to operate every single burger place. That would be bad. Because the burgers would all be the same. But with health care, you *want* the health care to be the same everywhere, for equity—"

"Remember," Mr. Danyon said. "There will be no rebuttal; your speech will stand alone. Emotion is a big part of this."

"Umm, and I guess people don't want universal health care because . . . you know, I don't know . . . I mean . . . yeah, I don't know. Okay, let me think."

"Boo!" Drew said. "Boo!"

I looked at Mr. Danyon, but he didn't say anything. Then someone threw a piece of paper at me. I bent down, but someone screeched, "They just flashed me!" I straightened up, kicked the paper out of the way.

The room was a big echoing basement room with linoleum floors. I gripped the podium again. The boys were sneering, the girls were staring stony-faced.

"You know, people don't . . ." I blinked a few times; tears had come to my face.

When the speech was done, I didn't go back to my seat; instead, I went straight to the bathroom.

I sat alone in a girl's stall. At least at St. George's the girls' bathrooms were never used. At Ainsley I always felt so embarrassed that I never used them, just used the single-person bathroom instead, even though everybody totally supported my right to be in the girls' room.

My parents' voices came to me: *Don't you want to be anything besides the trans girl?*

I'd dreamed for years of standing up in front of people and just . . . telling them the truth. Telling them, like a character in a video game I used to play, *Why are you doing this? What you are doing is wrong.* And telling them with so much emotion that they finally believed me and understood it. And I was pretty good at talking in class, or with my friends, but facing other people—anyone who disagreed with me—I was just *awful*.

Like, George Washington once was faced with a bunch of mutinous officers, and when he was reading their demands, he asked for his spectacles, and he said something like, *Excuse me, I have grown old in the service of my country*. And that was enough to shame them and make them back down.

Coming back out, I had a new plan. I waited until my turn was called again. And this time everyone was bored, openly yawning.

Handy shouted, "Wrap it up."

Mr. Danyon said, "Okay, this will be our final talk today. Tara, how about you discuss . . . the importance of free speech, even if it's potentially offensive."

Drew Handy was making offensive gestures with his mouth and hands, licking the split between his fingers, which meant, I don't know. Oral sex or something.

"Aren't you ashamed?" I said. "Drew."

"You're the one in a dress."

71

Mr. Danyon didn't respond. Didn't do anything. He was probably the nicest teacher at St. George's, but even he was afraid to speak up. This is what people didn't get about St. George's. It wasn't fake liberal. It wasn't liberal at all. It was a horror show.

"See," I said. "Offensive speech right there."

"You're the offensive speech," Drew said. "You're pathetic, man. You're just doing this to get into college. I heard you're even going for a scholarship over there. You're not queer; come on, admit it, man."

I put up a hand. "No, Mr. Danyon," I said. "You know he says shit like this all the time. Don't stop him now. Don't pretend you care."

Mr. Danyon's big eyebrows furrowed, but then I realized something. I had them. I had everyone looking at me. Even the guys and girls in the far corner, they paused their debates.

Drew's eyes were small and beady and dark. "Drew," I said. "Everything you say—"

"Boo!"

A devastating attack was forming inside me, if only I could get it out. "Everyone here can see, Drew, that you—"

"Boo! Boo! Get off the stage!"

"That's enough, Drew! Detention! Now!"

"Drew, everyone can hear that you—"

"That is enough!" Mr. Danyon blew a whistle, and a few

minutes afterward he yelled that the practice was over for the day. When I left, he was busy dressing down Drew.

I got driven home by a friend of mine, Henry, and he hung around my house afterward, playing a first-person shooter on split screen. Henry was short, with bleach-blond hair gelled into spikes. He tried to slouch and look cool when he walked.

"Drew is an asshat," he said.

"No, yeah," I said. "He is."

"If I were you I wouldn't even come back."

"But I want to debate."

"Yeah, except you kind of suck at it, no offense."

Out of everything people had said to me over the past few days, that stung the most. I blinked a few times to clear the tears, and we kept playing our game.

I couldn't figure out how to talk to Felicity. We only had Latin together, but I made sure not to look at her. Mrs. Gimbel breathed over my neck as usual, but even she seemed happy with me, and she said one of my translations looked good. I kept wondering if she'd want us to work in class on our Sibyl presentations, and what I'd say if we did, but nothing happened.

Going directly from a boys' school to a girls' school was weird. Like, yeah, it was incredible to see girls around everywhere, to see them talking, laughing, to watch their faces move and ponytails bob. To see the flash of their legs as they ran, and their high voices joking and laughing.

And yeah, I was more attracted to girls than to guys, so I was in this constant starstruck state, like I'd died and gone to heaven. The guys at St. George's would always make the same non-joke—*Doesn't a lesbian get distracted by all the breasts in the locker room?* Well, it was kind of true. I was excused from gym (for reasons we didn't talk about; I'd just asked and they'd said, "Yes, sure"), but at school I did sometimes get overwhelmed, and I even got an erection once, which was crushingly awful—I had to weigh it down with my bag (there's no way to hide one in a skirt). And my body tingled all the time, and almost always, almost every second, I felt like a fake: a real girl couldn't possibly love being at Ainsley so much.

I was part of an online group for trans girls, which met every Thursday night, and the group had girls from different backgrounds—it actually had lots of drama, because some of the girls were rich, TV-trans types—the kind of girls who become actresses on CW shows, whose parents had accepted them and who'd gone on hormones right away and transitioned pretty easily. They complained about the usual teen-girl stuff (but with a trans twist), like boys being mean to them and asking about their dicks—stuff that *was* pretty bad. But the other half were, like, in serious trouble. Some were homeless, calling

74

in from a car parked in a McDonald's parking lot to use its Wi-Fi. Or they couch surfed with friends, or lived in cars, or had weird dating situations that they didn't talk about much but which sometimes seemed pretty gross. They used drugs or turned tricks, got fired from their jobs, got expelled from their schools, bought their meds illegally online.

And it wasn't that the two groups hated each other—the girls who'd had it tough, they were proud of their lives, of what they'd survived. They envied the richer girls but also felt like they were soft. And the richer girls tried to be nice, but they also knew, that, well, their problems were different.

Lailah, the girl I was closest with, lived way out in the Maryland suburbs somewhere, in Prince George's, so I hardly ever saw her in person. She lived with her grandma and got her drugs from an older friend while they waited to see if the government's health insurance would cover her. She went to an arts high school, so she knew lots of snotty white girls, and I guess she felt that me at Ainsley and her at her school were really the same.

As our group meeting was going on, I opened a chat window and I told her, Hey, I think I've got a crush on another girl at school. I'm gonna bring it up when it's my turn to share.

Lailah: Nice! You've never said that kinda stuff before.

Lailah was perfectly done up, with contoured cheeks and purple holographic patches under her eyes and on her forehead.

She winked into the camera—she was in a red-lit room with a trippy painting on the wall—and I winked back. The whole group could see us, if they cared, but one of the rich girls was talking, talking about how *stressed* she was over these new laws and how she'd been crying every night.

Tara: You think that's real? That Shelly cries about shit the Governor is doing?

Lailah: Nah. She lives in DC. That's safe. She's just being dramatic.

Tara: I don't worry that much about him. I don't know, maybe there's something wrong with me.

Lailah: You're just tough. When're you gonna start on blockers? I can probably get you some.

Tara: I don't know.

Lailah: Just take them secretly. Nobody'll know. It's not like estrogen, you won't grow breasts or anything.

Tara: Yeah. How's your insurance stuff?

Lailah: Got Obamacare, so now I've got an appointment at the Johns Hopkins teen clinic, like six months away. But whatever. I think I'll just start on estrogen on my own. I can get it online pretty easy.

Tara: I don't know.

Lailah: If I'm gonna audition, I need an edge over the Shelly types. You know her parents won't let her get started before sixteen? I saw an article that it's fine— pretty safe, even—they just wait to make sure we won't change our minds. But most cis girls are on estrogen way before sixteen.

Tara: That makes sense.

What people didn't get about being a trans girl was how much it was about your body. How you just wanted to look like a girl. To be able to walk through a door and not seem like a boy in a dress, to not stand out, to have a crush and think, *Well, there's no reason for him not to like me. I don't look different than a cis girl.* And yeah, there are nonbinary and gender non-conforming kids who are out and proud and play around with gender and don't give a shit. But that wasn't me. I just wanted to be ordinary.

Then I heard a voice call my name: it was the facilitator, a college kid named Madison, who had fantastically long and lush fake eyelashes, and whose preppy name was clearly a joke, because she was pretty dark-skinned. "Tara," she said. "Do you have anything to share?"

"I, uh, yeah." I jerked my voice up, like the voice tutorials on YouTube said, and then I tried to talk through the front of my mouth, to avoid straining my throat, to create resonance and pitch using breath instead of my vocal cords. "There's a girl at school—I like her. We, uh, she's a year older. But . . . it's kind of awkward, right? I'm not on any kind of drugs, and I had, I guess, an earlier puberty. So I basically look like, you know, a boy. I even have some facial hair. But I don't do the things that make a boy hot. So if she liked me, how could she like me as a girl, when I don't look like one, or like me as a boy, when, if I'm a boy at all, I look like one who's super gay?"

"Okay . . ." Madison said. "That's a lot to parse. Have you asked her whether *she* likes you too? You're at a good school— the all-girls school, right, so I assume it's safe? What are her parents like?"

"Yeah, but come on, does anyone really do this *Are you into me, check yes or no* stuff?" I said. "Isn't it supposed to be natural? Like, you flirt and build up to it?"

"I think lots of people are more direct," Madison said. "Why not just ask her out?"

There was a cacophony of raised hands. Madison was always telling the girls to just ask the other person out (assuming it was safe), and we were always like, *That's just not how things work.*

"I guess what I'm asking you is something you can't answer," I said. "Which is, like—is it possible that she could like me? Because it seems impossible. Like, I guess you're supposed to say yes or you're a pretty bad counselor."

"This isn't hot or not," Madison said. "I can't rate your looks. I am sure there is a girl out there for you."

Nobody said, *You're beautiful! You're so wonderful! Obviously it's not out of line to think she would love you.* Because we all knew that wasn't necessarily true—that a lot of people, maybe most people, wouldn't want to be with us. Sometimes you crushed on someone even though you knew in their mind the whole idea of being with you was revolting.

But I still had the interview: I'd spend time with Felicity there. I didn't really think I'd be made a Sibyl, but for a little while, for a day, or maybe even an hour, I'd have her full attention focused on me and nothing but me.

6

I WAS GETTING INTO MY mom's car when someone pushed into the space between me and the door.

"Hello, Mrs. Rituveni," Mrs. Gimbel said. "You haven't been answering my calls!"

My mom seemed older than usual—older than Mrs. Gimbel, at least—with dark patches on her skin and rumpled clothing and hair she wearily pulled back into a ponytail as she came out of the car.

"You are Mrs. Gimbel?" she said. "You wanted to speak?"

"Uh." I looked between them.

"Just follow me."

And Mrs. Gimbel led us, not back the few steps to Ainsley but down the path I'd gone with Felicity. Did she want us to meet in the gazebo? I walked along with her, holding my backpack, and my mom put a hand on my shoulder and squeezed.

"How was class?" she said. "Are you learning everything?"

We were preparing for finals week.

"Uh, yeah," I said.

"You hardly ever study," my mom said.

"That's sort of my thing though," I said.

We hurried down the path, and then up the hill. St. George's had a different parking lot, and not a lot of people walked on the path between schools, but I saw two middle school boys look me up and down, and then whisper something, and my face went red. My mom hadn't noticed.

"Excuse me?" she said. "Will this take long?"

"Not long," Mrs. Gimbel said, looking back. "Sorry, but since Tara is still technically a St. George's student, I thought we should involve their administration in this."

"Uh, is this about me . . . ?" I stopped. She hadn't mentioned me missing the lunch meeting. Maybe she'd forgotten.

"Is this woman from the school?" my mom said. "I got some calls from someone, but I was too busy—"

"I am the faculty adviser for the Sibyls." Mrs. Gimbel looked back, and she frowned. "The organization that your daughter is trying to join. And now there is a situation to sort out."

"What situation?" my mom said. "Is this something to do with her gender? Perhaps she was not born female like the other girls, but many of them have other privileges she has not had. My girl had to struggle much to figure herself out at an early age, and I think even the cabinet secretaries and senators within your club could appreciate that."

My skin crawled. My mom was praising me, I guess, but something about it made me sick, and I hated her right then.

Mrs. Gimbel led us to St. George's.

Drew stood in the doorway, leering at me with that acne-ridden face. He was in a crisp dress shirt, not wrinkled or anything, and he surreptitiously slipped a finger toward the hem of my skirt. I reacted without thinking, pushing him away.

I was about to take over and show them the way to the conference room, but my mom said, "It's right here. God knows I've visited enough times."

Then, after nodding to the head secretary, Mrs. Fellman, we were in the main conference room: a drab room with blue walls and darker blue carpet. Outside, we saw sad, gloomy trees waving in the wind and a bunch of middle schoolers listlessly waiting to get picked up.

"Hello again," said the assistant headmaster, Dr. Eagleton. "This must be a record; it's been a whole four months since I've had you in my office, Tara."

My mom rubbed the bridge of her nose. "Now what is it? Our payments arrived on time."

I was still technically a student at St. George's—we paid tuition there and my scholarship came from there—I just happened to eat and take all my classes at Ainsley.

Mrs. Fellman shouted, "We've got Ms. Beaumont on the line."

My stomach dropped. It couldn't be. . . .

The screen at the front of the room flashed, and my heart dropped. She was on-screen: Evangeline Beaumont. Felicity and Liam's aunt. She had bookcases behind her, and she was sitting on a couch in a crisp white dress, smiling at the two of us. A glance off camera, and she held up a finger: "Just a minute, please."

Her face was luminous. I'd studied what made a girl's skull different from a boy's: all the stuff about proportions and brow ridges and cheekbones. And her face had it, almost like she'd gotten surgery. High, full cheeks, and a narrow jaw. She showed acres of eyelid when she blinked (my eyes were so recessed I didn't bother with eyeshadow; it just didn't show). Her hair was long and wavy and brown, and I tried not to stare at her narrow shoulders and smooth, slender arms.

"Hello there, yes, thank you," she said. "Oh, can I ask who's on the other line?"

Everyone seemed starstruck, except my mom, who whispered, "Who is this? Does she work for the school?"

Dr. Eagleton tripped over himself, thanking Evangeline for all her donations and her time.

Then Evangeline got smaller and took up only half the screen, which was somehow a lot more manageable. Dr. Pearson, an old woman who wore rimless glasses and had a very short haircut—she was gnomelike, in height, face, and voice—appeared on the other half the screen. She was the headmistress of Ainsley.

"Evangeline!" she said. "How are you doing? Sorry I couldn't attend your last soiree."

"Come up any time," Evangeline said. "That goes for you too, Headmaster. I'm almost always in. Visiting hours are Wednesday afternoons, but really just call ahead. I can make time."

"Evangeline, that's absurd," Dr. Pearson said. "You have *work* to do. We can't intrude on a whim."

"You can only work so much." Angel's voice was high and pure, like she was tapping on a crystal glass.

I put a hand to my throat, trying to imagine how to make that sound—no trans woman could do it, at least none who'd gone through male puberty.

"All right," Angel said. "Let me see . . ." She put on a pair of dark-rimmed spectacles, then brushed her hair to one side. Leaning forward a bit, she said. "Tara, is that you? My niece has mentioned so much about you! Both my niece *and* my nephew, actually. You're quite popular."

"Th-thanks," I said.

"I'm Angel," she said. "I'm on the board of the school, and I'm the main donor for the trust that maintains the Sibyls' scholarship. You must think it's the strangest thing on earth for an adult to take so much interest in her old high school."

"No," I said.

"Yes, yes," she said, laughing. "I see it in your eyes. Don't lie. You start out, and you're a fresh-faced alum, just entering college, and you go back to say hi to your favorite teachers. And they ask you to be on some panels or groups or do interviews. And before you know it, you're thirty-six and you realize the kids look at you as if you're inconceivably ancient—as if there's some Rubicon between you and them that they can't imagine ever crossing. Let me tell you, Tara, are you interested in public service work?"

"Y-yeah," I said.

"Trans rights, I assume," she said. "All the kids love to work on LGBT issues these days."

"N—" My mind was empty. "I don't know."

"Many, many good organizations do that," she said. "But remember to have fun. Life happens too quickly: it's very easy to get prematurely old in the service of your country."

My eyes shot open. That was—that was George Washington. I was about to mention the reference, but Dr. Pearson had taken over and was smoothly talking about all the institutional difficulties caused by my attempting to be a Sibyl despite not being enrolled at Ainsley. The scholarship fund was locked to one school. Taxes. All kinds of difficulties.

"What do you think about this, Tara?" Angel said. "My niece and nephew think I'm insane. They say these aren't real problems. I tell them the government would be very interested in catching me and this school in a tax violation."

"I, no, that seems right," I said. "Caesar's wife must be above reproach."

"Ahh," Angel said. "But can you say it in Latin?"

"Umm. Caesaribus uxorem— No, wait, it's from Plutarch. It's a Greek quote."

"I was only kidding," Angel said. "I'm not a Latin whiz like my niece. But being a Sibyl isn't really about classical knowledge, is it? And it's not exactly about a scholarship either, right? Would you take up the position even without a scholarship?"

"Sure," I said.

"Even if it meant the money was wasted, and some other girl didn't get it?" Angel said.

"Umm . . ."

"Dilemmas," Angel said. "I'm sorry, my lawyers will try to figure out the situation, but we might not be able to give the money to you. I wanted to apologize personally. . . ."

"I, uh, that's fine—"

"Excuse me." My mother had leaned in. "What is this nonsense? You are rich, are you not? Who cares where my son is enrolled?"

I hissed. It was okay for my mom to misgender me in private. I knew it only happened when she was emotional. But it looked really bad in the meeting.

"You can simply give her the money if she wins the award,"

my mom said. "We have no money. You in this room represent lots of money."

Dr. Pearson said, "I'm sorry, Mrs. Rituveni, it's all tied up in specific bequests, and—"

"That though is not true."

I made a nervous laugh, and I pulled on my mom's sleeve. Everyone was looking awkwardly at me.

Angel looked at her watch, gestured off-screen. "Excuse me," she said. "I have another meeting in—"

"These are lies," my mom said. "They are simply lies. The money is not all tied up in bequests. I've spent significant time at universities. I know how these things go. There is always some money in the general fund. Now, Dr. Eagleton, you made a promise to our child. Over the summer you made a promise that if we did not complain, she would be treated exactly as if she attended the school for girls, and now you renege on your word!"

"Nobody is owed this money," Mrs. Gimbel said. "Before this year, nobody even knew about the money."

"Just be honest," my mom said. "It is because she is trans. Simply be honest. Be honest with everyone. She is trans. So fine, we will hire a lawyer."

I coughed, convulsively. Angel frowned. Mrs. Gimbel's mouth went open, and she looked around the room. Everyone else was gritting their teeth. I'd heard my mom say "Fine, we will hire a lawyer" so many times this summer. I think that I actually heard the phrase in my sleep sometimes.

"We will sue you," she said. "You have deep pockets. My b—girl is one of your best students."

"Actually—"

"Even if she has poor grade performances, that is due only to mental suffering from the stigma and the trauma of being marked out as different."

"Mrs. Rituveni," Angel said. "I really have to go, but I absolutely feel for you, and we will do everything we can to—"

"Do not lie to me."

"To get the legal access to—"

"You are worth tens of millions," my mother said. "And yet you are chiseling pennies from a poor family. This is—"

"I'm sorry. I'm so sorry. Goodbye."

Her box went black, and Dr. Pearson grew to fill the whole screen.

Later, in the car, my mom was furious. She slapped her hand against the horn of the car, and she called my dad on speakerphone to relate the story.

"Are you surprised?" he said. "They will not give him a scholarship for rich girls."

"Her," she said. "You always get it wrong. The word is *her*. We cannot be fighting for her rights and be getting it wrong."

"Arai," my dad said. "Sorry, sorry. And you are playing a

dangerous game with *her* life. They know we live in Virginia. They can easily report us to the police if we make trouble."

"She is doing nothing wrong," my mom said. "She is on no drugs."

"Even the social transition is illegal now," he said. "You talk endlessly of the Governor but do not pay the slightest attention. A child in Fairfax was taken from his family for wearing a skirt to school. That will be us if people find out."

"Mom, Dad," I said. "Angel wouldn't do that."

"No, no, I am not saying that will happen," my dad said, his voice crackling over the phone. I was holding it between us, microphone side out toward my mom, as we drove through the wet, sticky streets. "But perhaps it is best to quit this club. We can pay for things."

"I asked the club adviser, and she said they will pay fifty thousand dollars," my mom said. "With that she can go anywhere. Otherwise, where will she go? The University of Virginia? No, that is not doable. She must leave the state, and that costs money. You are not thinking ahead."

"Actually, I wanted to see about using the money maybe for surgery," I said. "If I passed better, I could go anywhere."

My mom squinted at me, and she shook her head, then looked back at the road. "If you do not improve your grades, you will not even *get* into college."

"All Ainsley girls get into college somewhere."

"They get into schools for rich children—some Bennington

College type of place. Not schools for people like us."

Back when she was working, my mom had a coworker—a white woman—who sent her daughter to Bennington. My mom looked it up, and she couldn't believe how rich and spoiled everyone seemed, so the school had turned into her main example of a college for spoiled kids.

"The only two colleges in the world are not Bennington and UVA," my dad said.

"She couldn't get into UVA perhaps," my mom said. "It would be Virginia Tech, out in Blacksburg, where they have the KKK. Or George Mason, where all the conservative thinkers are headquartered. No. No, no, you must leave this to me."

"We will talk later, in private," my dad said.

"Umm," I said. "So your theory is that Ainsley actually *could* give me the money but is choosing not to? Because I'm trans? You don't believe their explanations at all?"

"What is the difficulty in giving money?" my mom said. "You write a check. It is that simple. There is no need for complications. Rich people pretend it is complicated, but it isn't. Perhaps you pay a little more in taxes, but if you believe in justice, then you pay the taxes."

My mom was actually making a lot of sense.

"Angel wouldn't—" I remembered what Liam had said, about Angel being a TERF and hating trans people. My stomach flopped. It just . . . I shook my head, like water was caught in my ear. "At least they're not stopping me from being a Sibyl at all."

"They will," my mother said. "You do not know how these people think. They assume we are shallow and only care for money. They will offer us a pittance for you to not join the club, and they will expect us to take it. But do not worry, I will negotiate them upward."

"Mom," I said. "I *do* actually want to be a Sibyl."

"Ahh, my girl, but that is not possible, I think."

"So . . . but . . . Maybe I shouldn't take money. Like . . . if . . . I don't want to set a bad example. I don't want to *prove* that we only want money."

"Right now there is no money," she said. "Nor will there be unless we are careful. For now, just keep quiet about this. Your father and I will handle the rest. And do not tell any of your friends about this conversation. The time for publicity is not yet. Your father is right; there are some dangers. But don't worry."

I hadn't worried much until that moment, but suddenly my heart started to throb. I forced myself to smile and say all right.

7

BEFORE OUR LATIN FINAL, WHITNEY sat down next to me in the hall, her shoulder touching mine, and she said, "I'm gonna die. I was up all night."

"Oh yeah?" I said.

"Come on," she said. "Are we still in a fight? Liam called me out, by the way. I apologize. If we're gonna be Sibyls together, we've got to be cool."

I shrugged. So much had happened since then. I couldn't remember what it felt like to care what Whitney thought about me.

"Yes," I said. "We're okay. Even though you lied about not having a famous Greek already picked out for the Sibyls."

Whitney laughed, and she looked up at me with a big smile, which made me remember why I'd wanted to be her friend in the first place. She was in tights, so she could lift her knees without worrying about exposure, and she lifted them, then planted them on the ground and swung herself upright.

"I don't know why I said that," Whitney said. "Hannah and I had been brainstorming for weeks actually. Just seemed weird to admit it. But then you thought about it for a second and gave her a much better one, so I guess we're the jerks."

"Oh! Is she still going to do Clytemnestra?"

"Yep," Whitney said. "She keeps asking if you sabotaged her, and I said you weren't like that."

"No," I said. "I just wanted someone who'd pair with Penelope so I could talk to Felicity."

"Oh yeah!" Whitney said. "We did do that exercise that day, right? Hannah was a wreck. We didn't discuss the pairing at all. Just talked about you, really, and whether you had it out for her."

"Felicity and I had such a weird talk that day."

"Hmm . . ."

I waited for a second, and I could feel Whitney's breath radiating through her chest, making her arm shake where it was touching me.

"You're not gonna ask me more?"

"Sorry! I didn't know if you wanted to talk."

"Of course I did," I said. "Like, do y—" I took a breath. I was about to get mad at her, have it all come spilling out, say something like, *Do you even care what's going on with me?* But, of course, I knew the answer was no, she didn't. She wasn't my real friend, and that was all right.

"Yeah, I really like Felicity," I said. "I'm gonna be a Sibyl, I think. I want to be one."

"That's good," Whitney said. "You deserve it. I'll be one too, I bet."

"Yeah."

"Hannah will be really disappointed."

"Maybe she doesn't deserve to be one," I said.

"Still . . ."

The hallway was full of chattering girls waiting for their finals to start. In a corner, a sophomore was quietly crying and another girl was patting her on the shoulder. Teachers were in the halls trying to move people along to their proper rooms, but nobody was moving.

"So do you like Felicity?" Whitney said.

"I, umm, I . . . no . . . yes? I think? But is she gay?"

"Who knows? I bet she is. She plays field hockey. So . . . that's usually a pretty decent clue."

Yeah, I'd seen her on the pitch, hitting other people with her stick. And she had the cuts and bruises on her arms that all the field hockey girls got. I'd imagined, in my daydreams, going to see her play, going, as . . . as her girlfriend, and rushing out to kiss her when they won the game.

"You really think so?" I said.

Then Mrs. Gimbel came into the hallway. Ever since our meeting, I'd started to reconsider everything she'd said and done around me. Like, wasn't she a bit hard on me? I hadn't mind getting picked on before—teachers were supposed to do that—but it seemed unfair, like she was trying to send a message that I wasn't good enough and should quit the Sibyls contest.

"What're you wearing?" Mrs. Gimbel said.

My hand went to my face. "Um, just foundation . . ."

"On your legs," she said. "What're those?"

I was in black tights. "Tights?"

"They're supposed to be Ainsley colors. Those aren't."

"Oh, uh, okay." I looked at Whitney, who was looking away. Her tights were actually brown and gold. Whoops. Since I wasn't officially an Ainsley student, nobody had ever fully told me the rules, given me the manual. "Should I buy some . . . ?"

"The uniform store will be out," Whitney said. "They always run out by the end of the semester. Here, take mine." She got up, and she tugged on them, pulling them off. "Wow," she said. "I bet this is something we'd never do if we were coed."

But when I started to shimmy out of mine, Ms. Gimbel said, "What're you doing?! Go to the bathroom and come back quick."

"Uhh . . ." I normally used the single-person bathroom, because it was less weird, but that was on the other side of campus from us.

"I'll go with you," Whitney said.

Then we were down the hall. She was still holding her

tights like a limp worm. "You can't be happy about getting interviewed by her."

"Oh, uh, yeah," I said. "But I bet Angel's vote counts for more than hers, right?"

"I guess," Whitney said.

We were in the closest bathroom—somehow it seemed all right with Whitney alongside—and Whitney was telling me about last year's process for the Sibyls. It took place, like every year, in the mansion up on the hill. Whitney said normally the interviews weren't a big deal. You went there and you talked for a day in a big conference room, and you got asked about classical civilization and stuff, and then you got asked to leave, and the Sibyls discussed who to pick, and the losers went home. Normally the discussion took about an hour, and it was unanimous, but last year, it'd gone almost the entire night.

"My sister didn't want Strife," Whitney whispered. "She knew something was off about her. And my sister went to Angel and asked her to step in, and after a lot of discussion, Angel let the majority pick: Hecuba, Andromache, and Thetis all wanted Strife for some reason, so she got in."

"What about Felicity?"

"Oh, Antigone was certain to get picked," Whitney said. "That was obvious. Everyone wanted her. Anyway, I guess the loser, Claire Cooper—do you know her?—I guess she had proof that Strife knew beforehand about the scholarship, and she told Angel and Dr. Pearson that Strife only wanted the money, and when they asked Strife, she said, 'Of course I wanted the money. Do you think I'm stupid?' And when they asked her how she'd known about the money, she mentioned that she'd overheard some parents talking about it during pickup, and she'd kept it secret so she could get the scholarship, but now she was going to tell everyone. And she did! It's so dumb. All Strife had to do was not admit she knew."

"Like you," I said.

"Huh?" she said.

"You must've known there was money. Even last year, you knew. That's why you studied to get the Greek and Latin prizes."

"What?" Whitney said. "No. I just love that stuff."

I nodded. "Mmm-hmmm."

"It's true!" Whitney said.

"Okay."

"My sister doesn't tell me anything!"

"No, no, you're right," I said. Of course, that was a clear lie, or how could she know about the deliberations from last year. But if I was going to call out every lie an Ainsley girl told, I wouldn't have any friends left (except, I guess, for Felicity and Strife).

"Anyway, here," Whitney said, throwing over her tights.

I didn't put on Whitney's tights, which were still uncomfortably warm, just threw mine in the garbage and went back with her. She noticed me clutching her tights when I came out but didn't say anything. When we got to the room, there were only two empty chairs, far apart, and she touched my arm for a second before taking the one in the front.

After finals were over, I had nothing to do. Whitney was going to visit her grandpa in Ohio for the few days before coming back for the Sibyl interview, so I couldn't hang with her. My dad was still working, and my mom was taking care of a neighbor's two kids, who ran around the house all day and even came into my room to jump on my bed.

"What the hell?" I said. "You let them in here?"

"Arai," she said. "Don't complain. They've even napped in your bed before."

She was worried they would tell the neighbors I was trans, so she asked me not to wear girls' stuff around them, which sucked. But the boy said, "Why are girl clothes in your closet?"

"Uh," I said. "My sister used to live here."

"What happened to her?" he said.

"She died when a lizard crawled down her throat," I said. "Now she's a ghost who haunts the place and wears these clothes at night."

I thought he would cry, but instead his eyes got wide, and he rushed off to grab his sister. I shook my head.

It's weird when people say they're bored. I can always find ways to have fun. Video games, of course, but books too, or memorizing my speeches, or just daydreaming. I'd been doing a lot of that last one. The Sibyls were important. If I won, it'd be in the news. Until her meeting with Angel, my mom hadn't totally realized how huge a deal this was. But instead of being intimidated, she was determined not to back down. That scholarship would change everything for my family.

But what it meant for me was that someway, somehow, I'd be able to go on blockers, and, in a few months, on hormones too. After all, if I was a famous trans, it wouldn't make sense for me to have basically the body of a boy. So I lay in bed and rubbed my legs and my shoulders and my waist, as if rubbing could make the flesh disappear. It seemed impossible that I could look into the mirror and actually see a girl. It *was* impossible, actually, because something I never told anyone was that when I thought of myself in a girl's body, I imagined being white.

Like, it wasn't a choice I made—it's just that the Indian girl version of myself didn't come. Instead, I was sporty and angular, like Felicity or Hannah or one of the girls at school. I'd be able to go outside, could date, could be trans whenever and wherever I wanted—choose to tell people instead of having it just come out. I could have a future.

One winter day, my mom asked, "Where would you go? What college?"

"Smith, maybe?" I said. "Or Wellesley? I guess they're saying I could get into an Ivy League if I became a Sibyl, but with my grades . . ."

"No, no, the Ivy League wouldn't want someone with your report cards, but these Seven Sisters are not too awful. Except are they not both schools for girls? Why go to another one? Even most cisgender girls go to coed schools. And it would be very constricting if you later decided to become a male."

"I just like girls," I said. "I know you think it's dumb, but being at Ainsley is great. Everything is so fun. Even when it's awful, it's fun. Like, Whitney and I gossiped in the bathroom the other day, and I almost insulted her, but then I walked it back. And that would never happen if there were boys around. Or maybe it would, I dunno. But I just don't need them, really."

"And wouldn't you date a boy?"

"Err, theoretically? But not any of the boys I actually know." I shrugged. Maybe when I was an adult, and the boys weren't so stupid and awful, then I'd want to be with one. But at that moment, I'd love never seeing one again.

"So you've been having interest in girls?" my mom said. "I know you have a girlfriend, but remind me who it is?"

"What?" I said. "No! I don't have a girlfriend. Where did you hear that?"

"Simply from around. From other parents."

I narrowed my eyes at her. My mom didn't know anything, I thought. Definitely not about Felicity. I hadn't even gotten up the courage to text her. Part of me kept thinking Felicity would text first, but I guessed that wasn't happening.

My hand went to my phone. The kids downstairs were still romping around. I got up, crossed my legs, and I went to a social app that the girls at school used to chat. I'd had a message to Felicity composed for days.

Hey, I wrote. I like you. Want to see each other before the interview starts?

With a single tap, the message went out, and I stared at it, my heart throbbing, thinking that was crazy. I'd done it. I'd done it. And, of course, I ruined things, sending a few more messages, offering stuff we could do, telling her I couldn't hang out in Virginia but didn't she live in DC anyway? And we could go to the mall or whatever.

Then I texted Liam about it:

Liam: Oh hey, that's cool! What did she say!

Tara: Nothing yet.

Liam: Let me know!

Tara: But you hate her.

Liam: I don't hate her. She's my cousin. And if you got together, I'd be happy. Would definitely protect her during the revolution.

Tara: But if we're not together then it's off with her head?

Liam: Oh yeah, definitely. Sorry, cuz, family doesn't mean anything when it comes to the revolution.

Tara: But dating your friend does!

Liam: Of course, because then she'd be one of us.

Tara: You're ridiculous.

Liam: Hey, so . . . are you feeling okay about the Sibyl thing? I've been meaning to reach out.

Tara: Yeah, I guess. What do you mean?

Liam: Just my aunt. I know she scratched you off the list. It's totally awful. I'm planning on protesting when they announce the new Sibyls. It'd be great if you could maybe record something to put online? But I know you wouldn't want to get exposed like that. Maybe Felicity would? My aunt loves her, so that would really hit home.

Tara: I didn't get scratched off. They mentioned I might not get money because of some tax thing, but that's not the same as being scratched off.

Liam: Oh. Maybe I was wrong. So you're headed to the interviews tomorrow?

Tara: What?

Liam: They're tomorrow. They didn't tell you?

Tara: No. We were waiting for them to call and fill us in.

My phone lit up with a call from Liam, and I ended it. Then I looked up, staring at the falling leaves without seeing anything, until my mom asked what was wrong.

I watched my parents from the stairs, as if I were a four-year-old who'd snuck down after bedtime.

My mom had the cell phone in her hand. "I will call the

Washington Post front desk," she said. "And I will say that a famous civil rights lawyer is discriminating against my trans child."

"They won't take your call," my dad said.

"Use Twitter," I said. "Reporters take tips off Twitter."

"Show me," she said, coming to the stairs. "Show me now."

"No," my dad said, standing up. "No, that's too much. The school will be locked into their positions if this comes out. They tried to pull something on us, but we caught them. One cannot have an outcry before the interview itself. Tara needs to win, to be clearly the best. And if she doesn't win, then that is the end of it."

"Well, there's no winning," I said.

"Do the other girls get a vote or not?"

"Yeah . . ." I said.

"And will they vote for you?"

"I . . . I don't know."

Felicity still hadn't answered my text.

"I think so."

"If we speak out now, they will simply say Tara is not the best. They will point to her grades or to some other little problem. The only way we have a case is if the other girls support her."

"This is absurd," my mom said. "You know it is not a fair competition. They will maneuver and cheat to make sure she doesn't win. The time to speak out is *now*. After the contest it will be done, and they'll say, *Oh, but she lost.*"

My heart was pounding, watching them argue. I was honestly just glad they were worrying about it. I'd do whatever they said. And then I had an odd out-of-body experience. I remembered them sitting down across the table from me, last year, telling me that I couldn't transition yet. They'd been calm but firm, with all kinds of arguments about how it was too hard, given the Governor. My mom hadn't offered to call a newspaper then.

"What do you think?" my dad said. "You are almost an adult. It was your skills that got us here. What should we do?"

"I just think . . ." My throat closed up. I imagined them saying last year, *Screw it, we'll get our girl her drugs.* Imagined not feeling so wrong and out of place and like my body all the time was being twisted and molded into something grotesque.

"I think that I want to be on hormones," I said. "When I turn sixteen. That's five months away. It's time."

"Ahh," my dad said.

And my mom looked up too, not really comprehending. The dog took this moment to creep up onto the couch, guessing that my mom was too busy to shoo him away.

"We will talk," my dad continued.

"No, it makes sense," my mom said. "After this news comes out, our position will be weaker if she's not on the hormones."

"Let us discuss it together, the two of us," my dad said. Then, to me: "Can you leave us alone?"

104

So I crept back up the stairs, feeling small and scared, and I repacked my bag for the interviews. They'd said to bring a sleeping bag, in case I was chosen and needed to stay the night, and I had an old one from my Boy Scout days. But no need to bring a uniform. It would be semiformal clothes, although we were supposed to bring hiking stuff and things for outdoors, and changes of clothes for dinner too. No devices—they'd be taken away once we were inside. Medications, if we needed them.

My phone chirped, and my heart stirred. A message from Felicity.

Hey, she said. I like you too! Would love to hang out. Am I gonna see you at the interviews tomorrow? Let's talk more then.

I looked at the phone, eyebrows knitted. *'I like you too'? What in the world did that mean?*

8

LIAM LAUGHED AND LAUGHED AND laughed and laughed and laughed (electronically).

Liam: Welcome to straight girl BS.

Tara: Okay. But what does it meeeeeeeaaaaaaaaaan? Should I've been more clear?

Liam: Nobody knows. Nobody can ever know what they mean.

Having Liam to laugh with me over the whole thing was kind of nice, and it made me think, *Well, at least if I lose and don't enter the Sibyls, maybe I can still be friends with Hannah and Whitney and the other Sibyls.*

And that made me remember Whitney. When I texted her she wrote back:

Whitney: Wow, that seems like a good sign!

Tara: Really?

Whitney: She said the same thing back to you that you said to her. That's good, right? But I don't have the most experience or anything.

Tara: Okay. I hadn't thought of it that way.

I wrote that to Liam, who said, That's one way of looking at it, but I don't know. . . .

Then I was like, *Wait, is this how group text chats get formed? Is this the moment?* I had heard so much about these mythical beasts—ongoing group chats—but had been afraid to ask if they were real. So I was like, *Okay, compared to asking a girl out, this is nothing,* and I roped both Liam and Whitney into a chat, being like, *Hey, blah blah, we're going to be seeing each other in a few days anyway.*

Whitney: Great idea! Let me invite Hannah!

Hannah: Hey.

Whitney: Hannah, you're used to ignoring people. What would you say this text from F back to T means?

Hannah: She's probably just busy. And she's like, we're gonna see each other anyway.

Tara: Yeah. But, like, at the interviews. With Mrs. Gimbel. Who hates me. At an old stuffy mansion with no heat.

Whitney: Does it not have heat???? I can't do that! I was worried there would be old creaky radiators that have toxic mold in them! But no heat??????

Liam: It's DC. You need heat, or the pipes freeze and burst.

Whitney: But isn't the house like two hundred years old????? Did they have heat back then???????

Liam: No, but there's heat now. There's running water. There's electricity. Trust me, guys, my aunt wouldn't live anywhere that wasn't nice.

Whitney: By the way, Liam, we should hang out! You promised to keep being my friend after you went up the hill, but you're hardly ever around!

Oh yeah, I sometimes forgot they'd all known each other before I did—I'd met all three of them at the same time, while we were doing the fall play at Ainsley last year. And they'd all gone to middle school together, so they actually knew each other pretty well. Kind of funny how Liam always hated on them and never mentioned those connections that he had.

Liam texted me on the side.

Liam: So you're going after all?

Tara: Yeah, if I can.

Liam: Because we should ask W and H to boycott. They probably wouldn't but you never know. Anyway I've been holding off on sounding the alert, because I didn't know if you'd want me to make a fuss.

Tara: My parents have some crazy plan to get the Washington Post involved.

Liam: Wow! Your parents are incredible.

Tara: I guess. Hope it doesn't end up w them deported!

Liam: Oh. Are they undocumented???????

Tara: No. But no permanent visas. And my mom can't work at all. That's why they're so worried about the government coming after us if I was taking anything.

Meanwhile the conversation with Whitney was still going on:

Whitney: Should I invite Robin to the chat, since she's gonna be with us too?

Hannah: Mmm, if you want.

Tara: I think that means no.

Robin was notoriously intense and weird, and she'd pin you down and talk off your ear for hours about, like, Davy Crockett or President McKinley—she went beyond nerd, into stuff that absolutely *nobody* cared about.

But Liam texted me privately, saying:

Liam: You should invite her. Don't get into this Ainsley mean girl shit. You're too good for that.

Tara: Oh fine. You're right. Wow, the mean girl thing really creeps up on you, doesn't it?

Liam: I wouldn't know, I don't play those games.

Tara: Ouch!

So we ended up inviting Robin, and she had a *ton* of information about the interviews, including a lot of pretty specific stuff.

Robin: What's most fun is there are robes and outfits

and everything is quasi mystical, and it's all based on ancient mystery cults. It's very pagan.

Tara: You're kidding.

Robin: The founder of the Sibyls was Winifred Coatesworth—she was obsessed with pagan stuff.

Liam: Yeah, and she was also super racist. She traveled all around the world and was really condescending about other cultures that she saw, and when she was a congresswoman she voted to limit immigration from Asia.

Tara: Yeah, but that's normal right? Basically everything white people say about India—even today!—is really condescending.

Liam: I dunno, it was pretty bad, I think.

Robin: And when she was in Congress she voted against the war! Said we had provoked the Japanese and that we had no business fighting the Germans, since they weren't fighting us.

Liam: Oh yeah, I saw that. She was one of only two people to vote against WWII. The other was another woman, who was an outright pacifist and didn't believe in war at all.

Whitney: So was she, like, a literal Nazi? Lots of Americans back then were sort of Nazis.

Robin: Like Lindbergh!

After a minute Robin added:

Robin: And JFK's dad.

And then she had a stream of people from that era who liked the Nazis. It went on for such a long time, and I was in my bed laughing. The chat just went on for hours, between us talking about Felicity and sharing details about the retreat and then Robin busting in with weird early-American-history stuff. And I was like, *Wait, I don't want to beat any of these people. I mean, I do want to, and I will. But I also don't.*

That afternoon I got a text from Felicity.

Felicity: Are you working on your talk about Alecto? I bet it's going to be awesome.

Tara: It really won't be. I'm actually a terrible speaker. Full of umms and ahhs, and I get confused and lose track of myself.

Felicity: No.

Tara: Err, I didn't ask a question. I'm telling you a fact. I do speech and debate. I know that I'm bad.

Felicity: Well you're just wrong. What can I say? You are Alecto. None of the other girls has that. They're still doing Penelope and Clytemnestra, I checked. And Robin is going with Tiresias.

Tara: Oh wow, that's one I was thinking about!

Felicity: My aunt and Mrs. Gimbel will hate that.

Tiresias was a man!

Tara: Not for those seven years! And anyway, they'll hate mine too.

Felicity: Look, I think it's not worth being a Sibyl if you can't be yourself. But I dunno, maybe you see it differently.

Tara: Becoming a Sibyl could really help with my trans stuff. My parents are really invested in it. But I need to actually get picked.

Felicity: Hecuba and Strife and I love you.

Tara: But don't Gimbel and Angel and Calliope have equal votes too? That would mean it was tied!

Felicity: Personally I wouldn't want to fake it and bring a name I didn't believe in. But whatever, who else were you thinking of?

Tara: I've been kicking around Sophrosyne. You know, the goddess version of what the Sibyls stand for.

Felicity: Ohh. Huh. Maybe they'd like that actually. I forgot she was a goddess too.

Tara: And I'd write about what those values really mean to me! How I'm not a troublemaker. How I value everything she stands for: restraint, wisdom, listening, tradition.

Felicity: That actually could be good.

Tara: See!

Felicity: And you'd be okay being called Sophrosyne?

Tara: Sure. It'd be fine.

I felt like that's all I did these days, tell people I'd be fine, or that I didn't care or wasn't bothered. And after all this time I had no idea whether or not it was true.

Felicity: Well if that's what you want, yeah it would probably help. But don't worry about not becoming a Sibyl. Like I told you, it doesn't mean what it used to. Unless you just care about the money.

Tara: No!

And in that moment, what I had written was true.

Felicity: Strife says it's dumb to pretend people don't want the money, and I actually hate that the money exists. But the point of the group is that we stand for something, that we think for ourselves, and say what we really think. You're so clearly the right person—I don't understand how people don't get that. Like all these St. George's guys told me that you only transitioned to get into college, and I was like . . . that's the dumbest thing I've ever heard. It really made me lose respect for them. I thought people at St. George's were smart! But a) nobody would ever do that, and b) Alecto DEFINITELY wouldn't do that.

I couldn't believe Felicity was texting me. We'd exchanged numbers a few weeks ago. I could've been texting with her all this time! I was in my room, listening to the faint sound of the TV downstairs. The wind outside made the trees scrape against our house, and our dog rustled and scratched at his bed.

Tara: Where were you talking to St. George's guys?

Felicity: Cotillion. It's this DC thing. Fancy balls and stuff.

Tara: You're joking. Like some Pride and Prejudice stuff? What did you wear?

Felicity: Exactly like P&P, yeah.

The three dots flashed, and I saw a photo of her in a light green dress, with bare shoulders, sitting impassively in a gazebo. Her long lashes were teased out, and she wore dark eyeliner that stood sharply against her pale skin. Only the scars on her knees and shins seemed the same. The guy next to her, in his suit, clutched her arm, and she looked stony-faced, into the middle distance.

Tara: Wow you're having LOTS of fun.

Felicity: It's alright. Tradition. Would be better with you involved. It's the only time Liam and I get along.

Tara: Liam goes too! You're kidding.

Felicity: Totally. The girls love him—he's one of the only guys who can lead.

Tara: I am dying. This is the greatest thing I've ever heard. I would kill to go to a cotillion.

Felicity: Happy to invite you sometime. It's queer friendly and stuff. Just weird. Lots of old people around. And St. George's boys, tons of them. I've gotta say I'm starting to get why you came to Ainsley. Our girls can be illogical sometimes, but these guys are way worse. I had a guy leave me in the middle of a dance, he got so mad.

Tara: You called him out!

Felicity: Of course, he was saying stuff that wasn't true. Like that he knows your neighbors, and they say you aren't really trans.

I could've talked to her forever, but she reminded me to go back to my speech about Alecto. Just remind people what she stands for, and why those things resonate with the values of the Sibyls: intelligence, ambition, courage, and wisdom.

So I wrote something down. And when I spoke the words, my ears burned—not out of embarrassment, but because it sounded kinda nice.

By the next morning we still hadn't gotten the information officially, although my mom had been calling and calling the school. But at around 8:00 a.m., my mom got a message on her voice mail. I saw her in the kitchen holding the phone in her hand, her face screwed up, looking like she was going to smash it on the ground.

"What's wrong?"

"Nothing," she said.

"Come on. . . . Is it—is it about me?"

She took a deep breath. "Oh, my baby," she said, putting out an arm. "Come here."

I came close, and she grabbed me into a hug, and she said,

"Bend down, bend down," and she kissed me on the head.

I didn't have feelings; my brain was full of static. "What's wrong?"

"It's not your problem."

I went upstairs, and I sat in bed. The interviews were starting in a few hours. And a picture came into my head of my mom the day she got her visa renewal rejected. I'd known something was wrong—I'd listened when my parents said it wasn't my business, but deep down I'd known! And still I'd waited for weeks, hoping it was okay, afraid to ask for the truth.

So I went downstairs, and I saw her on the phone talking to my dad. I stood straight, and I took in a breath. I said, "Mom, this is about me. I want to know."

She looked at me, and she said, "One minute, I'm playing the message for Tanay, and then I'll get back on the call."

"Tara," I said.

"Tara, I mean. Sorry."

She got off, and she turned the phone to speaker, and I heard Mrs. Gimbel's voice: "We've come to a decision about Tara's eligibility. We're hoping you'll call so we can discuss more in person. So just, uh, give me a call. . . ."

"Now is the moment," my mom said. "Right now, it might almost be too late, but we need to try. I can see if any reporters will answer our call. This woman, Angel, she is famous. She has won the Presidential Medal of Freedom, for God's sake. If we get publicity she will back down."

Our kitchen was drafty and cold, and I was in socks and pajama pants, bundled up in an Ainsley fleece. The winter morning light streamed through the bare branches of the trees, but the December sun wasn't very warm.

"We—" I stopped myself. I was about to say something like, *We don't know what she means.* But my mom was right. We knew. Mrs. Gimbel wouldn't have left a message like that if she just wanted to invite me to have a nice time at the interviews.

"The question is," my mom said, "whether to threaten them first with bad publicity—to get some money in return, make a settlement—but I bet they will think we're too cowardly and will try to bluff us out. We should instead go to the press right now!"

"I . . . I . . . but . . . what about the Governor? The government will find out that I'm trans."

"You're talking now like your father," she said. "We cannot let this go. It's for your future."

Some power above stopped me from screaming at her that going on hormones was about my future. That this was just a dumb club—that the real thing was the thing she always put off, telling me I'd be endangering our family if it went ahead. I took a deep breath and said it calmly instead.

"I want to go on hormones."

"What?" she said. "That isn't—"

"It is that," I said. "If you go to the press, then I go on the drugs. . . ."

"It's not so simple," she said. "Doctors are scared. They don't prescribe—they don't want—"

"Then I'll order them illegally online. We'll get someone to see me secretly. This is insane. You'll fight the Governor for a scholarship but not for my hormones?"

"Tara!" she said. "I am doing this all for you. In two years you'll be eighteen."

"My body will be *ruined*," I said. "I'll be a boy."

"You were a boy for many years and never complained."

"I did, but you didn't listen."

"These exaggerations of yours are ridiculous and tiring. You pretend as if every trans teen in the country is on hormones, but it isn't true. There are fewer than five thousand teens beginning any sort of drugs or hormones for transitioning every year. Five thousand in the whole country! That is much less than the number of transgenders. You can wait until eighteen and be perfectly fine."

And that was true! Of course it was true! Everyone said it. Everyone on Reddit was like, *Fifteen is really young, and it's okay if you need to wait. In fact, you're lucky! I didn't even suspect I was trans until I was twenty-five. I can't believe you get to go to college as a girl.* And they were right! I was unbelievably lucky!

But I still couldn't stop staring at my forehead and thinking:

I'm already hideous and broken and marked forever by the wrong puberty.

"So please," my mom said. "Enough with these emotional blackmails that you—"

We were interrupted by my dad calling us back, and my mom looped him in, telling him more about our argument than about anything else, and he weighed in, taking the opposite view, saying maybe we can do the drugs illegally, but we should not complain to the press—the government could easily get his visa revoked too, and then where would we be?

I never told people about my mom's visa because white people wouldn't get it. They'd be like, *Oh, so you're undocumented*, or *Oh, so it's bad luck*, or they thought we'd broken the rules somehow. No. There was a program so the spouses of people on H-1Bs, like my dad, could work too, for as long as their partners did. And my mom had worked under that program as an engineer for fifteen years, renewing it every three years, which she could do because my dad's green card application was still in the process of going through. But then they ended the program and there was just . . . nothing to do. Nobody to talk to about it. Some people in my dad's category were getting their renewal requests rejected too, and if that happened, he'd have to go back to India and neither he nor my mom would ever get a green card.

The phone in my mom's hand chirped, and she put it to

her head, speaking to my dad in a stream of Hindi. Then she tapped a button, and his voice emerged, hoarse and distant.

"They have us trapped," he said. "We cannot do this. Cannot fight. Let's call them and get some money out of them at least."

My mom was about to argue again. I sat on the couch, listening to them. I'd heard these kinds of arguments so many times. My mom was angry. She didn't want to live like this. She'd been all set to just go back to India with my dad the moment I turned eighteen, but they were like, *Well, Tara will need our insurance, and she will never be able to come to India if she's trans, so we'll need the ability to stay here somehow.*

I texted Felicity: Hey, I'm having an emergency, can we talk?

"Don't do anything," I yelled. "I'm talking to Felicity, Angel's niece—she's a member of the Sibyls."

My phone immediately rang.

"What's up?" Felicity said.

My hand clamped tight around the phone.

"Hey," I said. "So, I'm not sure you knew, but, uh, your aunt is pressuring the school to not let me compete. To become a Sibyl, I mean."

"Oh," she said.

"Huh," I said. "So . . . you did know?"

"Not really," she said. "She was mad, yeah, but . . ."

"So you *did* kind of know."

"I didn't," she said. "Not really. I told my auntie you're the best and you deserve to win."

"Okay," I said. "Well, Gimbel left a message basically saying they're gonna make me withdraw."

"Wow," Felicity said. "That's . . . that's not right."

"Yeah," I said. "So what're you gonna do?"

I could almost hear her blink.

"I, uh, I'll talk to my aunt . . ." Felicity said.

"Antigone," I said. "Talk won't do it. If you don't want to help, that's fine. But if you do, then you can't be like these other kids and just do something that feels good. Now is the time to prove what you are, whether you're a true friend."

"Okay," she said. "Okay. Don't do anything. Hold on. Do you trust me?"

"Yeah."

"Nice reference, by the way."

We'd had to read *Oedipus Rex* in English class. Antigone was a character in another Sophocles play. I'd read it after learning Felicity's name, and I'd underlined the lines Antigone spoke to her sister, Ismene, which began, "Now is the time to prove . . ."

Antigone's brother had died in a rebellion, and the king had orders that he be left unburied to rot in the field, but Antigone defies him, buries her kin, and is executed for her actions.

"Where do you live? I'll come to you."

After I gave my address, the phone went silent.

After I filled them in, my mom said, "Okay, your dad is almost home. Let's order some dosas and discuss with him."

9

WE SAT QUIETLY IN OUR cold house, waiting for the Indian food to arrive. Do other people of color order out their own kind of food? We order Indian food all the time. People are always like, *Mexican food tastes different in Mexico, Chinese food tastes different in China*, but that's not true for Indian food, at least not our kind. I've been to restaurants in India where they serve idlis and dosas that look exactly the same.

My mom said, "When the food comes, let's discuss hormones. Maybe it's time."

"Huh?" my dad said, like he'd forgotten that entire part of the thing.

"Maybe we should go to India," she said. "There are trans people there. And we can definitely get any drug."

"Now you are just being crazy. You are the one who always

insisted she could not be trans in India, and you were right!" my dad said. "America is the place for her. She just needs to live in California. Or even DC. We need to sell our home. I'll discuss with a Realtor."

"Tell me," she said. "What's this about your body being ruined? I have googled it, and plenty of trans girls take the drugs at eighteen."

"It's different for everyone," I said. And yeah, I'd exaggerated. Eighteen was still young. And I saw how unfair it was to put things that way, to make my mom think it was life and death, and that I'd never have a normal life if I didn't go on right away.

"But I just want my real life to start. Like . . . how can I date, looking like this? Or be at all normal? Like, if I looked different, don't you think the school wouldn't be so against me? What they care about is how strange it looks—a hulking boy getting a girl's scholarship."

"She has a point," my father said.

"They will always find a way to discriminate," my mom said. "That's what it means to live here. America isn't like India; it doesn't reckon with its own past."

"Arai," my dad said. "Not this. That man has turned Kashmir into a giant concentration camp. Is that a reckoning?"

That was another fight my parents sometimes had. Neither of my parents liked India's Hindu nationalist prime minister, but my dad thought India was a terrible place to live, while my mom thought the country was a lot better than it was when they'd left. Before I'd come out as trans, my mom had talked a lot about moving back as soon as I got into college. She hadn't mentioned that in a while, but I suddenly thought, *Maybe she wants me to get this scholarship because if college is cheaper, they won't need to earn as much and can go home sooner.*

"You are beautiful just how you are, of course," my dad said. "And you look surprisingly like a girl, I'll say. But maybe you have a point. . . ."

"I've been waiting twenty years for my real life to start," my mom said. "It doesn't work that way. We must decide what in life is truly important. For us, it's making sure you are safe and taken care of. Plenty of people transition at eighteen, with drugs, and they are fine. But if we are deported, you will lose your school, lose everything. You are lucky you were born here. If you weren't a citizen, you would *have* to leave if you turned twenty-one before we gained permanent status."

That'd happened to a friend of ours from temple. They'd been born a year before their parents arrived, and now they'd aged out and weren't covered under their parent's visa—legally it was like they hadn't grown up in the States at all. But I was a citizen, thank god.

My parents' problems were so big. Part of me was angry, like, couldn't they just *handle* this? It was their job to take care of me. But they'd tried to keep me out of this, and I'd bullied my way in.

"In any case, your transitioning will be benefited if you get this scholarship. You can go to some other school in some other state, where things are friendlier, and you'll have much less debt. Otherwise, you'll need to attend a college in Virginia, like it or not."

"Actually," I said. "That's another thing. I was thinking with the money we save, maybe we could hire someone to, er, to work on my face? If I need to?"

"Work on your face?" my mom said. "What is this? What is wrong with your face?"

"It's a boy's face," I said.

"Nonsense," she said.

"No, but boys can get these features that make it really hard to—"

"We'll figure it out," my dad said. "Will your friend call, or what?"

Just then my phone rang.

"Hey," Felicity said. "I'm at your house, I think? Someone else is trying to get in?"

I ran to the door, where the food guy was walking away, and Felicity waved at me from beyond the fence.

Felicity wanted to just whisk me away, but my parents insisted she come in and eat. I was gonna explain to her what everything was, but she was like, "Oh, I love idlis and dosas. Is this the sambar?"

Cutting up the idli with a fork, she introduced herself to my parents, called them Mr. and Mrs. Rituveni.

I said, "You mean Dr. and Dr. Rituveni."

But my mom rolled her eyes and said, "Just let her speak."

"Well, I talked to the other girls," she said. "And we were like, *Okay, we can't allow this to happen*."

"Even Calliope?"

"Well, no, not her. We didn't talk to her."

"Shh, beti," my mom said. And I looked up sharply. She'd said beti instead of beta—used the feminine ending for the word. Used it automatically, without thinking. "Let your friend talk."

"You've got your speech?" Felicity said. "We can't vote for you if it's awful."

"No, no," I said. "It's great. Sophrosyne."

"Okay . . . Yeah, that's safe," Felicity said. "I miss Alecto, but I get it."

"What are you talking about?" my mom said.

"Just that you have to give a speech about a woman you like from antiquity, and I was gonna choose this angry, furious avenging spirit, but eventually I decided to go for a calm, quiet, demure goddess."

"Good," my mom said. "For the other they would have rejected you for sure."

"I'm sure it'll be good," Felicity said. "Anyway, ironically I had an idea, based, on, oh my god, I can't believe I'm saying this, but based on that Cleopatra reading we had to do."

"Really? I thought you hated Cleo."

"I just hate that we're supposed to worship her. Anyway, you'll remember, Cleopatra got carried in to see Caesar while wrapped in a carpet."

"So you'll just sneak me in?"

"Yep," she said. "And right as things are starting, we'll be like, *Oh yeah, Tara is here*, and you'll say, *Oh, I didn't get the memo I was barred*, and what'll Gimbel do?"

"But what if they evict her for trespassing?" my dad said.

"Then we get video and put it online and it goes viral," she said.

"And why would you help?" my mom said. "What interest have you in our daughter?"

"Umm." Felicity's face went slightly red, and she looked down. "Err, it's the right thing to do?"

"For most that doesn't go too far," my mom said. "People often say something is right when it's what they want, and if they don't want it, then they say it's wrong. Your aunt thinks she's doing the right thing."

"No," Felicity said. "Right is right. Tara is an Ainsley girl. If she doesn't deserve to be a Sibyl, nobody does. Now it's possible my aunt won't give you the money . . . she almost withdrew the entire scholarship last year when the Strife thing went down, and I had to argue with her really hard, say it wasn't fair to Strife and Hec, but still—"

"That's fine!" I said.

"No, it is not," my mother said. "If you win the award, we will go to court to force them to give you the money. But let us focus on winning first."

"Okay . . . I'll pretend I didn't hear that," Felicity said. "You don't want to face my aunt in court."

"I do, and I will," my mother said. "She is a liberal icon; let her explain to a judge why my daughter is so unworthy!"

I laughed. That sounded a lot more Alecto than Sophrosyne. Felicity was about to argue, but I waved my hand across my throat, cutting her off.

"So," Felicity said, "are you packed? Should we go?"

"Where?" I asked.

"To the mansion. I've got the key."

Felicity drove a silver sedan—the same color as the clouds above us—and seeing her behind the wheel of the car was a totally different experience from being in class. She was bundled up in a coat, wearing a big fluffy hat that made her face look even narrower and paler.

"Uh," I said. "This is really brave of you. . . ."

She shrugged. "It's fine. It's no big deal. What's the worst that can happen?"

"They end the Sibyls forever?" I was thinking of one school

that had closed its girls' soccer team instead of letting a trans girl compete.

Felicity tightened her grip on the wheel, and I thought for a second that I'd done something wrong. "Then I guess I'll be in the last generation. That would be so weird. Nobody would've ever thought I'd be a civil rights hero."

"Yeah, you're not gonna be popular at the cotillion."

"No." Her eyes were still distant. "My aunt and grandma and all their friends would be really pissed. But it's okay. So I don't get into Harvard. I'll be fine."

I rolled my eyes a little bit, but she didn't catch it. Maybe if I hadn't been so attracted to her that even looking at the smooth curve of her thigh under her jeans made me delirious and sweaty and almost faint—maybe I'd have been annoyed at her for focusing on what this meant for *her*. I'd been joking about the cotillion, but she was *actually* worried they wouldn't like her! Meanwhile, there was like a nonzero chance that if I won this contest the Governor would try to take me away from my parents.

But you know what? I didn't know any other people at Ainsley who were literally afraid to go outside because the government would take them away from their parents. Like, even the idea of that happening, in America, was so absurd that I couldn't believe it—but we'd read news reports that other trans kids were being investigated.

So whatever, if I wasn't gonna sympathize with rich-girl problems, then I should just go to a different school. And besides, Felicity was cute. Maybe that's shallow, but whatever. I dunno, sometimes I thought that cis girls were different, somehow. They claimed if somebody did or said something privileged or problematic that they instantly weren't into that person anymore. I wasn't like that at all. For me, looks were a big part of it. I liked how Felicity looked—her body was long as a knife and just as sharp, and something in the way she moved—in the way her hands turned the wheel, end over end, just like they taught in driver's ed, made my heart thump.

"What is it?" She glanced at me, then back to the road. We were on the highway, driving past the airport. "What's going on?"

"Nothing," I said, smiling. "Just . . . thanks."

"No problem, Sophrosyne," she said. "How does that sound?"

I forced a smile.

"Or . . . Alecto?"

My heart thumped. It was stupid. I just liked the second name more. It was more me!

"Okay, Whitney knows all this, so there's no harm telling you about the interview," Felicity said. "I should've done it earlier. You've got five minutes to speak, then there'll be questions; it'll be pretty intense. And you might need to do a comparison.

Can you do all that for Sophrosyne?"

"Uh," I worked my throat. "Uh, yeah. She's not in many myths though. . . ."

"That's fine. Just be quick on your feet."

My stomach was tight. I wasn't quick on my feet! I was terrible at this.

"What questions do they ask?"

"Uh," Felicity said. "Shoot, we sent around the email this morning. Let me remember. Oh yeah: How have the values of your chosen person inspired you in ordinary life? Blech."

My mind was completely blank. I couldn't think of anything. "What did you say?"

"Oh, umm. You know Antigone symbolizes reverence. First, she follows her dad into his disgrace and takes care of him. Second, she's willing to die in order to honor her brothers and bury them, even though they weren't good people. I believe in honoring our traditions— Oh, but they threw a curveball at me, and they said, what about traditions that are evil or need to be dismantled?"

"What did you say?"

"I was just honest. Ainsley girls don't really get that powerful. The Sibyls is a club for girls. Yeah, if you're a guy, then valuing tradition can be wrong, because it turns into something to hit people over the head. But for us, it's mostly our job to bear witness."

"Holy shit," I said. "You said that? That Ainsley girls don't get that powerful?"

"Why not?" she said. "It's true. My grandma is basically our most famous grad, and she was a senator for one term. St. George's has had a president, five Supreme Court justices, and a ton of senators and governors and congresspeople. At Ainsley, our most successful people are like . . . a newscaster. Or a journalist. We don't train people to be real leaders."

"And they let you be a Sibyl?"

"They laughed," Felicity said. "Because it's true. And that's what being a Sibyl is about. Saying what others won't say. So, okay, Sophrosyne, shoot . . ."

"I . . ." My ears were red.

We had crossed the bridge, and we were about to head into Georgetown, where our school was. She turned hand over hand, going around the circle around the Jefferson Memorial, which stood lonely on a little hill surrounded by traffic. It was far away from the other memorials, so hardly anyone ever visited.

"I . . ." I couldn't think of a thing. Sophrosyne was so fake and bland. She just wasn't me. "Can I change and try Alecto?"

The punch hit me square in the arm.

"Ouch!" I said.

"Finally," Felicity said. "Okay, go, Alecto, how blah blah blah, how did the values help you and stuff?"

"Well, I read the play *The Eumenides*, and what I loved was that the Furies were from some ancient era. They were totally different from Athena and Apollo. They were ugly, born of a union between the earth and the sky, and they were dedicated to these ancient laws of right and wrong—stuff so elemental that nobody had ever needed to write down these rules. And I think that's what gives me strength: the idea that there are rules that even a king has to obey, and that if you break them, even a god can't save you. And that's a woman's job too. Like you can go out and slaughter whomever and say what you want, but women know what's right. Women reverence right. That's why women used to be early Christians. That's why they helped convert men. That's why women started Prohibition. Like, we didn't get to write down all the religions and philosophies, but we still understood right and wrong."

"You don't think that the cis white woman is the oppressor?" Felicity said. "That's what Liam always tells me."

"Huh," I said. "I think everyone is responsible for themselves. If you oppress people, then you're an oppressor. But I don't think you are. People like Liam forget there's good and bad, right and wrong, and that people can choose to do the right thing."

"Yes!" Felicity said. "Angel is gonna love that. That is incredible. Like, my aunt is going to love this. You're literally talking how she talks."

"I love her defense speeches," I said. "She's a genius."

"Wow," Felicity said. "Wow, this is going to be great. You

know what? I think this is all gonna work out really well."

I settled back in my seat, smiling widely. Her hand went forward and stabbed the radio, and she found a classical music station—I laughed at how unbelievably stuffy and Waspy that was, but she didn't say anything, and the violins played us toward our school.

10

THE MANSION STOOD TALL AND narrow like a stake jammed into the ground. I'd always thought the place was ugly and lopsided, with its two wings that didn't balance, and its high, tottery center. Members of the Coatesworth family had lived there since before the founding of the school, but Angel, who was just a distant relative, lived in an apartment upstairs and ran her law firm out of one wing of the house.

Felicity drove right up and parked her car in the gravel lot. It was the holidays, so I guess nobody was around. We went past the shiny plaque announcing the Law Offices of Evangeline Beaumont, and we went around to the back porch of the house and climbed its steps. This side was covered in potted plants and looked over the long grassy walk between the mansion and St. George's. The trees had all lost their leaves, and their bare branches made dark streaks against the white sky.

"This is really creepy," I said.

"You think?" Felicity said. "I like it here."

She swiped a key card to let us in through the doors on the portico.

"Wow," I said. "So if you're a Sibyl, you can come in here whenever you want?"

"Not really," Felicity said. "Just during my aunt's visiting hours. But all my cousins and I used to live here a week each summer when we were kids."

The mansion *looked* like what it was, which was a museum to a lesser-known founding father (the same guy who'd endowed the land for the schools). Everything was gold gilt and red velvet and overstuffed furniture. Lots of little standing exhibits and pictures walled off by ropes. I stood in front of a huge one depicting the founder sitting on a horse at a big battle.

"This is kind of insane," I said.

"Oh yeah," she said. "That one's really old."

"So you can really just wander around here?"

She shrugged.

Then, as if she'd done so all her life, she went up the grand central staircase, and we were in a more regular, normal area— still old, but with furniture that looked as if someone had sat in it this century. She went to a big sitting room, which had a chandelier above, and lots of couches and chairs, and a fireplace. She turned the dial, making a fire come up, then threw down her duffel and sat on the couch.

"Wow," she said. "This brings me back."

I sat down on a chair, perching on the edge, and my heels hit the little wooden claws that held it to the floor.

My phone was blowing up. My mom said that Mrs. Gimbel was calling her again and again, and I wrote back, Just let it go to voice mail—don't talk to her! Don't pick up any strange numbers today!

Felicity opened her duffel, put away her coat, and pulled the laurel wreath from a little hatbox. I moved to the window seat, watching her go through the leaves, looking really intense, inspecting each one.

My breath made a mist as I exhaled, and I breathed again. Felicity seemed not to have noticed the cold. She sat there for an extremely long time, not looking at her phone—just going through her wreath and then looking at her blazer and her badge. Then we heard voices downstairs, and someone calling her name, "Antigone? Antigone? Are you already here? Have you heard at all from your friend Tara?"

"Shoot," Felicity said. "It's Mrs. Gimbel. I thought we had time. All right, come on, get your bag."

I was sitting in the window seat, my heart still frozen. I grabbed my duffel bag. We walked out, and there was a woman holding an armful of bedding. She was middle-aged, brown, probably a member of the staff.

We looked at each other blankly, and Felicity grabbed my hand and said, "Come on."

We went down a back staircase, and she got out a big skeleton key and stuck it into a door that looked like it ought to be creaky but that actually swung without a sound. My eyes went wide. It was a little museum exhibit, with a marble bust in the center and some bookcases and little placards around the edges. The foyer led into a bigger sitting room, like the one we'd been in at first.

"Hello? Hello? Did I hear somebody?"

There was a knock on the door. Felicity looked blankly at me. Then she went to a big divan in the sitting room, and she sat on it, her legs out, looking at the statue.

The person at the door was clearly Mrs. Gimbel. She knocked a few times more. "Is anyone else in here? Felicity, I saw your car. . . ."

Again, Felicity put her finger to her mouth. She was angled sideways on the couch, the wreath in her hair, looking haughty and languid like a neoclassical portrait. Eventually the knocking stopped, and we heard footsteps.

The chaise or divan or whatever was the only comfortable-looking chair in the room, which was dominated by a huge window that seemed almost to radiate cold, as if it was a portal into a bleak, gray alternate dimension.

"Don't stand near the window!" Felicity said. "Go over there. Try to stay low."

I walked around the edges of the room, reading the

placards. This was a little exhibit room devoted to Winifred Coatesworth, the founder of the Sibyls and great-granddaughter of the person who'd originally owned this house. It had a bunch of her actual papers and notebooks. Her writing desk. One nook was curtained off. I went behind it, and it was a bunch of shelves and racks of clothes and lots of notebooks, almost like yearbooks. I picked one up—it was marked 1924, and I saw old photos with flapper haircuts—they were wearing togas and standing in weird positions—one was lying on that divan, lounging just like Felicity.

"They were re-creating old paintings," Felicity said. "Something Sibyls used to do. The 1920s version of being a total nerd. Look here . . ." She took the book from me, and she slipped down between the racks of clothes, and I noticed there were some rugs stacked up in a corner.

"Come on," she said. "Come on." She tapped the ground.

I opened the curtain, letting in some of the cold light, and then, my heart shivering, I crouched next to her.

"Sit," she said. "Just be comfortable."

So I sat down, our shoulders touching, and she went through the photos, showing me the old Sibyls. The book had been updated in places—usually in elegant italic cursive—with notes about various girls. She pointed to a girl in slacks, with long, curly hair, her hands in her pockets, smiling next to a car.

"She drove her own car," Felicity said. "It was a big deal. All the journals mention it. I think she took the photos too—like, it was her camera—but I'm not sure. Ariadne, they called her. And look." She went to a page at the end, and she read the entry from 1954: *"Ariadne dead, perhaps at her own hand. Perhaps it's not wise to be so clever."*

"What happened?"

"Not sure. Ariadne was a professor, not married. Maybe a lesbian."

"Liam should see this," I said, looking at the photo of the short-haired girl. "He'd say maybe she was trans. Or something."

"Yeah," Felicity said. "Well she was definitely out of step with the rest of the school. People talk about the Sibyls like we're these rich girls who wear pearls and vote Republican, but that's not true at all. We're just a bunch of weird girls who've convinced the world to leave us alone."

Our shoulders were touching, and I had an urge to take her hand, but I didn't.

"Do you like any of this?" Felicity said. "I used to spend hours reading the books."

I took down another one: 1965. I sighed. Another group of girls, their arms around each other, this time in full color, sitting on the portico of this house. This book was more organized: the handwriting was boxy, not careful cursive.

We just had our interviews, the writing said. *And I suppose that I made it. My friend Lianna didn't. She cried in the end, and I said we'll be friends always, but I don't think that's true, and*

saying it just made her mad. I already feel quite distant from her.
The note was signed *Medea.*

"Oh, her," Felicity said. "She's great. Everything she writes is so depressing."

"It's so cold," I said. "Like, just because one person gets picked and another doesn't, that doesn't mean the person who gets picked is *better.*"

"No, no," Felicity said. "Calliope certainly isn't better than anyone. But you'll think I'm being weird. . . ."

She went quiet, and I shivered. We were right next to each other, and I felt so gross and sweaty and large—I wanted to put a hand on hers, but the idea also made me sick. "Oh," I said. "Were you gonna keep talking?"

"No, just . . . sorry," Felicity said. "I don't mention this stuff to people who aren't Sibyls, because they get offended. But . . . there's something about us. After you join, you change. You become better. More interested in the truth. And in doing what's right. You didn't have to call me—you could've called Hecuba or Strife, and they would've helped you too."

"Angel was a Sibyl. So was Mrs. Gimbel."

"Yeah, I don't know. Maybe it only lasts while you're still at Ainsley. But I've read these journals," Felicity said. "You know how people at the school seem really shallow and impersonal and fake? Like your friends Hannah and Whitney. They're great examples."

Suddenly I thought of the time they'd come over, and how

we hadn't been able to talk about anything real. Or about how they'd spent the whole time pretending like they were bad and not smart and didn't deserve to be Sibyls. "Y-yeah," I said. "I sort of know what you mean."

"Sibyls aren't like that."

"Except Calliope," I said.

"I already said she was a mistake," Felicity said.

"Maybe you and Strife and Hecuba are just good people," I said. "Have you ever considered that? And Calliope and Mrs. Gimbel are bad."

"And my aunt?"

"She's not bad," I said. "I think she's just busy or something. Like she's an actual civil rights hero. And she's worried about the government coming after her for tax stuff. It must be frustrating to have to deal with all this teen girl drama when you're trying to free people from prison."

"Wow," Felicity said. "So you're really into her."

"Ummm, I wouldn't say I'm into her. But she's basically the perfect human being. She's gorgeous. She wears high-fashion clothes. Knows famous people. And she's effective and brilliant and fights the power. She's even taken on some trans cases, so I don't know why Liam says she's a TERF."

"She's definitely a TERF," Felicity said. "Everybody is. Like everyone in the old DC families. And all the alumni of the school. They all hate trans people."

"Come on," I said. "Everyone? Liam does okay."

143

"It's really hard for Liam," Felicity said. "He gets people questioning him all the time, asking him whether he's not just a lesbian. Our grandma is the worst. And I hear what people say when he's not around. They totally think he's just a trans-trender. It's awful."

"Ohhh," I said. My bottom lip quivered. I hadn't really taken Liam seriously somehow. Thought he was just a rich kid.

"His mom is really brave," Felicity said. "She almost got cut out of her inheritance because she let him go on hormones. Liam hates her, of course, because she pushed back in the beginning, but my mom never would've done that. She'd have sent me to boarding school."

"That's nuts," I said. "So . . . everyone? Like . . . why did they even let me into Ainsley?"

"I don't know," Felicity said. "What were they gonna say? We don't believe being trans is real? We think you're just sick? I think their view is it's okay having a few really queer boys at Ainsley; it doesn't do any harm. And they're happy you agreed to not play sports. Sorry . . . is this hard? I'd never tell Liam stuff like this, since that's his actual family. But your parents seem really cool and supportive."

"Yeah . . ." I said. "I guess they are? I'm not on hormones. But . . . I don't know. I don't know. . . ."

"You're not?" Felicity squinted. "So . . . oh no. That really sucks. That must be really hard. You must feel . . . kind of . . . not yourself."

"I don't know," I said again. "Wow. You know a lot about this stuff. I figured you were just . . . like you didn't care about politics at all."

"Liam's my cousin," Felicity said. "I'd die for him. We fought about the Sibyl thing last year, but he knows I'm on his side. Anyway, politics is too complicated. You can't win. I wanna be like these girls: I'll go to college and major in literature and be, like, a professor somewhere and never get married and disappear."

"Kind of like Angel," I said. "She's off by herself up here."

"Maybe . . ." Felicity frowned. "I'd love to live here someday."

We were whispering, and I still couldn't believe how close we were, in this little corner. Felicity felt small next to me, even though she was tall, and she was so beautiful I could hardly bear to look at her. But, glancing at her wide mouth and pale pink lips, I thought, *I could kiss them. I could kiss them.*

I reached forward and picked up a book, flipping through. Here and there old photos were pasted onto the pages. Snapshots of white faces. "Has there ever been a non-white Sibyl, besides Strife?" I said.

"Yeah. Olympias. She was from some rich Iranian family. A few people like that, rich girls, the kids of ambassadors and kings, in the forties and fifties, then, weirdly, nobody until Hypatia in the eighties—a Black girl. And then nobody again, until Io, six years ago. I think her family was from China. I barely remember her, but she was cool."

I knew I was supposed to say that nobody in these year-books looked like me, and that these were a bunch of privileged white girls who did nothing to challenge the terrible society they'd been born into. But I *never* saw anyone like myself. I could read books and watch TV all day, every day, and never see another girl like me. The trans girls on TV made me feel the worst: they were slender and light-skinned and beautiful, and I always changed the channel when I caught a teen show with one of them.

So looking through these girls, reading their words, hear-ing their fears and sorrows, knowing they'd suffered, that they couldn't do the things they'd wanted, that they'd felt weird and out of place, and they'd found something in this house—it just made me feel grateful. I wanted to be like them, and being in the mansion, it meant that was actually possible. It was a thing I could do.

"You really like them," Felicity said, touching my hand.

I looked up.

She had kind of a shy expression, and for the first time she looked almost human. "You *actually* like them."

I turned the pages again, looking at the long-past girls, see-ing their careful handwriting. "I love them," I said. "This is the dream."

"I know!" Felicity said, leaning into me, then pulling back, sitting cross-legged, her face gleaming. "That's so cool. What do you like?"

"Just the girls, all together like this. Happy, but not—"

"Not stupid," she said.

"Right," I said. "Not empty. Not faking for the camera—maybe they were, I don't know. Not . . ." I turned the pages, and I saw a note. *Eris fainted today after her ride on Clio's motorcycle. Went into a swoon, just like a girl in a novel would.*

"Is that a euphemism?" I said, pointing to the line. "'Rode her motorcycle'?"

I blushed, and there was a second of sweaty silence between us. Felicity jumped in, talking fast, ignoring what I'd said.

"Hey, what're you reading these days?" Felicity said. "What're you thinking about? I'm afraid to ask most people that. But not you."

"Here," I said, pulling out my bag. "I brought the book. It's dumb; it's this giant, expensive tome of speeches I got for my birthday. Look."

"Ooh, book darts," she said, going to familiar pages. "Wow, Eugene Debs. You'll get along with Robin, I guess."

That was one of my favorites: Debs in 1918, speaking to the court that was sentencing him for opposing WWI. He was a socialist, and I knew some of his words by heart: "In this nation, the most favored beneath the bending stars, the most blessed and fruitful in its lands, if even in this nation, men and women are bent and broken under the wheel of Mammon—basically to make money for the rich—then it is not the fault of God, but of Man."

Her eyes went down the page as I spoke, and I thought she was wincing because I hadn't spoken them exactly correct, but after a second of silence, she said, "Wow, and Winifred Coatesworth was living in this house. She was against the war too."

"But for different reasons," I said. Winifred wasn't a pacifist or a communist. She just thought the world wars were stupid and we shouldn't have been a part of them.

Felicity looked up, shy. Like I was about to attack. The giant book sat open in her lap, and I reached over, said, "Here, it's a speech by Sojourner Truth, the, I don't know what to call her—'abolitionist' feels not strong enough."

She took the book, and her eyes went down the page. "I love it."

"You've read it?"

"Not until just now," she said. "I love it. This is great. I think . . . I feel that way too sometimes. Like, I'm a girl too. Even though I'm strange."

"Of course you're a girl."

"But I had to learn how to be one," she said. "Or something. I don't know. It's weird, to not care about what I'm supposed to. Not have friends, at least until now. Not get angry like other people do. Not be as intense. Like I'm in a different world, and

I'm the only thing that's real and everything else isn't, and it can't possibly affect me."

"You're incredibly intense."

"I don't know," she said. "I don't know how to say what I am."

"What about you?" I said. "What've you been reading?"

She pulled out her phone, called up the e-reader app, and she was leaning close again, pressing into me, and I could smell her hair. "Look," she said.

"What's that?"

"A poem, from a Russian mom, going to see if her son was still alive after the Soviet police took him away. 'Seventeen months I've pleaded / for you to come home.' My mom recommended it. She does stuff like that. But it's good."

I read the lines and shivered. She was so hopeless and heartbroken, and yet she stood in line with all these other women, of all ages and all classes, and they shared food, while waiting to hear if their men were dead.

"That's cool," I said. "So you don't just love ancient Rome."

"No," she said. "I love all kinds of stuff." And for a second, and I know it was a hallucination or a dream, and I thought she was on the edge of saying *I love you*.

But that made no sense, clearly, and we pulled apart. She handed me back my book, and she looked at her phone, and we were feeling kind of awkward when suddenly we heard a single knuckle rapping at the door.

"Are you decent?" said the voice. It was high-pitched and elegant, and I found myself using my tongue to form a little sound chamber under my nose, wanting to imitate the voice.

"Shoot, it's my aunt," Felicity said.

"I can hear her in there," her aunt said. "Please, I can *hear* you. How could you think . . . No, I'll just go in. Of course I can go in. This is my house."

The door swung open, and we both shot to our feet, looking guilty.

Angel had her phone in one manicured hand, her French-tip nails draped over the screen, and the other hand went up, waving at us. In person, she was genuinely beautiful. She was in a gray dress, cut to the hip, with a green belt, and she wore high-heeled black shoes. Her dark hair came down in waves, shiny like in a shampoo commercial. Her nose was straight and slender, and her face was narrow, with high cheekbones and a tapering chin that made me want to rub my jawbone, to tug and pull at it and make its sharp angles go away.

I squinted, and suddenly I saw Felicity, if she didn't always dress in her school uniform and tie her hair back in a ponytail. Felicity if she wore makeup and high heels.

"Hello," Angel said, raising two fingers, "Tara? I don't think we've met in person before. I'm Angel."

I stepped forward, put out my hand, and she offered me her hand, palm down, like I was going to kiss it. But then she grabbed my fingers, and her warm hand covered mine for a second. Her eyes were set off by dark eyeshadow and light mascara, and she looked at me with a smile—a genuine sort of smile, one that touched her face.

"However this Sibyl business went, I meant to connect with you," she said. "So I'm glad you've come."

Staff members were bustling around behind her, but she didn't pay attention. She had a quiet girl off and behind her, looking at a phone.

"Hey, Mindy," Felicity said.

The girl looked up, smiled, and then her eyes swept over me, and she gave a slight wink, before going down to her phone.

Angel took two steps and then was in the mess of journals. She bent down, from the knee, squatting on her heels, and she poked through the journals. "I haven't looked at these in years," she said. Then she pulled down a black one, and she opened it to a middle page: a shot of six girls, arms around each other, in front of this house. It wasn't that old a photograph: it was in color, and not stained or faded. She smiled, and then she closed it.

"Mindy," she said. "Can you lock up this room? You and I can put everything in order later. Maybe Felicity would help?"

"Sure," Felicity said. "Sorry."

I was left standing in the doorway, feeling kind of at odds. I stepped out into the hallway, where I saw tons of people carrying folding tables and other stuff up from the basement. One of them looked in, and he grabbed my bag. "I'll take this downstairs?"

"Good," Mindy said.

Then I felt a hand on my shoulder. "Are we ready to go?"

The hand squeezed, and Angel's voice said, "I have a quick call. Can you take her to our waiting room? Felicity, they need you downstairs."

Then Angel was gone.

11

THE LAW OFFICE PART OF the house was through a set of narrow corridors, so I got lost pretty quick. But I heard people's voices, and Felicity said, "Oh, okay, here."

We came out into a huge anteroom with curling staircases and a big chandelier and a marble floor. I saw a bunch of girls—other hopeful Sibyls—and their parents. Strife rolled her eyes at me and Felicity. She was with Calliope and Hecuba near the stairs. They were all in dresses and short heels, as if they'd gotten the same message about what to wear. The room wasn't too big, but the voices echoed inside it.

"Oh, hey," Calliope said, breaking away from the Sibyl candidates. "It's you. Where were you?"

"Just in Winifred's room," Felicity said. "With the old journals."

"Who? Where? Okay, I think you— Wait, there's something

going on with you, Tara." She looked me up and down. I was in slacks and a blouse that was barely long enough for my torso. My makeup felt cakey and oily, like I'd run butter over my face and dipped myself in flour. My hair itched, and I was desperate to pick off a peeling bit of lip but couldn't because I had lipstick on.

"Sorry," I said. "I don't look great."

"No, you're fine," Calliope said. "But Mrs. Gimbel was looking for you."

A parent came up, thrusting out her hand. "Hello! Tara, right? I'm Hannah's mom!" The woman was tiny, just like Hannah, and she was dressed like a normal person, in a T-shirt and jeans and sneakers. "Can I just say how brave you are?"

"Mom!" Hannah said.

"What?" her mom said.

"That's offensive!"

"Oh," the woman said. "I am so sorry. Did I offend you?"

"No." I squinted, thought about it for a second. "No, I'm brave. I agree."

"You're funny!" Hannah's mom said. "Anyway, we're so happy you're here and happy you're at Ainsley."

"Mom!" Hannah said.

Mrs. Gimbel descended on me and hissed, "Come on."

Hannah's mom picked up on something. "What's wrong? Hey . . . what's wrong?"

"Nothing," Mrs. Gimbel said. "Some questions about eligibility."

"Oh!" Hannah's mom said. "Do you need help? I'm a lawyer. No Evangeline Beaumont, but I do work for the school sometimes. What's happening?"

The arm on my shoulder was guiding me back between the stairs, and I walked into the law office part of the house. It was beautiful. Bright open windows, with a little rotunda, looking onto the back gardens. Lots of desks, arranged in a sitting room, with phones and computer screens, and then glass-walled offices at both ends of the room.

Felicity trailed behind, and Mindy poked her head out of an office, where we could hear Angel's voice. "Right . . . there," she said, pointing across at another office. I took a few steps, trying to get away from Mrs. Gimbel's touch on my upper arm, but she sped up, so we were almost running to the room.

Inside it was ice-cold, as if the air-conditioning was on, even though it was December. I sat at the small circular table and Mrs. Gimbel sat with me. Felicity hung around outside, looking doleful.

"I'd like you to call your parents and tell them to come and pick you up." Mrs. Gimbel pushed across her phone.

"I don't have their numbers memorized," I said.

We waited for a few seconds, staring at each other. Every time I saw her, I remembered Mrs. Gimbel was a lot younger than I imagined. She was younger than my mom, definitely. Her face was smooth, and she wore cat-eye glasses and eyeshadow. But something about the way her lips pursed and how she pouted gave her an ugly look.

"I've been trying to reach them all day," she said. "And you're trespassing, you know."

"Okay."

"You could go to jail," she said. "That was a room with valuable things. I could easily call the police right now."

"Call them," I said.

She blinked, and there was a moment of silence.

Oh shit, maybe I'd made a mistake. But I was just tired of adults not telling me the truth. For months they'd told me I couldn't come to Ainsley because Ainsley didn't accept transfers in the tenth grade, and I was like, *But that makes no sense. That's a rule you made. You can change the rule.* And they were like, *But rules are rules.* It was happening again.

"Felicity let me in with her key card," I said. "You guys told me I could compete to be a Sibyl, and I'm here for the interview. So, call the police. My mom is talking to someone from the *Washington Post.* I'm sure they'd love that."

"Uhh . . ." Mrs. Gimbel looked at her phone. She typed something, then she put it down and stood up. Looking at me, she said, "Stay here."

I watched her rush out. Suddenly I was alone in the room. My phone was full of texts from my mom, but I didn't write her back. Something had collapsed in me. I didn't feel good about this. Like, needling Mrs. Gimbel was one thing. But why was I at the mansion? Why was I doing this? If they didn't want me, I should leave.

I looked through the windows at the other conference room, where there were drinks and snacks set up. I opened the door a little, and I heard the voices of the other girls and their parents.

"Hey," Felicity said. "What's going on?"

"Nothing," I said.

"We're gonna start the interviews soon," she said. "Come on, you've got your Alecto spiel, right?"

"I . . ."

Then I looked toward the office on the other side of the room, where Angel was talking into a bright ring light. "Wow," I said. "She uses that for all her calls? It must be blinding."

"She likes to look good in case anyone is recording," Felicity said.

Hecuba's voice resounded through the stone halls, and all I heard clearly was the final sound, "—igoneeeeeeeee."

"You should go," I said. "I'll wait here."

"But . . ."

The call came again, and Felicity yelled back, "Hold on."

"No, it's okay," I said. "I'll come find you guys in a sec. I just want to talk to your aunt."

Then I closed the door. Felicity put her hand against the glass, which made me wince, because I could see it'd leave a mark. Then she pushed off and headed down the hall.

I watched as Whitney, Hannah, Robin, and the other girls

slowly came into the room, and they were directed by a member of the staff into the other conference room, along with Calliope and Hecuba and Strife and the other Sibyls. Strife looked at me and shrugged her shoulders slightly, mouthed the word *sorry*, which made me feel better. I didn't want anyone to lose their scholarship just to help me.

Angel closed her laptop, and the ring light went off. Then she looked at me and beckoned with a finger until I got up.

"Don't worry about them," Angel said.

All the other girls—the Sibyls and the applicants—were in the conference room with Mrs. Gimbel, talking. But there was a solid wall between them and us, and when the door closed, all sound was cut off.

Instead, I was sitting in a seat that was bolted to the ground by one big piece of metal. Angel was behind the desk, in another stylish, futuristic chair. Her desk was all glass, with items placed neatly around it as if according to a grid. She had one leg crossed over the other, and I kept having to jerk my gaze up to look into the eyes that burned behind her mascara and kohl.

She smiled at me through deep crimson lips, and she adjusted her glasses.

"Let me ask you something," Angel said, still smiling. "Do you understand the portion of the US tax code regulating nonprofits?"

"No," I said, narrowing my eyes.

"To award you this money to someone who is not formally an Ainsley student would be in clear violation of the terms of the bequest. And it makes no sense to consider you for the scholarship if you can't get the money. You must understand that."

"Umm," I said.

Angel met my eyes. She was in front of a huge window, and the sky loomed blindingly white behind her, so sometimes she seemed like a stark silhouette, not a person at all. She passed forward a bottle of water, one of the expensive kinds in an aluminum bottle. I unscrewed it, and the soda water—it was carbonated—spurted out.

"Oh!" Angel said. She looked around, but Mindy had seen through the door, and she ducked inside with a napkin, which she swabbed at the table. Meanwhile Angel had grabbed her laptop and placed it on a shelf.

"But . . ." I said. "Umm . . ." My eyes drifted to the high collar of her dress, which was closed across the throat. Every inch of her was powerful.

"Take your time," Angel said, looking up, her large eyes catching mine.

The room was really bare, with just one wall of reference books, and then windows all around. Angel didn't fidget. She didn't pull out her phone. Instead, she held her pen, with its tip poised over a writing pad—just like Felicity did in class—and my eye traveled up her smooth arm and took in her contoured cheek and wavy hair.

"I just think . . . it's not really fair," I said. "You know? Nobody told me I couldn't be a Sibyl. They just said you can't have the scholarship."

"But the two things are one," Angel said.

"The Sibyls came before the scholarship though," I said.

"True, but not really relevant," Angel said. "Why do you *want* to be a Sibyl, can I ask? What does this mean to you?"

"I just . . . I like Felicity."

The moment I said the words, I wanted to take them back. Something terrible appeared in Angel's eyes. She leaned forward, and I thought *I've lost.*

"Tell me more," she said.

"Just . . . I think she's really cool. All the Sibyls. They're all great. Hecuba and Strife. They're such good friends, and so genuine and honest. Not like other people. And they seem to like me."

"But do you really think becoming a Sibyl made them that way?" she said. "Don't you think they were that way always? Why do you need the name *Sibyl* to be their friend?"

"It's just . . . they're insular. I read in the journal, this girl, about her trying to be a Sibyl with her friend, and how she got to be one and she stopped being friends with her— Okay, sorry—" I'd noticed Angel's eyes flicking down to the phone lying on the table.

"Anyway," I said. "I want to compete. I really do. I deserve it."

"Well, you know I make the final decisions," Angel said. "Have you considered . . ." She tapped the pen on the pad. "Have you considered I'm saving you from embarrassment?"

I squinted. My knees were pushed tightly together, and I twisted around in the chair. I couldn't even look at her.

"Feli—" My voice squeaked. "Felicity and Hecuba and Strife will vote for me."

"You're misinformed. They don't get a vote. They only get to advise. After last year, we decided that since money was publicly at stake, it was better for adults to have more control."

"Why are you even doing this?" I said. "Can't you just do things like they were always done? You didn't have all this trouble when *you* wanted to be a Sibyl."

I was pouring sweat from my face and arms and butt, and I could smell myself in the air. The room had a faint sound, maybe the hum of the monitor on the wall for video-conferencing calls.

"Tara," she said.

And that word, my name, made me shiver.

"Tara, look at me," she said. "Can you meet my eyes? I'm your friend."

I blinked a few times, looking up, doing my best to avoid snot gathering in the back of my throat; I quietly harrumphed down a glob. Looking at her, I saw Felicity in the cotillion picture I'd seen. Except not grumpy like Felicity had been. Angel was glamorous, smiling, ready to take on the world.

"Tell me, do you know about my work?" Her voice had a slight accent, the sounds were softened a little, rounded off, like an actress might say them in a play. And I repeated the word to myself *waaaahrk*.

"I'm a lawyer, as you know, and I represent—"

"Death penalty cases," I said.

"Among others," she said. "I specialize in applying pressure to governments that are infringing upon people's liberties."

My eyes dropped to her thin arms, and I forced them back to her face. Her gray dress was like a uniform, and it was almost hard to believe this person was sitting with me. I'd watched her give a speech on TV once. She'd moved across the room, making eye contact with each member of the jury, smiling and then going suddenly serious when she had a point to make.

"The government is very anxious to make an example of me. Have you ever heard the phrase 'Caesar's wife must be above reproach'?"

I'd used that quote with her before! "Umm, yeah, in our last—"

"I cannot afford to have a gap, cannot afford a misstep, cannot have this gift examined, cannot have people saying I am anti-trans. The government will come after me with anything it can. You know the Governor of Virginia? I am facing his attorney general in a case in a few weeks. He would love to get his friend the president to investigate me. I have trans clients, trans cases. I'm challenging his legislation in a court of law."

Her voice was beautiful, and I let it wash over me. She was so far removed from Ainsley, and from everything I knew. Listening to her was so enjoyable if you just ignored the words and listened to the trills, the rise and fall—I'd heard it was hard, with a woman's voice, to speak in a way men didn't find whiny and shrill, but she managed it, and everything she said sounded emotional and at the same time clearly thought-out and reasonable.

"Okay," I said. "You win. It's fine. You're right. I was stupid."

"No, no," she said. "I don't feel good about that. Because besides everything, I have learned a lot about you. And you're a very smart and courageous girl. I do think you're a girl, regardless of what Liam has said about my opinions. But have you considered the optics? What are your grades?"

"Bs," I said.

"Bordering on a B minus / C plus average," she said. "Felicity has a four point oh. Her friend Strife, for all her faults, has an even higher GPA. All the girls competing have higher GPAs than you."

"Okay."

"And what other honors do you have?"

"I debate."

"Have you won?"

I didn't say anything.

"All the other girls are at least the best in the school at what they do. Felicity is being recruited to play field hockey for some of the national leaders in the sport. I'm sorry. I think you're very courageous, but think about how it will look."

"That's not what the Sibyls are about!" I said.

Her eyes got wide. Her pen stopped writing, and she edged back. I guess that I'd spoken loudly. But she was talking over me!

"So what is it about?" she said. "My great-grandmother founded the club, and I was one myself, but you tell me: What is it about?"

"It's about . . . being honest," I said. "Being . . . different. Finding your people."

"It's about using the knowledge of classical civilization to preserve our nation and help the people of this country and the world."

"That's not what Felicity says! She says Sibyls almost never do great stuff."

"My niece has a moody, romantic temperament. But fine, if you insist. Let's do it. Tell me. Give me your speech. Who are you?"

"I . . ."

I understood for the first time why I couldn't really look at Angel. It was because she was too beautiful. She was like when you went over to a friend's house and their sister was home from college and you snuck looks at her and your friend made fun of you and then later you went home and thought about her constantly and worshipped her and dreamed of saving her from a car crash so you'd have an excuse to know her. Angel, with her smooth skin and stylish shoes and great-fitting dresses and wavy hair, with the little pen in her hands, and, sitting in the office chair, she was like a literal goddess, like something from Roman or Greek myth. In a single instant, her mind could think through a billion things, come up with a billion arguments, handle so many cases, stare down so many powerful men.

"My person is Alecto," I said.

"And who was she?"

"A Fury," I said. "Unceasing anger."

"Why did you choose her?"

"She was the final boss in a video game." Actually, the boss of the first stage, but this didn't seem the moment for that detail.

I expected a laugh, but she didn't smile; instead, she cocked her head, and her eyes softened, like she pitied me. "Why would you say that?"

"It's the truth."

"But you know more about her, surely. She's featured in a play by Aeschylus."

"N— Yeah!" I said. "And I read it. And I really liked how she pursued justice. And how she wasn't bound by the law of the gods. Or by their whims. She pursued a deeper justice. I admire that about the Sibyls I know—especially Felicity—how

165

she has her own sense of right and wrong. And that's what I really like. I'm very into great speeches—"

Again her face didn't budge.

"And what I most admire is that sense of righteousness people have. The sense that they're saying something very obvious, even though it's not. Like Clarence Darrow to Leopold and Loeb . . ."

I said part of his speech, and for the first time Angel seemed receptive.

"You like Clarence Darrow? Do they still teach him in school? You don't think he's some old white man?"

"He's incredible," I said. "I loved *Inherit the Wind*. But I like William Jennings Bryan too."

"Really?" she said.

"The Boy Orator of the Platte," I said. "Do not crucify me on a cross of gold."

"Ah, but that's not my favorite line from that speech," she said. "Do you know—"

"Me neither! Mine is 'You come to us and tell us that the great cities are in favor of the gold standard; we reply that the great cities rest upon our broad and fertile prairies.'"

"Fascinating," she said. "So you enjoy rhetoric."

"I love it," I said. "But only when it's paired with what's right. I don't like sophistry. I think that's why I do badly in debate. I don't believe in what I'm asked to argue."

Suddenly something shut in her eyes, and my heart stopped.

She capped her pen. Then she leaned back, and she shifted in her seat, and the full sight of her body was terrible, like a dark queen enthroned.

"Tell me, then," she said. "What do you believe? How is your joining the Sibyls the right thing to do? Explain it to me."

"Because . . . because I love it. I love Felicity. I love Hecuba and Strife. I love every inch of what they stand for. I love the secrecy and the mystery. I love that it's *not* about your grades—it's about something deeper, something you can't explain, but which has something to do with being strange, not being in touch with other people. I love how the Sibyls are the weirdest people I've ever met, but they're powerful too. I love that they're all girls. That they hide out in rooms together and are such good friends and wear these crowns, and that guys aren't a part of it at all. They don't talk about guys, aren't even opposed to them. It's just their own little world, with everything that's great about Ainsley, everything I ever wanted, all the friendship, all the community, all the honesty, all the . . . the . . ."

"So that's it?" she said. "Simply because it's all girls?"

"N-no, because—I love you too—and you're a Sibyl—and you're incredible. You're so smart. And you talk really well, but you've also got power! It comes, from, like—"

"But."

"Huh?"

"You said 'but' I have power. You don't think my power flows from being smart and speaking well?"

"No . . . yeah," I stammered. "Those things are part of it. But . . . I mean . . . you're not like a male lawyer."

"How so?" she said.

"I . . ." My face was red, and I saw the trap. "You're not like Clarence Darrow. You're not William Jennings Bryan. You dress really well. You're sharp. You're, I dunno . . . you're . . ." My throat caught. "Err . . . you're really femme."

"That isn't a word I use for myself."

"Okay," I said. "But I just mean . . . being a Sibyl is really gendered. It teaches you how to use, you know, a girl's power. I love that."

"Hmm," she said. "That's certainly an opinion to have."

"Sorry. I didn't mean to offend you."

"No." Her hands came together, clapping solidly. "What a wonderful talk. Very refreshing." But she didn't blink, and there wasn't any softness in her eyes. "But it's simply not possible to give you the award."

12

ANGEL LET ME LEAVE THROUGH the back exit. Felicity texted to ask what was going on, and I said I'd decided not to join after all.

Felicity: What? Why?

Tara: I'm just not good enough. It was crazy. I hope we can hang out sometime though.

Felicity: No . . . come on!

But I didn't stay at the house, I hiked out beyond the walls, into Georgetown. It was one of my first times out in public, in a shopping area, around strangers, looking like a girl—usually I was only at home or at Ainsley. I sat in a diner, getting weird looks from every person who walked in, until my mom picked me up.

At home, she asked what had happened, and I said, "You

know . . . it just really didn't make sense. I was putting Angel and the whole school in danger, because of the tax thing, and if I was, like, really great, with really great grades and something really outstanding about me, then it would make sense. But right now it didn't."

"Oh, beti," she said, reaching out and brushing aside my bangs. "What happened?"

"Nothing," I said. "But Angel gave me a fair chance, and I didn't say the right things. I tried my best. You know, I always thought that my being bad at debate was because I couldn't go against my beliefs. I thought that if I was really speaking from the heart, I'd find the words and convince the other person. Like, you're always asking what my ambition is, and I never worried about it, because I was like: knowing the truth, that's my superpower, knowing and explaining it. But that didn't work."

"Ah, beti," she said, her lip turning down a bit. "I am so sorry. So, so sorry. You *are* truthful and passionate. But some people cannot be reached either by emotion or reason. They only respond to strength. Someday they will come back begging you to join their club, and that is when you can speak the truth to them, and they will be forced to listen."

"No," I said. "I'm just not good enough. You knew that."

"Tara," she said. "I never . . . that is never what I wanted you to think."

I went upstairs, thankful it was the winter holidays. Liam texted me to ask what had happened. Felicity texted to say she was sorry.

I got an email after two days, saying Whitney and Hannah had gotten picked. I saw a few comments online asking what had happened to me and how had they picked two white girls *again*, especially during a year when a trans girl of color was running. I got some more messages, asking, and I couldn't help texting back: I wasn't eligible. But then people got really angry and excited, and I got scared, so I didn't write back anymore.

My mom still wanted to sue, but my dad thought that it wouldn't work, and I heard the two of them arguing while I was in my room.

I stayed out of it, and neither of them asked my opinion.

Henry was on break too, and after a few days I hung out with him. We were in my basement, playing games, and he said, "Hey, I saw your name online."

"Yeah? What about?"

"Don't remember."

"Probably this Ainsley scholarship thing," I said.

"Oh yeah, what happened with that?"

"Didn't get it."

"Shoot, I'm sorry."

He stayed the night, and we slept in the same room, and it wasn't weird at all. In the morning he didn't talk about going home. I knew that something strange had happened to him at St. George's. It'd been hard on him when I left. But I kind of hadn't hung out much this semester, so it was weird to ask if he had any new St. George's friends.

Around lunchtime I got a text from Felicity.

Felicity: Hey, are you home?

Tara: What?

Felicity: Are you home right now?

Tara: What's going on?

Felicity: Shush. Just pack a bag.

I ran upstairs. Henry was still tired, rubbing his eyes, looking up a strategy guide for our game. I started throwing things into my bag, and he said, "What's going on?"

"This, uhh, this girl, Felicity. She texted me."

"All right, man! What's going on?"

"No idea, she said to pack a bag."

"Whoa!" He got up, looked over my shoulder, then wanted to high-five. I slapped his hand.

"Oh shit," I said. "How're you gonna get home?"

"Naw, naw, don't worry," he said. "You go and get it, son."

Yeah, he really talked like that for some bizarre reason. He'd picked it up this year at St. George's. Finally, my bag was packed, and I stood at the window, staring out like a dog. I didn't even ask my mom if I could go out, because I was afraid she would say no. She'd want to know if it was anywhere in Virginia where I could get reported for being trans, and honestly I didn't care. I just wanted to get into that car. Luckily, she was out shopping, and my dad was at work.

The car pulled up, and my heart exploded: Hecuba stood up through the sunroof, and she waved, her red hair streaming behind her from under the beanie. They were playing music really loud: some kind of trap rock, not the kind of thing I'd ever expect them to listen to. They parked the car, and then the horn sounded, going again and again.

"Whoa, is that her?" Henry said. "She's old."

"Gotta go, gotta go," I said, and I ran down the steps, my backpack hitting my bag, and I burst through my front door, into the cold. Our street was loud and fast, with cars whizzing by. I waved wildly at the girls through my fence. My fingers almost froze trying to work the latch. Strife turned sideways in the passenger seat, and she gave me a tired smile. Then the back door slid open, and I hopped inside.

The car was a mix of every temperature, with hot air blowing from the vents and cold air streaming from the open windows. A sucking sound filled all our ears, and we had to yell to be heard over that and the music. I sat in the dirty back seat, with someone's bag down at my feet. The car was filled with old wrappers and empty cans of energy drinks.

"None of us have slept in, like, three days!" Felicity yelled.

"Why?" I yelled.

"Can't hear you!"

"Why?"

"Initiating the new Sibyls," Hecuba said. "Lots of rituals and stuff."

"Oh."

Felicity turned down the volume. Strife reached for the knob again, and Felicity slapped the top of her hand, yelling "Queen of the Radio!"

"Yeah, if you can change the volume without someone noticing, you're Queen of the Radio and can choose the song and the volume," Hecuba said. "But if you get caught, you can't try again for the rest of the day."

Strife twisted around in her seat. None of them were in their semiformal Sibyl clothes. Instead, they were in jeans and T-shirts, with bulky coats and hats. Strife's was a fur hat with flaps on the side. She squinted at me. "Hey, sorry we didn't follow you out. Antigone said we should, but . . . I didn't want to. I like you and everything, no offense, but not fifty thousand dollars' much."

"That's totally okay," I said. "I would've been mad if you had."

"Thanks," Strife said, putting out a hand.

I took it, feeling the weathered skin.

"It's nice to meet someone else at Ainsley who's normal."

If I could've bottled that moment and lived inside it forever,

I would've. The four of us together in a car, whipping down an expressway, with leafless branches waving overhead. I'd literally never been in a car with so much girlhood, and I couldn't help shivering at the sight of Strife's tired eyes and Hecuba's grin and Felicity's long fingers on the wheel.

The initiation had been terrible, apparently. Normally this was a bonding time, when the Sibyls got to know each other, and they picked each other apart, made fun, looked through the journals and learned the secret rituals. It's also when Sibyls usually heard the first details of the scholarship, which usually made their eyes go wide and started them talking for the next few hours about how nuts it was that something this big was such a secret.

But after I'd left, Angel and Mrs. Gimbel had selected Whitney (Penelope) and Hannah (Clytemnestra). The household staff brought them tea in the museum room, and the girls brought out all the journals and wrote in them. Then they got dinner, and their rooms were prepared for staying the night. When Calliope, Whitney's sister, caught the other three together talking about how weird and ridiculous this was, she got mad at them, and then they had to have a big meeting with Mrs. Gimbel about how they weren't upholding the honor of the school.

"Antigone said some really unforgivable stuff," Strife said. "Like . . . you might be kicked out of the *school*, Tig."

"Like, what did you say?"

Felicity punched Strife in the arm. We were at a fifties-themed diner in Alexandria, near where Strife lived. The diner was crowded with families and with people talking loudly at each other behind the counters. The table had a tiny jukebox that Strife kept fiddling with.

"It doesn't work, Strife," Hecuba said.

"But I got it to play a song that one time."

"It's just a decoration!"

"Then why are there buttons?" Strife said.

"What did you say, A-Antigone?" I said.

She shrugged. "Umm, nothing special. Just that we hadn't picked them, so they weren't real Sibyls."

The other two girls erupted into laughter. It wasn't that funny, but their shrieks were so loud that an older guy leaned in and said that other people were trying to eat, and suddenly we all got quiet. My ears went really hot as the older guy looked at me. He walked behind me, and I wondered if he was calling child protective services to report a trans girl on the loose. I craned my head, missing the conversation, but he didn't pull out a phone, just went back to his table to eat alone.

The girls had suffered through two days of the retreat, and the moment they were done, the three of them met at Strife's house (which was where they usually hung out) and stayed up all night, toasting to the end of the Sibyls, and then they'd hatched a plan to snatch me up and elect me to the club. So there we were, stumbling into the woods behind Strife's house, my feet sinking in the cold leaves. The giggling was really loud, and all of them were slurping on canned coffee drinks.

Then we were in a clearing, at a place where a tree had fallen and rested in the crook of another tree. Nearby a stream burbled, moving sluggishly over some stones. Then Hecuba opened up her bag, and she took out a hatbox. I looked inside, and I saw four flower crowns. She placed one on her own head, and then one each on Felicity and Strife, who'd both taken off their hats.

We stood in the windy clearing, everyone's hair flapping a little bit, and their pants and shirts sticking to their bodies. The trees loomed above as Hecuba scratched a cross into the ground with a big stick.

"What happens now?" I said.

"You took a photo of the letter, right?" Hecuba said.

Felicity opened her phone. And she pulled up a picture of a piece of paper with faded typewritten text. I looked over it, reading through the lines under my breath.

"Say them aloud," Hecuba said.

I looked at her. She was bigger than the other two, and she *looked* older, and somehow very sad. The other two were giggling, but Hecuba took a breath. I remembered Felicity saying Hecuba and Calliope had once been friends. And I wanted to ask Hecuba if she really wanted to do this, to be with me at that moment, but I thought, *What if the answer is no? What would I say then?*

So instead I read the words. "'I pledge—'"

"Normally you put your name there," Felicity said. Her voice was high and soft and got carried by the wind, so she seemed far away.

"'I, Alecto, pledge to uphold the secrets of the Sibylline order. To . . .'" I started to smile, but even Strife looked dead serious.

The three of them were arrayed in front of me, making the other three points of a square.

"'To resist everything new. To ignore whatever they teach at school. To listen to my fellow oracles above all. To never forget my cruelty, my courage, my ambition. And to enjoy the freedom that our namesakes were denied.'"

"Witnessed under the first gods, Earth and Sky," Hecuba said.

"Witnessed under the elder gods, Chaos and Chronos," Felicity said.

"Witnessed under the lesser gods, the Uranians, the Titans and Olympians and whoever may come afterward," Strife said.

"You should do it, Antigone," Hecuba said. She handed over the flower crown. Felicity walked up to me, and then she frowned, pulling on the lapel of my coat.

"Bend down."

I half curtseyed, half knelt, and she tucked the flowers

into my hair. When I pulled away, she said, "Shh," and messed around with it, I guess making everything look nice.

"That's it?" I said.

"Mm-hmm," Felicity said.

"So now what?"

"Sleep," Strife said.

"But *I* slept last night."

"Sleeeeeeeeep."

So they ended up sleeping all together in Strife's bed, while I lounged around her house, watching videos on my phone. Her mom came in and offered me lunch, and I took it. Eventually I got tired too, and I crept back into Strife's room with a blanket and curled up in her chair.

13

TWO WEEKS LATER I WAS in the car with my mom, on the way to school, and completely stuck in traffic going over the Chain Bridge, when my mom touched my arm: "Who are you texting? You are always texting! Do you have a boyfriend?"

I texted the Sibyls group chat:

Tara: My mom asked me if the person I'm texting all the time is my boyfriend!

Felicity: Wow. What'd you say?

Tara: Nothing. She just said it.

Hecuba: Like right now? Like she's waiting for an answer?

Tara: Just now. I'm in the car.

Hecuba: So . . . shouldn't you answer?

I looked up. My mom was frowning. "I'm texting my friends," I said.

"Every second of the day," she said. "What can you possibly have to talk about?"

"Just stuff that happens?" I said. "Like you asking if I had a boyfriend."

"Show me."

Traffic was totally stopped. I gave her the phone, and when she started scrolling up, I grabbed it back.

"Sensible," she said. "I suppose they are good girls. Older than you though! Don't you want to befriend some girls your own age?"

"I tried that," I said. "I'm just too mature."

"So many jokes," she said. "You don't do drugs with them, do you? Or drink?"

I shook my head. I think what people like me don't get is that everything our parents understand about the average American teen girl *also* comes from TV shows and movies. So they have no idea what's normal, just like we have no idea what's normal. We're sitting around going, like . . . do people have sleepovers with their friends? Do people date? Do they talk about their crushes? And meanwhile my mom is like: *ALL AMERICAN KIDS GO TO KEG PARTIES WHERE THEY TRASH THEIR PARENTS' HOUSES!*

I texted the Sibyls this observation, and they texted me

back the funny stuff their parents did. Felicity was from the most traditional Ainsley family, and the weird thing about these old Waspy DC families was they *expected* their kids to be crazy. Like, her mom would ask Felicity whether she wanted to bring alcohol to a party and had told Felicity there was Narcan in a cabinet at home, and Felicity was like, *What's that?*, and her mom was like, *For fentanyl overdoses*, and Felicity was like . . . *What? None of my friends use heroin.*

Tara: Guys, I am insanely nervous.

Felicity: Why?

Tara: Not sure. Just that things will be different. That we won't be friends.

Hecuba: C'mon.

Tara: I dunno, it's just been so good, hanging out, learning to be a group.

Strife: So dramatic! But we love you too.

The last two weeks had been amazing. Everything seemed to happen automatically, like it's supposed to. You get a text like *We're doing such and such, wanna come?* You go over on the Metro, you get picked up in Hecuba's car. You see the movie, you go to lunch, you browse in a bookstore or mall, just passing time, you go to someone's house, and nobody's parents says a thing—or they're even extra nice—because Sibyls can do no wrong. You talk and talk and the words flow like water, and you're not sure where they come from or where they go, but everything feels so natural. And every moment she's there:

Felicity, touching your arm or shoulder, leading you around, whispering in your ear. And when you're alone, you wonder: *How could this be possible? I don't deserve to be this happy. I don't deserve anything this good.* And then you wake up and text your friends, and they go, *That's so silly, of course you do.*

Except, of course, for Strife, who, true to form, texts you privately.

Strife: When're you gonna tell Felicity that you like her?

Tara: Should I?

Strife: Never know until you try!

Tara: Just feels like it could be awkward.

Strife was the only one who'd apologized about them all going to sleep and leaving me by myself. She'd woken up first, and she'd crept out of bed, and we'd spent an hour or two alone. She'd noticed how I looked at Felicity and made me confess.

But somehow, with Strife, everything came tumbling out. She assumed she knew what she didn't, and she pushed and pushed, and it was exactly what you'd always wanted. Of the three, I sometimes thought, Strife was the person who I liked best.

Strife always managed to maneuver it, too, so that I could be left alone with Felicity. The other morning, Strife had rolled her eyes at me when she found Felicity and me asleep at opposite ends of the couch.

And then I was sitting in the car texting them like we were best friends.

"Hey, kid," my mom said, grabbing me by the shoulder. "I'm proud of you."

"Yeah, the Sibyls are great," I said. "But it was them who chose me."

"No, for everything. For knowing who you are," she said. "For sticking to it and being brave. It is clear that under the rules of any other year, you would've won this contest and that it was simply stolen from you. But I am proud you are not embittered."

"It's okay," I said.

We were in the parking lot of Ainsley, I suddenly realized. And a crowd of girls were gathering by the front door. The laurel crown was sitting at my feet. I reached down and picked it up, nestled its leaves in my hair. I hadn't planned on wearing this or a blazer, but, weirdly, Hecuba had taken me aside and said, "I think you should."

I shivered, remembering sitting in her sunroom, weaving another crown from a bucket of laurels we'd unpicked from Christmas wreathes. The power of the moment, how I'd wished to live inside it forever, to not go out into the world. These people, these girls, I loved them—they were special—and if people didn't—if they didn't—

"Are you okay?"

"Fine," I said as I opened the door, leaving the crown and blazer inside the car.

* * *

Liam found me in homeroom, saying, "Hey, everyone is so mad you're not a Sibyl. Are you ever gonna tell us what happened?"

"Nothing. I didn't get it."

"Why not?" he said.

"Your aunt interviewed me. I just wasn't good enough." I noticed other girls turning around, looking at me. One of them, Kylie, another queer girl, had touched me on the shoulder, saying she was so angry for me.

I'd known Liam was stirring people up online, but it all seemed so distant and weird. "Actually, can we not do this?" I said.

Through my first few classes, all I thought about was Felicity: a slideshow of her laughing, of her serious face, of the sadness she sometimes showed. I remembered too the chills I'd felt, reading those vows. I couldn't believe they'd been written a hundred years ago, by the first Sibyls, and that everyone: Mrs. Gimbel and Angel and Calliope and Hecuba, had all taken them! They'd seemed so crazy. I tossed the words over my tongue, "To resist everything new." I guess that I should be offended. Being a trans girl was definitely new, but Felicity had told me that to Persephone, the founder of the Sibyls, *new* meant a "trap," something designed to lure the girls into doing stuff against their own self-interest. She'd seen the whole school as a trap, designed to make them good and safe little girls, so she'd built the Sibyls to protect a chosen few.

The new Sibyls were announced over the PA, and someone

hissed at Hannah's name. Both of the new Sibyls were wearing their crowns and blazers, and they looked scared. Nobody would look at them.

"Hey," Hannah said, while we were walking to a new class. "You're not mad? You kind of disappeared."

"No, I'm fine, you deserved it," I said.

"I feel really bad," she said.

"Don't."

"No, no, you're always doing that emotional labor for me. I can't take your forgiveness."

"Umm, okay . . ."

All the Sibyls were getting tons of hate online, even Hecuba and Antigone. It was weird to think nobody knew they were my friends. Strife found all this hatred incredibly amusing. She said that four members of her civ class had cornered her, asking how she could participate in this unjust system. She'd flipped them off. She'd got mad only later when she discovered nobody had physically confronted Hecuba and Felicity. "Of course they pick the Black girl to call out."

Hecuba and Felicity were quiet, but when I asked if I'd meet them at lunch, they said, "Of course. Just wait for us. We've got to let the Other Two into our room."

Lunchtime came with a burst of shouting. "No more Sibyls!" I grimaced, looking through the cafeteria. The six Sibyls, including Calliope and Hannah and Whitney, were standing by the door to their club's room. They unlocked it, going in.

Felicity's face was completely blank. Liam stood up, waving at me. Every step I took in his direction stretched out infinitely.

"Hey," he said. "So what happened? You talked to my aunt and then you disappeared? Not even Hannah and Whitney know what went on."

I shrugged. "Can I not talk about it? Everything went okay."

"Sure, but if the Sibyls can't give money to somebody like you—who could really *use* the protection the scholarship would offer—then why does it even exist?"

"Because your aunt is rich," I said.

"Sure." Liam nodded, moving his cafeteria spaghetti around with his fork. "But it's just not right. They clearly did something to you. Everyone is so pissed. I think the Sibyls don't know how much people really hate them."

"Strife does," I said.

"Well, yeah, but she's the best of them," Liam said. "At least she's not rich and white. And she broke the news about the scholarship."

Just then the door opened, and Felicity came out. Through the open door, I saw the Other Two leaving, out into the door that went into the hall. I got up and waved to Liam, who had a really confused expression on his face, and walked over.

Then I was inside the room, and I burst out laughing. "This has been the weirdest day ever."

"Yep," Strife said, sitting down.

The Sibyls got a newspaper delivered—a real newspaper just for them—and she hunted through it, looking for the style section.

"What happened?" I said. "Where are Calliope and Penelope and Clytemnestra?"

"Gone," Felicity said. Her voice was quiet. "We told them they can have the mansion. Go there for visiting hours. Hang out with my aunt. But this room is for real Sibyls only. I guess we'll have to be in the same room for Founder's Day, but that's it."

In February, the whole school would have a day off to celebrate our founder. And that's when a lot of the alumni Sibyls usually came to meet the new Sibyls in a big gathering up at the mansion.

I pursed my lips. "That's really harsh."

"Yeah, I felt sorry for them," Strife said.

"They deserve it," Felicity said.

I sat at the small table, across from Hecuba, who had her computer open and was chewing on the eraser end of a pencil. I opened my lunch, which my mom had made at home, and instinctively apologized for the smell.

But Strife said, "What smell?" and Felicity was still quiet, looking through a book.

"Wait?" I said. "Why did they deserve it?"

"Because they're not real Sibyls," Felicity said. "Right? If they were, they would've cared what we were doing through the holidays."

"I guess," Strife said. "It's not a crime to not be friends. It's a scholarship, not a gang."

"Stop it, Strife," Felicity said. "You know it's more than a scholarship."

"Hey." Hecuba put up a hand. "Can someone read over my supplemental essay for this scholarship?"

"You're *still* applying to scholarships?" I said. "Why?"

"Because applying to stuff is like her drug," Strife said. "What're you writing about now?"

There was silence. And then Hecuba's face was bright red. She crossed one leg over the other on the couch and put up a hand, pushed her hair back over her ear. My eyebrows went up.

"Don't hate me, Alecto," she said. "I hate myself."

"Uh, what?" I said.

"Alecto?" Strife said. "What's happening?"

Felicity was on the armchair, reading some dusty old book. She had her own chair in the corner, and another stack of books. One weird thing about the Sibyls was that although all three were studious and got good grades, Hecuba and Strife weren't really bookish. They were like, *I don't have time to read outside class.* But Felicity really loved books the way I did. And she liked when the books were physically *old*, with yellowed paper and musty covers. She turned another page, not looking up.

"Hecuba," I said. "Are you writing about me? Can I see?"

"Stop, it's embarrassing, it's for a diversity supplement, and I'm so boring, I never know what to say in these things."

"What do you say?"

"Blah blah blah, hadn't realized how insidiously transmisogyny operates, blah," Hecuba said. "It's really awful. I'm sorry, Alecto."

"I don't mind," I said. "The idea that I could care about or want anything else is just . . . it doesn't even make sense to me right now. I cannot believe I'm here. It's absurd."

"Well, don't thank us," Strife said. "We're followers. Thank her." Then she pointed to Felicity. "With your lips."

My face went a deep red, and I turned away. Felicity didn't say anything. I wasn't sure she even heard.

"Oh, hey," Hecuba said. "Alecto. As oldest to youngest, can I take you out tonight? Just us two?"

Having relationships with all three girls was weird. Strife texted me all the time, asking me questions, making fun of the other two, maybe because she sensed that the two of us were both more cynical than them. Felicity was always interfering in my life, wanting to know things, giving me advice, and complaining about the other girls at school.

I knew Hecuba the least. I thought she seemed sad. Felicity and Strife would've been or could've been friends anyway, but Hecuba was with us only because we were all in the group. She really was like Hecuba, the character, someone who was destined to be a witness to other people's wrongdoing.

We went out that night to a bookstore/coffeeshop in Dupont

Circle, just far enough from school. I was a bit nervous—I still wasn't that used to being out and about as a girl—but it was fine. Nobody harassed me or was weird, and anyway we were in DC, not Virginia.

We were at a table in a corner, and the room was full, with lots of people shouting, talking loud, some even drinking alcohol.

"Hey," she said. "So you're okay with my essay?"

"It's fine," I said. "It's funny. I don't know if it'll get you the scholarship—it just highlights what you're not. But it doesn't bother me."

"Good," she said. "Let us know if you feel weird. Or, I don't know, maybe I should check in sometimes, to see, so it's not just your responsibility to speak up. I'm not sure. Oh, also, I can tell Strife to stop bothering you about Antigone."

My stomach dropped. "Would she?" I said. "Like, is that possible? Or would it just be a challenge?"

"I think she'd stop," Hecuba said. She was poised on the edge of her seat, with her elbows under her, looking almost like an adult, and not quite looking into my eyes. "Probably."

"No, it's fine," I said.

"Is it?" Hecuba said.

"Look," I said. "I like lots of people. It's fine. Even if I liked Antigone, if she said no, it'd be weird, or if we broke up, I dunno. It'd ruin the group."

"Well, if you two got together, I'd definitely worry about

Strife," Hecuba said. "Take care of her. Take care of them both. You'd be fine no matter what, but Antigone gets, like, really angry at stuff. And so does Strife, but not in the same way. Strife bottles it up, gets bitter and weird—we're good now, but it took a month last year after she joined to get her to stop sniping at Antigone for being rich and white and out of touch."

"I can see that."

I gave her a weak smile, and there was a pause. I liked her a lot—she was a natural leader, and a nice person. But the two of us still didn't fit together quite right. We had silences.

"I'm really gonna miss you guys," Hecuba said. "It doesn't feel good. To, like, let you go. And you and me, we've just started! It's sad."

"Yeah, I know . . ." I drew out the last word, not sure what to say.

"So . . . what's going on with you?" Hecuba said.

"I don't know. My parents have been on me lately: they're like, *You should do more extracurriculars, decide what you're interested in, you cannot just be the trans girl*, and I'm like, *But I do debate!* Except I don't win. I think they're asking what I can win at."

"That's what parents do, at least at Ainsley. It's all about specializing, showing them who you are, having a brand for colleges, jobs, internships, life."

"I guess the Sibyls are like that too. Antigone, Hecuba,

Strife, you all have a brand, even if nobody else gets it."

"Sure," she said. "So what're you gonna do?"

"With Felicity? With the Sibyls? For my parents?"

"All three?"

"I just . . . I want . . ." My hand moved up and down just under my throat, like I was working a pump to bring out the words. "I just . . . I feel . . . I feel really *happy*. You guys picking me, that was the best thing that's ever happened in my entire life."

"You deserve it," she said.

"But why?" I said. "Angel thought I was so clearly not good enough."

"She's got to worry about whether you can, like, become a senator or something. And you probably won't. But you're one of us. Like I knew if I left Strife and Antigone together with the Other Two, then they'd fall apart. That's why I suggested we come get you."

"What? You?"

"It was my idea. Don't get me wrong: they really liked it. But I don't know if you've noticed that Strife and Antigone are a little . . . socially awkward?"

"No kidding."

"Yeah, they don't have friends outside the Sibyls. They don't really get how friendship works. They were complaining about the Other Two, saying how much better you would've been, and I was like, *Okay, so let's get her.*"

"Thanks," I said. "I totally believe you. It feels like the two of them can be a little . . . theoretical. More talk than action."

"And I don't care about being canceled and stuff," Hecuba said. "But it would be amazing if Princeton didn't retract my offer? Like . . . is that too much to ask?"

I laughed. "No. Should I post online that I love you guys?"

"Maybe? Yeah?"

"Done."

"You're not upset?"

"No."

"I have to say, until we started hanging out, I never would've known it, but people stare at you constantly," Hecuba said. "You are so brave."

"They do?" I said. "I don't know. I don't notice, I guess."

"It's intense," Hecuba said. "And after you left the interviews, when Strife and Felicity weren't around, people thought I agreed you weren't any good. I heard what Angel and Mrs. Gimbel and Calliope and the Other Two said. They acted like you'd *done* something to them. As if you just applying for the Sibyls was hurting them somehow. They didn't want to be forced to even consider you—they just wanted you to reject yourself."

I was almost getting unhappy. I didn't want to hear any of this. "Well, I guess transmisogyny *is* real."

"It is," she said earnestly. "It really is."

Hecuba put a hand out, squeezed mine, and pulled back. She wasn't as touchy-feely as the other two. It was weird that Felicity could be so cold, so mean sometimes, but she was always touching us, kissing us on the head. Even thinking of it made my heart melt, but I told myself no. Trying to get with her would ruin everything.

14

LIAM WAS POSTING A PETITION online asking Ainsley to ban the Sibyls, and maybe even stop teaching Greek and Latin totally because they were racist and sexist right to their core. Each day he raised the temperature, saying more and more about how the Sibyls were transphobic and gendered and how the club made him sick and how it was everything wrong with single-gender education. He was causing trouble about Founder's Day, saying we should crash the gathering of all the Sibyls that happened every year up at the mansion.

Liam wrote that before the retreat his aunt had come to him, pushing for him to join the Sibyls to keep me out.

I wrote on a few of his posts, "Hey, I actually like the Sibyls. They gave me a fair chance."

Eventually he wrote back, "Look, this isn't about just you

anymore. It's great that you've made your peace, but they're a regressive, conservative club that has no place at our school."

One day in mid-February I found Liam standing in the entrance to the Sibyls' room right as lunch was starting. He was passing the petition from hand to hand, talking closely to a girl I didn't know.

"Hey," I said.

When he didn't answer, I grabbed the clipboard. "Can I sign?"

"Umm," Liam said.

The most annoying thing about this petition was that Liam could've picked a half dozen reasons for wanting the Sibyls to get stripped of their official recognition. He could've said their founder was racist, or that it was really colonialist to favor Western culture over the East, or even that it was unfair to let a little clique of girls distribute a huge scholarship to people they liked. But instead he'd gone for the throat: he'd said the organization was transphobic. Said his aunt was deeply transmisogynist, that she had tried her hardest to stop Ainsley from admitting me and stop me from attending the interviews. The petition said the Sibyls encouraged binary thinking and conformism and fear of men. He even wrote about the quote on the door, and about how the whole concept of Sophrosyne was designed to keep women trapped by the patriarchy.

The statement printed on the cover sheet of the petition wasn't new to me—I'd read it online—but I was surprised by the number of names on the next sheet: maybe fifty or sixty in all.

Wait, then a new page started, and I looked through: over a hundred names—boys at St. George's.

"You're asking them?" I said.

"It's their campus too; what Ainsley does reflects on them," Liam said. "It's not fair you're the only St. George's kid who got to compete. There could be a lot of guys or GNC or enby kids at St. George's who'd appreciate being part of Ainsley activities, but you're the only one who gets to be, and why? Because you accept the gender binary."

"Liam," I said. "Look at me. Do I look gender conforming or binary to you? I'm like every Ainsley parent's nightmare—a boy in a dress among their precious girls. You're being *super* unfair."

He grabbed the clipboard again, and I swiped it away, holding it high. His face got red, and he stood there with both fists clenched, shaking—I towered over him, got up close, and I wanted to say: *Did you want to be a boy? Well, this is what it is. Being so angry you feel like you could explode, and having other people see that and take pleasure from it.* Saying that would've been unforgivable, but still, I thought it.

"Liam," I said.

"Can you give that back?" said the girl.

"Yeah," said another girl.

Suddenly they were all around, and my face went blank. I let the clipboard fall.

"Pick that up," said the girl. "The pages are everywhere."

I looked at her. She was in one of my advanced classes. Tiffany. I turned away, stalked out into the gray cold of the woods. I kept walking and walking until I was out of sight of the school and stayed away until lunch was over.

After that confrontation with Liam, I'd been afraid to go back to the Sibyls' room. It suddenly seemed like a trap—a place people could find me. I knew from the other girls that Liam was usually outside it, that he'd nailed his petition to the door like Martin Luther's Ninety-Five Theses.

Felicity had texted, Let's be real black lipstick kids and go hang out with Persephone.

So there we were, just the two of us, at the family cemetery. Although it was forty years old, Winifred Coatesworth's marble mausoleum was the newest thing there, and the epitaph still shone crisp and clear.

> *The Goddess now in either empire sways,*
> *Six moons in Hell, and six with Ceres stays.*

We were both freezing, sitting on the simpler gravestones of Persephone's two friends (I'd said, "Is this okay?" and Felicity had said, "For a Sibyl, sure, they'd want their graves to give us succor"—yes, she did rhyme the line, which was awesome).

"What's her epitaph from?" I said.

"Ovid," Felicity said.

"Kind of dark," I said.

Felicity shrugged. She was on her phone, scrolling through one of her social apps. I looked over her shoulder, watching her look at pictures, like them, move to the next one. Lots of cute animals, some rings and necklaces, and many photos of very extravagant hairstyles.

"This is what you like?" I asked.

"Not everything can be all serious."

"Would you pin up your hair like that?"

"No," she said. "This is, like, a lot of work. Days and days."

"I'd help!"

She raised an eyebrow. "Hmm . . . you do always look good." She put the phone facedown against her hip, and I shivered, though not with the cold. I was poised on the edge of the headstone and simultaneously sort of wrapped around her, but without actually touching. It felt like a true contortion, and my body was cramping up, but I stayed still.

She pushed back against me, rubbing her shoulder against my chest, and my heart stopped. Instantly I was outside my body, which was good, because hot sweat broke out all over my face and back, and that body was looking pretty uncomfortable.

Her voice went low, a little sultry, and I had to choke off a laugh at its weird tone.

"Hey," she said. "Do you want me to quit the Sibyls?"

"What?" I said. "No."

"Because I would," she said. "Maybe Liam is right."

"If the Sibyls had never existed, you'd have been the loneliest girl at this school. And so would I and so would Strife. That's enough reason to keep it around."

"I think so," Felicity said. "But maybe it's not the thing we need anymore. That oath we take—you know Winifred Coatesworth would've hated you."

Winifred's Wikipedia page was full of the weird positions she'd taken over the years. After graduating college, she'd spent a long time visiting India and China and Japan during the twenties, and then she'd been a war correspondent in the forties. She was always writing about the Asiatic temperament and how it contrasted to the European one.

"Maybe, but so what? She's dead."

Felicity was quiet for a long time, and then her shoulders heaved. I put a hand on her shaking back, felt the bony shoulder through her Ainsley fleece. My hand looked way too big on it, almost gross. I craned my head around, trying to see her face, and, yep, she was crying.

"What's wrong?" I said.

"Nothing," she said. "Just worried. I don't know. Really, really worried about everything."

One thing I still wasn't used to was how girls cried. They said it was the hormones—it unlocked something inside. But whatever it was, I didn't have it yet.

"Err," I said. "Literally nothing is wrong."

She stopped. Then she frowned and looked up. "What?"

"Nothing is wrong," I said. "Everything is great. I am super happy. So Liam thinks you're a transphobe. So what? I know you're not."

"But how do you know? He's saying we became your friend to use you as *window dressing*. You don't worry?"

"No," I said. "Because I have a brain."

Felicity snorted. "Wow," she said. "You make it sound so simple."

"Yeah . . . I don't know what else we might be," I said. "But we're definitely friends. And . . . and I know you see me as a girl, Antigone. Meeting you is what made me realize most people *don't* see me as a girl. The way you treat me is just . . . perfect."

Her lips tightened and quivered a bit. "What else?" she said. "Huh?"

"You mentioned you don't know what else we might be?"

"Yeah . . ." My stomach tightened, and then I had a great idea. "We're friends, definitely, but we could also be lllllllllllll"—I drew out the letter for a long time—"lab partners. If we take the same bio class."

She hit me on the shoulder, and I caught her arm, and we sat like that for a second, smiling at each other.

"You're lucky I like you so much," she said. "You're really lucky."

"Why?"

"Because I don't like most people," Felicity said. "It's like with Liam. He's great and everyone loves him, but he's *boring*. Never anything new with him."

"No, I meant why do you like me?"

She frowned. "Umm, because you like old stuff."

"What?" I said. "Come on, that's not the reason."

"Yeah, it's definitely the reason. You were *into* all that Latin stuff. Nobody else really cares about it. Not even Whitney, she just does it to win awards."

"Felicity," I said. "Err, Antigone . . . that's . . . that's not a reason to be friends."

"*What?!* You're friends with Liam just because the two of you are trans!"

Her voice went high and got a bit screechy while we were saying that, and I laughed. She seemed small, and kind of young, and without thinking about it I hugged her close and kissed the top of her head.

15

I SMILED CRAZILY FOR THE rest of the week, looking up things like how to flirt, and how to ask out a girl, and texting a bunch with Strife, telling her my plans—

Tara: You know, I guess that I just realized: she's just a person. She's not a goddess. But then the next second I'm like oh my god how could she possibly like me?

Strife: Antigone is a weird one. Nobody knows what makes her tick.

Tara: What? Of course you do—she's told you—she's like a person from another world. She believes in, you know, honor and justice and stuff.

Strife: Except she doesn't actually do anything honorable or just.

Tara: So what? She will someday.

Strife: Wow. I have no idea what form of disaster you

plus her will be, but it's going to be absolutely wild.

Tara: Shush.

My entire body felt different. I'd done my best to cover up or ignore my body. I wore makeup and put on skirts and leggings and other girls' clothes, and I stared in the mirror long enough to see if I looked okay, but then I wiped the image off the hard drive of my mind, saying, *This is just my temporary form.* I knew that I looked ridiculous: a gigantic broad-shouldered dude with big arms and calves and a strong jaw, dressing in schoolgirl clothes.

But I tried sometimes to put myself back on that tombstone, with my arm around her shoulder, and see myself as someone not ridiculous, as, like, someone cool and mysterious: a giant person with flowing hair and an androgynous body and slick makeup—someone from outside of time or space, someone unlimited and great.

Then one day when I got home, a woman was in front of our house, arguing with my dad. He was on his tiptoes, moving his hands, with wisps of hair escaping from the sides of his head.

I hopped out of the car and ran up: "Uh, what's going on?" I said.

"Hello," the woman said. "Very pleased to meet you?"

"Uh . . ." I'd stopped wearing the big coat I'd used before to hide my girls' school uniform when I got out of the car—I just wore an Ainsley fleece like everyone else. But something about the way she looked at me made me pluck off the hairband Felicity had stuck today on my head. "I, uh . . ."

"Hello, are you Tara?" the woman said. "Can I speak to you alone for a minute?"

"Let me talk for a moment to him," my dad said.

I stood there, not sure who they were talking about, but then my dad waved at me, and the woman came in, wandering in behind. I was in the living room, and she was hovering there, saying, "It's just routine."

Toys were strewn all over the floor, and I instinctively kicked a toy truck to one side. The woman said, "Do you have a younger child?"

"No, just Tanay," my dad said. He raised an eyebrow, looked at me, and I got the message: We needed to hide things from this woman. Like the fact that my mom was illegally taking care of other peoples' kids.

"Who's she?" I whispered.

"The government," he said.

"Like, but from what agency?"

"Unsure," he said. "She didn't identify herself."

"But she has to."

"Actually, no, I don't," she said. "It's the law. I'm entitled to enter any home if we have probable cause."

"That's a lie," I squeaked.

"You can check with a lawyer," she said.

"We don't have a lawyer!"

"They're worried that you're trans," my dad said. "I told them that's absurd. You just dress differently, but you're a boy, not on any drugs or anything."

"I'm just here to collect some information," the woman said, moving to our kitchen table. "We've gotten some disturbing reports that you might be feeling pressure to identify as a different gender, and we're here to help you, so that you can be your most authentic self. You know . . . I can come back, but it would be with the police, and we'd have to take you into custody. . . ."

My mom got home then, rushing inside when she saw us. "What's wrong?"

I tried to text Hannah, because her mom was a lawyer, and the woman said, "Who are you talking to?" And I said, "Just some friends from school," and she said, "That's St. George's Preparatory Academy for Boys?"

"Uh—uh."

"Yes," my father said. "That's where she goes."

My father didn't even notice what he'd said. He was looking me over, then he told me to go upstairs, and change, and the woman said, "Actually, that's fine. That checks out with what we know. Is this what you wear to school?"

"Uh, yeah," I said. "I know important people. Have you heard of Angel Beaumont? She's the friend of a girl—of a friend of—she's my friend's aunt."

"I'm not familiar with her, no," she said. "Please, please, just take a moment to talk to me. Tara, is it? We just want to help you."

"N-no, it's Tanay," I said, trying to lower my voice, feeling the growl deep in my chest.

Everything was disordered and confused. My mom and dad both looked at each other and at me, panic-stricken, and I knew nobody had any idea of what to do. The woman sat at our table and pulled out a tablet with a little keyboard and started to take notes.

I went to the table and sat down, not able to feel my body or my legs. My parents sat down by my side.

The woman said, "Nothing will happen now; we just have questions. I have to say, I'm already quite concerned that we've caught you in some lies. As it stands, right at this moment, that's more than enough info for more investigation."

My phone chirped. Hannah said:

My mom says just talk to them, don't worry, and call us afterward. Just tell the truth. She says these visits are super common for trans kids in Virginia. A neighbor probably reported you. Don't try to lie. They already know you are trans. The most important thing is you tell them you didn't get pressured into being trans or into taking drugs or anything. It's crazy, I know. Just tell the truth.

"Uh, okay," I said. "But everything is fine. What's the problem?"

The woman said, "Can I speak to your child alone?"

The woman pointed at me, and then my parents, reluctantly, got up, and they went to the kitchen. The woman—she *must* be a social worker—looked at them, and she said, "Do you have a bedroom where you could maybe wait? Don't worry, your child will be fine."

I was glued to the chair, and I watched them walk upstairs with hangdog eyes. They shouldn't leave! I should run away. I suddenly understood how anarchists felt: smash the state! I hated this. It was so absurd. But Hannah sent another text, and I read her advice.

I'm calling an attorney I know who deals with family practice law, they'll be in touch. Can I give them your number? This is Hannah's mom.

I took a breath, tried to remember some of my heroes, what they'd felt. In ancient Greece, the most heroic ancient figure was Socrates—sentenced to death for blasphemy slash corrupting the youth. Today they'd probably have called him a "groomer," but he was really just a teacher. His friends begged him to escape the trial, but he was all, *No, if my state wants to put me to death, then I cannot say no. All my life I've been proud to call myself a citizen, and if my people say I must die, then I have to subject myself to their judgment.*

"I, uh, did you have questions?" I said.

"One moment, please," she said.

She asked my name, and since Hannah's mom had said not to lie, I said, "T-Tara."

"That's better."

Then she asked my birthdate and for a copy of my school ID and made me sign a statement that I was speaking of my own free will, and I said, "Don't my parents need to consent," and she said, "But they already did," and I thought, *Did they? I don't remember that.*

But after all the intro stuff, she said, "Tell me, in your own words, about your understanding of your gender and sexuality."

I took a deep breath. Weirdly, almost nobody had asked me this before—I guess because my parents were in denial, a little bit, and everyone else was just like, well she says that she's a girl—I guess they all figured someone else would handle it.

"Umm," I said. "Well, I guess, like, when I was thirteen, I realized that maybe I was a girl. Like, I was . . . I don't know . . . I was talking to my friend Henry, at St. George's, and some other guy friends—we were at his house—and they opened up and talked about girls and stuff, and I was, like, *Wow, I don't feel that way at all.* And it just made me think, and I—more and more, I was like, *I don't feel like these other guys,* and I think in the old days, I wouldn't have known what I was—but obviously I know about trans people now, and I did research on the internet, and I was like, *Okay, maybe this is right for me.* And

I told my parents, but they were like, *No, probably you're just gay*, and I thought, *Oh, okay*, but I dunno, I really liked girls. Freshman year I did a play at Ainsley, and I was around girls all the time, and I was like, *This is it. This is where I belong.*" I smiled. "And I sort of came out to Liam, who was on the stage crew, and he tried to make me feel included with the other girls, and I met Whitney and Hannah, who I thought were nice, and it just felt so right, and Liam gave me his old girl clothes—he's trans, but his mom still buys him girls' clothes in his size just in case—and he encouraged me to wear them and stuff, and on Halloween I went as a girl, and it just felt amazing, like my brain was melting, and I guess Liam let some other people in on the secret of who I really was, and I told them to call me Tara, which was the name I used when I played a girl character in online games, and it was so absurd. It was—I dunno. And then this guy, Drew, he saw pictures online, and he was like, *You're gay, you're queer, you're a fag, just admit it, just have the courage to admit it, just don't be a closet case, and . . .*" My throat was closing, and I blinked. "And, uh . . . I was like, *No. I'm a girl*. And then everyone at school knew, and one teacher at St. George's—Mr. Danyon—he said, *You shouldn't be here*, and I said it was okay, and he said, *No, you should not be here, Tara—it's not right*. And . . . I dunno, that was just like . . . I dunno . . . he talked to everyone, and this was, like, February, so I did remote school for the rest of the year, and then they made a new schedule for me for the new year where I'd take classes at

Ainsley, and it all worked out!"

During this, I'd heard the constant clatter of typing, and her eyes finally darted up then to meet mine. She asked how my parents were about it, and I talked a little more, and then there was a long pause, and I said, "But I am so happy. And I love it. And I'm not on hormones, or even blockers, so you *know* it's real."

At that she looked up. "I'm sorry. You haven't seen a doctor? Or the doctor has recommended no treatment?"

"I, uh, no. Like, my parents were worried about legal stuff. So we haven't seen anyone."

"And you're not on any drugs?"

"No."

"Because I'm warning you, the drugs leave a trace. In fact, I'll want a drug test."

"Why?"

"According to your internet provider, people at this address have browsed websites for buying estrogen and for getting sex change operations."

"I mean . . . how can you see that?"

"The commonwealth of Virginia takes protecting children very seriously. Have you been encouraged by anyone, by your friends or schools or doctor or even your parents, to take medical treatments? It sounds like after you came out as gay, you were almost forced into attending classes with girls. What did you think about that?"

"But I wanted to. And I'm not—I haven't done any medical stuff at all! So how could I get pressured?"

I took a breath. She asked about school and how it was all going, and I said it was fine. She asked about grades, and I said they were good. She asked my favorite subjects, and I told her about Roman stuff and the Sibyls, and she said, "We've heard there are some complaints at Ainsley about you competing for this award."

"Oh, uh, yeah," I said. "But it's okay that I—" I was going to say it was okay that I didn't get it, but the woman interrupted me:

"Some people are saying you claimed to be a girl just so you could get the scholarship?"

"Yeah," I said. "Drew. Some of the guys."

"Not just them. Some of your female classmates as well."

"Who?" I said. "That's totally wrong. I don't care about the money. I—"

"Then why did you compete? I heard that you made a scene, and that you needed to be ejected from the interview by security. Did your parents put you up to it? Did they suggest the idea of you identifying as a girl?"

"No!" I said. "They're so against it!"

"I see," she said. "Were they against you being gay?"

"Huh? No."

"Did you think being a girl might be more acceptable than being gay? Because to me it sounds like you only thought you were trans after meeting this other boy."

"What? Uh, no," I said. "I told my parents when I was a kid."

"That's not what your father said. He said there was no mention of it before last year, and he was surprised when it came up."

"Well . . ." I shrugged. "Come on . . . you can't trust that. Parents remember only what they want to."

"And wouldn't your parents remember you bringing up something so major?"

She probed at me, not letting go, and my ears burned, remembering how my dad and my mom and I had talked all those years ago. I'd told them about the sleepover, and the guys had talked about fantasizing about sex and all the hot chicks and what they would do to them, and I'd told the guys, *But don't you ever imagine you* are *the girl?* And they'd been like, *What, no, gross.* And they'd reacted so badly to it, that I'd been like, *Huh, weird, I thought that was normal,* so I googled it, and it wasn't!

"You never thought that simply meant you might be gay?" the social worker said.

"Well, yeah," I said. "But . . . you know . . . boys are . . . they're nothing. I hardly think about them."

"You had a crush, your father said, on your friend Henry, during eighth grade. And when you told Henry, he said not to tell anyone else about it and that he didn't think anyone else at

St. George's was gay. How did that make you feel?"

"Sure, well . . . you know . . . it was a phase." I tried to smile, but her eyes were hooded. And yet, the weird thing was, although I was drowning in this conversation, I realized I also enjoyed it, a little bit, because nobody else in my life had ever understood this stuff.

I took a breath. "Look," I said. "If you're trying to say that I started identifying as trans because I'm gay and didn't want to admit it, that makes no sense. Being trans is a thousand times harder than being gay."

"I think . . . sometimes boys think being a girl is the only way to fit in, to live a normal life. It's especially common in some immigrant societies, where traditional beliefs make gender an easier barrier to cross than sexuality."

"Yeah, maybe for Muslims—I know there are lots of trans girls in Iran—but I'm a Hindu," I said. "And Hindus would never ever let their kid become a hijra."

"That's not something I'm familiar with. What's that?"

"The point is, Hindus are so anti-trans. It's, like, an extremely low, almost outcaste thing to be. My parents would be a thousand times happier if I was gay."

"I don't know," she said. "I'm just investigating. It strikes me that maybe it solved some problems for them. You avoided bullying at your school. You kept your scholarship. You could compete for this *new* scholarship, which you almost won. I'm not saying any of this is your fault—just that you were maneuvered into this place by teachers, administrators, and parents who all had their own interests."

"That's . . . insane," I said. "Like that is awful. That is sick."

"Exactly why I am here," she said. "But someone needs to look out for you! Someone needs to make sure you don't make choices you regret."

My hand drummed against the table. I wanted to yell. My heart was locked up inside me, and my skirt and polo shirt and makeup felt like abominations. I hadn't felt so much like a boy in almost a year. But I couldn't make it stop! My phone beeped helplessly on the counter as the woman typed away.

16

I WANTED TO STAY HOME from school the next day, and my mom seemed okay with that. But halfway through the morning I found myself in makeup and a skirt anyway, thinking, *What's the point? Wherever I am, I'm not myself, so why not be at school.*

"You look nice," my mom said.

My eyes filled with tears. I'd spent a year not on hormones, just so we'd avoid the attention of the Governor, but it'd come anyway! In fact, we'd seemed more suspicious.

"I want to be on hormones."

"We will talk—"

"No!" I said. "Call the doctor! Call the clinic! This is stupid! Call them!" I was shrieking.

"You're emotional."

For the rest of the car ride, I simmered, and she tried to give me that "We will talk about it after the investigation is done" BS, and I snarled, "That's never gonna happen. It's never gonna be safe. We just need to do it!"

"You aren't wrong . . ." she said, which meant it was hard even to be mad. I hated my parents for being so smart and so reasonable. They knew just how to talk to me, to make me agree with them.

In Latin we were translating Cicero, which I'd already done last year, at St. George's. These were his speeches against the Catilinarian conspiracy, and I translated mentally: *Oh the times, oh the people. Though the Senate is aware of this man's crimes, he still lives!*

Mrs. Gimbel droned through her talk, reading directly from a notebook, and I wondered who had turned me in.

When I'd told Liam about the woman visiting us, he'd written back:

Liam: Probably Whitney's mom. She's been getting really upset about the protests. See, this is the kind of entitlement Sibyls have.

Tara: Liam. I don't care about the protests.

Liam: Well, it's not really about you. Did you know Winifred Coatesworth supported eugenics? And imperialism?

Tara: I know that's on her Wikipedia page. But she founded the club when she was fifteen. And she's dead. Come on. If you care about me, you'll stop it. I mean what if you're right and this protesting is why people are targeting me, isn't that reason enough to stop?

Liam: No. That's exactly why I should keep going.

Thinking about those messages, suddenly I wasn't mad at Hannah or Whitney or Angel or my parents or even the Governor. I was mad at Liam. He was spending his time talking about how the Sibyls were racist and transphobic, and meanwhile the Governor of Virginia was thinking about taking me away from my family!

The woman hadn't said when we could expect an answer to the investigation. She hadn't even said what crime we'd committed or what the punishment could be. She'd just said that we might hear from her office again.

As I went through the doorway into the Sibyls' room, I grabbed the sign-up sheet for the petition to have us banned. I clawed it off the wall and tore it up and threw the pieces onto the ground.

"Hey!" someone shouted. But I let the door swing shut.

Inside, I saw Felicity in her usual chair, crouched over an old dictionary, using a magnifying glass with a light embedded inside. She looked up and gave me a wave and then went back to her book.

"What's that?" I said.

"Old, old, old dictionary," she said.

"What're you looking up?"

"Nothing," she said. "Words. Just seeing what's going on."

I stood over her, not sure what to do, wanting to put a hand out, to touch her neck. She looked up and smiled, then looked down.

A fist pounded against the door.

"What?" Strife said. "What's going on?"

"That's been happening all day," Felicity said.

But the pounding came again, and then the door opened, and Liam stood in it, flanked by some of the other queer kids, and by another guy.

The other guy looked at me. Then he walked inside. I stood in front of him, blocked him with my big, broad hands. "What's going on?"

Abruptly he sat down, his legs crossed, and then I almost heard the smirk.

Behind him I saw Drew Handy, slouching against a wall, grinning at me through his freckles and laughing deep in the back of his throat.

I nudged Liam with my foot. "What's going on?"

Drew came into the room, and more kids followed him. A girl was in the back, filming on her phone. Suddenly there were ten kids sitting all around us, on the floor.

Hecuba looked at Strife, and Strife looked at me. Felicity calmly put down her magnifying glass and closed her book. When she got up, a girl swooped in and took her seat.

"What's happening?" Felicity said.

Then, as if on cue, Liam said to Drew. "How'd you do on

the precalc test?" And the room burst into conversation, with people talking to each other, and then there were more people in the door, more people waving their phones, and the four of us, standing, were crowded by the other kids. And I stood there, my lip twisting, and I thought about pulling my foot back, and kicking Liam's head like it was a soccer ball.

"What is wrong with y—?" I yelled.

The last word had been cut off by a sob. But the room had gone quiet, with my voice reverberating through the room. "I don't accept this," I said.

"Nobody cares what you accept," Drew said.

"Liam," I said. "This guy called me a shemale and a faggot for half a year. Don't you even care?"

My voice was creaky but still loud. Liam didn't look away, he made eye contact. I suddenly felt panicky, with all of them on the ground and me wearing a skirt with no tights or leggings—worried that Drew would somehow reach into my underwear.

"Stop it, Liam," I said. "I *don't want this.*"

"Hey, calm down," Drew said. "We're just trying to change stuff."

"And him," I said. "This guy, you're gonna let *him* speak for you!" I raised a hand, wanting to slap Drew, let my arm stay back, like the cocked hammer of a gun.

"Drew's good," Liam said. "He's been collecting signatures at St. George's."

"The boys?" I said. "We're gonna care what they think?"

"I'm a boy," Liam said.

I whirled, feeling trapped with them crowding the floor, making it hard to leave. "What is wrong with you?" I said.

"No what is wrong with *you?*" Liam asked. "Like, just because they're your friends you're letting them get away with hurting your people? It's pathetic."

I screamed at him again. And what was almost hilarious was that I *had* the words. I had the words that would destroy Liam and call him out. And they were simple enough, though they'd work only on him. I'd say, *This is a girls' space—so why are you interfering?* That would be enough. And it would be unfair, sure. Because I knew the answer: he was interfering because his parents forced him to attend Ainsley even though he was a boy. But the words would still destroy him, because they'd cut right to the heart of what he was and was not—the way only a trans person could cut another trans person.

The way he had just cut me, by saying I was helping the transphobes.

So even as Mrs. Gimbel appeared and grabbed me by the arm, yelling at me for making a scene, I laughed inside, knowing I'd shown Liam more consideration than he'd ever shown to me.

I was taken to a room at Ainsley. And the headmistress, Dr. Pearson, got a call. At first she was gonna punish me over yelling and making a scene in the Sibyls' room, but then they found an easier charge. They looked up my list of demerits and read them out to me. Dr. Pearson acted horrified and asked, "Why didn't you work these off?"

I shrugged.

"But didn't you care?"

This was the headmistress, Dr. Pearson, who I found ten thousand times scarier than Mrs. Gimbel, sitting across from a desk.

"Did you really think you could just not report them?"

"Nobody ever gave me the school manual! And I figured all that stuff about the honor system was BS. And that teachers report demerits themselves anyway, which they clearly do. And in that case, why am I reporting them myself? And that if anyone really cared, they'd come talk to me."

"Do you know how entitled you sound?"

I shifted around in my chair. Mrs. Gimbel was to one side of us, in the conference room. The assistant headmaster, Dr. Eagleton, from St. George's, was also on the phone.

"Why would you flout our rules this way?" Dr. Pearson said.

"You're always telling me I'm not really an Ainsley student. That I'm still technically enrolled at St. George's."

"Please," she said. "That is pure sophistry. You know the spirit of the law is above the letter. You had a moral duty to report these demerits and work them off. Now, why didn't you?"

I shrugged again. "It just didn't . . . I don't know . . . I'm used to St. George's. Over there, we wouldn't . . . we'd never . . . we wouldn't expect people to report themselves. It's just . . ."

"Did you ever consider that perhaps girls are held to a higher standard than are boys?"

I hung my head, and they pronounced a sentence on me, not just for my outburst in the Sibyls' room but for my sixty demerits. I was going to get an out-of-school suspension for one week, and they would consider expulsion.

So what. Maybe I'd leave this school, or go to public school. Or be homeschooled. My mom was home anyway and she could do it. Or I'd run away, be homeless, live on somebody's couch. Drink pregnant mare's piss to get my estrogen, like they'd done in ancient Roman times when someone wanted to transition.

When the tribunal was over, I was left in the office with just Mrs. Gimbel for company.

"Would it surprise you if I said that I have known plenty of trans people over the years?" she said.

I rolled my eyes.

"No, no, I have. I live right near here, in Dupont Circle. I've been there a long time. But every person I knew also felt a sense of responsibility to everyone who might come after them. You're the only one who's said, *I don't care, I'll act how I want, and I'll take what I can get.* And . . . I just don't get that. I just don't—"

"What about *your* sense of responsibility?"

"I'm sorry?"

"Don't you feel like you have a sense of responsibility? To not be hard on me? To not jam things up for me? I'm a kid. What did I ever do to you? Everyone else in the whole school is nice to me, except for you."

"Everyone else is *humoring* you," Mrs. Gimbel said. "You must know that in their hearts none of them truly see you as a girl. That's not prejudice. That's just biology. We all do our best, but we cannot make ourselves disbelieve the evidence of our eyes."

"That's not true. Lots of people treat me like a girl. I know, it's hard for me to believe too someti—"

"Even your friends routinely slip up. I remember during a recent meeting with Antigone, she used the wrong pronouns for you. And that isn't the only time it's happened. It's almost more common than not."

"See, now you're just lying. Felicity wouldn't do that."

"I don't care whether you believe me or not. But I doubt there is a single person in your life who genuinely sees you as a girl. Maybe someday, with drugs and surgery, you'll be able to pass visually for a girl, and people will have an easier time remembering. But right now you are simply not there yet, and it's disrespectful to our intelligence and to our sense of tolerance to expect us to go against what we clearly see to be the truth."

My brow furrowed. "I . . . Why would you say this?"

"Because somebody needs to. Because you are living in an illusion. Because—"

"Stop."

"No," she said. "Your people have tried to silence mine since day one, but I will not stop."

"You are a— What is wrong with you?"

"I am not the one who—"

"You're just an awful person. Nothing. Nothing . . . What did I ever do to you? Nothing. Nothing ever."

She wanted to argue some more, so I got up, and she kept speaking. Not in a yell, but not in a whisper either. And her voice followed me out of the room.

Later on, my mom and dad took me home and yelled at me, saying first I'd lost the Sibyls scholarship and now I had permanently endangered my college chances and put myself at risk when it came to the government assessment of our family.

I went to my room. They'd taken my phone and computer, leaving me with just paper books.

My head was heavy. I sat in my bed, still in my uniform and makeup, trying to sleep. I imagined hitting the streets, like some of the girls from my trans group. That's another thing people didn't get. You didn't always become homeless because you were kicked out. Sometimes you did it because life at home was just too unbearable. You decided that whatever happened, you just couldn't bear another minute in this house. And sometimes you did things—got into drugs or stealing or fighting at school or whatever—just to raise the temperature, make things harder for your parents—because you *wanted* to get kicked out.

My parents were the ones really at fault. Worse than Mrs. Gimbel or the Governor. They should've protected me! They shouldn't have put all this *weight* on me.

But the thing was, I still couldn't hate them. Because you know what I'd never said? I'd never said to anyone that my parents wouldn't *let* me go on hormones. Because it wasn't true. I'd always sort of known that if I pushed and cried enough and told them I was absolutely dead certain, then I probably could make them do it. Like, they weren't *really* against it. They just weren't sure. They didn't know if it was right. They were asking me to tell them.

And I owed it to them to be sure, so I'd waited. They'd trusted me, and I'd repaid that trust, and that was an honorable thing to do. Way more honorable than obeying our school's stupid honor code.

I went to the desk and opened the drawer. The blazer was folded up in there with the crown on top.

The thing people didn't get was that I *was* a Sibyl. The school might not recognize it, but that didn't make it untrue.

17

ONE MAJOR PROBLEM WITH SPENDING so much time brooding is that when really bad stuff happens, all your brooding is used up, and you end up feeling kind of cheerful. Like, oh, okay, I'm kicked out of school and the government is considering taking me away from my family, but so what? I'm still alive.

And anyway, my phone was blowing up with texts from the Sibyls. Mostly from Strife, who was positively gleeful over how out of control the school had gotten.

Strife: Where did you go? It's gotten pretty incredible here. The latest thing is Hannah and Whitney gave up their awards and said they don't want to be Sibyls anymore! Has Angel called you? Everyone's saying she's gonna give you the award instead.

Tara: Oh. Why would they do that?

Strife: Because they got it unfairly and everyone hates them?

Tara: Well yeah, but if they don't think they deserved it, why would they even compete?

Strife: They realized how unfair it was.

Tara: But *was* it even unfair? There are pretty good reasons to give it to them instead of me.

Strife: Maybe you should be Strife instead of me. Come on. You're winning! You're gonna get the scholarship! Can you talk to Antigone though? She's not responding to my texts.

I texted Antigone.

Tara: Hey, Strife says you're upset.

Felicity: I've been trying to talk to Liam. He's so out of control! He knows our aunt. He should know that she's not gonna back down. She might even rescind the scholarships completely.

Tara: So? What can she do? Sue him?

Felicity: Tara, maybe you don't care, but everyone will lose their scholarships.

Tara: Yeah and maybe not get into Harvard either.

The moment I wrote the text I felt terrible. If I was about to lose a guaranteed shot at Harvard, I'd be upset too. Or maybe I wouldn't. I actually wasn't sure anymore what it would be like to be an ordinary person.

I apologized to Felicity, and she took my apology, but then we didn't talk anymore. In fact, the whole Sibyl group chat (or at least the group chat with the four of us) was quiet all night.

The next morning, when my mom came to knock on my door, saying, "Enough self-pity, it's time to . . ." I let the door swing open, and I curtsied.

"Ahh," she said. "You look . . . interesting."

I was in a sundress I'd bought in a thrift store in Dupont Circle, and I'd put on a bra and used the inserts I'd always been afraid would look ridiculous. And I'd gone all out with my makeup, drawing on the contour lines on my cheek and chin to slim down my face. I had in full earrings instead of the little studs I normally wore in my pierced ears. My lips were a dark red, and my eyes were drawn out in a dark black. And, finally, I was wearing a pair of high-heeled shoes.

"It's okay if you hate it," I said.

"Let's not fight," she said. "I've prepared breakfast. We need to talk."

My dad had a bag of bagels from our nearby bakery, and he unwrapped them, putting them on the table. My fingernails were painted too.

"Doesn't this seem like a bit of an overreaction?" my mom said. "I know you want to be read as a girl, but . . ."

I shrugged, not finishing her sentence or butting in to argue.

The dog came over, groused around my feet and settled down. Normally he was my mom's dog, but today he was on my side.

I closed my eyes and took a deep breath.

"Can you give her the everything bagel?" my dad said to my mom.

I took the bagel, opened the wrapper, and stared down at it, wondering how to eat without getting cream cheese on my dress.

"Now, then, we would like to sue your school."

I coughed. My mom had spoken the words while looking directly into my eyes.

"Excuse me?" I said.

"A civil rights lawsuit, based directly on the Supreme Court's sex discrimination rulings. Title Nine. They cannot discriminate by gender. You ought to be treated fully as an Ainsley girl for all purposes, both disciplinary and for scholarships."

"Okay . . ." I said. "And how much money would we be talking about?"

My mom looked at my dad. "It is unclear. But at least thrice damages. If we count losing the scholarship as damages, then that is one hundred and fifty thousand dollars. If we name that Angel woman in the lawsuit, our lawyer thinks we can get a settlement."

"No, it is not fair to make her choose whether to sue her friend's aunt," my dad said. "We should just tell her *our* choice."

"But she has to choose," my mom said. "She will live with this decision for the rest of her life, whether we do it with her input or not."

"Umm," I said. "Okay. . . ."

They waited, looking at me. I picked up the bagel, smushed the two ends together, and a bunch of cream cheese squished out.

"I think that I want to be on hormones."

"We aren't discussing that now," my mother said. "We cannot—"

"No, but you have time to call lawyers. You don't have time to call the clinic? We're already being investigated. Even the transphobes think it's weird I'm not on hormones yet. Come on. I'm one hundred and ten percent ready. It's time."

The two of them looked at each other. My dad nodded slightly. "Okay."

"Do that, and maybe we can talk about suing."

When I woke up the next morning, there were two hundred texts on the group chat. Felicity and Strife had been arguing for hours about whether or not the Sibyls ought to be ended. Strife was saying that Liam was right, and the group was 100 percent terrible and classist and racist and transphobic and awful in every way, and Felicity was saying she'd been brainwashed and that she was just causing trouble mindlessly again, like she always did, and that it was so exhausting to be friends with someone who wanted to stir things up all the time. And I could tell Strife was just barely holding back from calling Felicity a spoiled white girl.

Hecuba had texted me.

Hecuba: Hey I'm sorry about what happened.

Tara: Yeah. It was really unfair, but I'll be okay. It's only a week.

Hecuba: What?

Tara: Yeah, it's only a week.

Hecuba: What's a week? Where are you going? Founder's Day is tomorrow.

Tara: Yeah, I can't make it, I'm suspended.

Hecuba: Why?!?!?!?! Is it about Angel's speech?

Tara: I don't know about a speech.

Then she sent me a video. I watched it once, twice, and three times. Then I texted the group chat, Uh can you guys come over? I'm feeling pretty upset.

18

THEY CAME BARRELING THROUGH THE door, giving little waves to my parents, and then sweeping me into a long hug. Strife and Felicity were fuming, I guess they'd argued in the car, and Hecuba was pulling long faces, frustrated with us all. But somehow sitting around the table with my parents melted them, and they all made fun of me—along with my mom!—about how outspoken and downright rude I could be in class, and how I'd just not gone and done anything about my demerits.

"Do you know *how rare* it is to get suspended for demerits?" Felicity said. "I've literally never heard of it happening. Normally you get suspended for, like, skipping school. Or taking drugs. Or cheating on the SATs."

"Yeah, not even plagiarizing on a paper gets you suspended," Hecuba said around a mouthful of pizza.

We were all at the kitchen table, with greasy pizza boxes sprawled in front of us. Felicity got up and reached over for another slice, stretching across the table, and I turned away, afraid to look at her.

"Did you just think nothing would happen?" Felicity said.

"Kind of?" I said. "Like if it was gonna be a problem, someone would do or say something. Also you've got to admit, I was getting a *lot* more demerits than anyone else."

"That's all the more reason to behave perfectly!" my mom said. "My daughter walks around with those books of speeches, and do none of them say not to offer provocations? Doesn't even your Jesus say to turn the other cheek? To walk the extra mile."

"Whoever forces you to go one mile, go with him two," I said. "It's based on an ancient Roman law where they could force someone to carry their pack for a mile, and—"

"Shhh," Hecuba said. "I'm Christian, and even I don't think your parents want to hear about ancient Roman laws. C'mon, Alecto, this suspension is BS. You've got to fight it. Write an open letter or something."

"It's really just a week. I can make it up."

"But it'll be on your record. Every college will hear about it."

Somehow the Sibyls and my parents had all gotten attuned to the same wavelength, and they crowded around me, telling me that it was really important to fight back. I closed my eyes, trying not to get mad. I didn't want to do anything. I didn't care about any of it.

"Hold on," I said. "Hold on. Hold on. Hold on. This video is bananas."

"Yeah, my aunt sucks," Felicity said.

"No, but it's wrong. Like, it's wrong. She's lying."

"Err . . . yeah. She got upset."

"These are lies," I said. "She's telling lies."

Now everybody was looking at me as if I was insane. I looked around the table. "Don't you guys care? This is a seriously important person. And she's telling lies about me. I just don't get it. Why would she do that?"

"I'm sorry, beti," my mom said, grabbing my shoulder. "We watched the video, but what were the lies?"

"All of it!" I said. "We didn't sue them. I didn't make any trouble. I didn't cancel anyone. I haven't hurt a single person *ever*. She's lying about me."

"It might *feel* true to her, beti," my mom said.

"No, no, no," I said. "You don't get your own truth. Not if you're someone like Angel. You only get one truth. *The* truth. And she's lying about it!"

Now the whole room was quiet, so I fished out my phone and started the video again.

Angel looked glossy and serious, with her hair pulled back and her face ashen. Still glamorous, obviously, but with a kind of undead look, made even creepier by her dark red lipstick. She was in a tan dress and white jacket and had a thick gold bracelet on one arm, and she stood in front of a microphone,

236

leaning a little forward, not smiling at all, looking very serious and a little scared.

"In book five of Herodotus's Histories, there's a story about Periander. After he became the tyrant of a small Greek city, he sent a messenger to his father—the tyrant of a much larger city—and said, 'What should I do now?' And when the messenger came back, he told Periander, 'Your father has gone insane. He didn't give me any advice. Instead, he went down to the fields, and he started cutting down the tallest and richest stalks of corn in the field, and he threw them away, until he'd destroyed the better part of his produce.'

"But Periander immediately understood what his father was advising. So he went through his city, and he gathered all his richest and most outspoken citizens, and he put them to death. And afterward everyone was afraid to speak up or show any independence, for fear they'd be punished the same way.

"Today we are faced by a horde of budding tyrants. Right here in Virginia, we have a governor with an astounding disregard for the law and for all principles of justice. He wants all women to be pretty, demure, and quiet, and all men to be brittle and violent, and he will destroy any who don't conform to that stereotype. It's not because he values those traits: it's merely a method of control. Anyone with the desire to chart their own course or speak their mind will be destroyed not because of what they say, but merely because of that very independence themselves. Make no mistake, it is not the message itself that he objects to—it's the fact that we are speaking at all.

"As you might know, my family founded a school many years ago. It's a little academy, not well-known."

At this point the audience laughed.

"And they did it because they knew that educating children, especially women and girls, to be independent-minded was a critical part of our democracy. I grew up on the grounds of that school, surrounded by the relics of our family. I was taught Greek and Latin and parables from Herodotus. We learned science. We learned history. We learned to think for ourselves. When Virginia began to build high schools, they came to Ainsley and St. George's to learn from our system. And our school has an unparalleled record of producing graduates who seek justice and equality for all. I was proud to think that no Ainsley student would ever seek to become a tyrant.

"The truth, and I know this isn't popular—but the truth is that the people who founded and ran Ainsley did not seek absolute power. And they taught their students to beware such power. They felt a sense of responsibility to this nation, and they steered it through centuries of prosperity. They fought a war and sacrificed hundreds of thousands of lives, so that everyone in this country could be free. And we have never been perfect. I know that better than anyone. But I have always been able to talk to people on the basis of rationality and truth. I have spoken to jurors in every state, I have spoken to the oldest of white men, and I have asked them to make decisions not on the basis of self-interest but on the basis of right and wrong, truth and untruth. Reason. Justice. These concepts still matter to average Americans.

"But whenever I walk the halls of that school, of Ainsley, where our future leaders are educated, I'm reminded how out-of-fashion those concepts are. The girls at this school do not believe in equality. Let me state this again. They do not believe in equality. They believe people *should* be treated differently on the basis of their skin. On the basis of their gender identity. On the basis of sexual orientation. On the basis of half a hundred other markers. And part and parcel of this new ideology of theirs is the concept of equity.

"Now, to these children, and to many of their parents and teachers, equity is nothing more or less than this: it is the process of cutting down and throwing away the tallest stalks of corn. You can disguise this however you want, but that's the core of it. They say that if a stalk of corn has grown tall, it must have some undue advantage, and it must be cut down, because that is unfair to the rest of the field.

"Now does this make sense? Does cutting down the tallest stalk help the rest of the field at all? Does it give them more resources? Help them to grow? Of course not. The thing to do is to figure out how to grow a field of tall wheat—in Greek times, corn meant wheat, of course, since corn hadn't come from the New World yet—"

At this point Felicity was getting bored, and she started

to push away the phone, but I said, "*Stop.*" I kind of loved the speech, in a way. I'd never noticed that slightly deep, hoarse quality in Angel's voice. Everything in her presentation was perfect. She spoke steadily, without using notes. With even cadences, without a lot of emotion. Just letting each word drop from her mouth into the ears of the silent, invisible audience.

"And it's not because they care about the underprivileged. If they did, they would want every person to be the best they could. They would want every child to be able to express their sexual and gender identity freely, without constraint. No! It's because they want power. They say utterly illogical things, merely to flush out those who are courageous enough to disagree, so that these people can then be chopped down.

"I've been aware of this tendency for some years now, but I hoped it was only a fad. I've simply refused to engage with these people and hoped that they would come to their senses. However, recently, a scholarship that I endow at Ainsley—a scholarship to support students who are well-versed in classical culture—came under attack when two white cisgender girls received it instead of a minoritized student. To be clear, I have no hand in awarding this scholarship. I originally wanted it to be awarded anonymously and to not be associated with my name, but word of it leaked last year, which prompted an influx of interest in the classics at Ainsley. By all accounts this student who didn't get the scholarship had every advantage, as they were originally a student at our brother school, where classics education is mandatory from middle school, so they had several more years of Latin training than the other applicants. And yet this student simply didn't have the grades!

"But that didn't matter. They claimed that they were *owed* the award because of discrimination they purportedly suffered. They claimed that the contest was intrinsically racist and sexist and queerphobic merely because they had lost.

"Now, I've heard from some that this person switched schools merely because they thought there would be an advantage getting the scholarship. I don't know if that's true. If so, it would be deeply sad, but we don't know anything about their home life or about what they suffered at St. George's. We don't know their financial pressures, or their culture and how that influenced—"

Now Angel was talking about how she would stand up for the rights of all girls and women and wouldn't let us be oppressed and blah blah blah. And in the rest of the video, she discussed how the other girls were being bullied and forced to recant their awards, and how the next day she was going to attend the Founder's Day celebrations at Ainsley, and unless the school officially disavowed all this bullying, she would end her family's two-hundred-year association with the school.

I turned off the video, and I looked around at the other girls. Strife frowned. She reached out and touched me. "Angel's a bitch," she said. "I'm really sorry . . . no offense, Antigone. . . ."

"She really is," Antigone said.

The girls drew in, trying to group-hug me, and I fought free. "She is *lying*," I said.

None of them spoke up.

"She awards this scholarship."

"Well . . . yeah."

"No, there's no confusion. She awards it. She's the person. She decided not to give it to me. And I didn't complain. Not *once*. I never complained! She knows I didn't complain! It's her own nephew making all the complaints, not me."

"Okay," Antigone said. "I know. It sucks."

"That's a lie," I said. "She's lying."

Again, nobody answered.

"How can she do that?" I said. "I just don't get it."

"Er." Strife put up her hand, like we were in class. "No offense, but I'm the one who's gonna lose my scholarship over this. Like, I'm trying to not be weird about it, but . . . yeah. So . . . it's okay. Whatever. She lied. She sucks. I'm sorry."

"I'm gonna call her out," I said. "Tomorrow. I've been writing the speech."

Now everybody scrunched up their faces, like I was speaking in a different language. "Excuse me?"

"I'm gonna stand up in front of all the other Sibyls at Founder's Day, and I'm gonna say: 'You lied.' Felicity, you can still get me in, right?"

The other girls all looked at each other, seeming desperately like they wanted to escape somewhere to discuss this plan. Felicity gave me a little grimace. "Er . . . I know Liam is planning some kind—"

"I want to talk to *her*," I said. "I'm gonna call her out."

19

AFTER THEY'D FINISHED EATING, MY mom said to my dad, "Let's leave them alone."

"But . . ." he said.

"Shh," my mom said. "Our daughter will want some time with her friends. Did you girls bring sleep clothes? Will you stay the night?"

Felicity and I exchanged a glance, and Felicity said, "We'll figure it out. Strife is close, and we keep some clothes at her house."

"Your parents won't wonder where you are?" my mom said. "Should I speak to them?"

"My mom kinda lets me do whatever I want, if I tell her it's to keep these two out of trouble," Hecuba said.

Something about the words *Whatever I want,* made my

mom narrow her eyes. "Can I ask, do you mind, do you girls have boyfriends?"

My stomach cramped, and I bent forward. "Mom," I said.

Strife laughed, a high and pure sound. I'd never heard her voice like that, so delighted—it was the kind of sound I'd make to myself, when I was practicing talking like a girl. "Hec does," she said. "And Felicity—she has a girlfriend. . . ."

"Oh." My mom's eyes opened wide. "So there are lesbians at your school?"

"Mom," I said. "They have a trans girl, of course they have lesbians."

"Be patient with me," my mom said. "My understanding was you were the only one."

"I'm, uh, I'm actually single—not sure what Strife is talking about." Felicity shook her head. "No, yeah, Hecuba, what's going on with Nate?"

"I dunno," Hecuba said. "Haven't heard from him for a while."

"Acha, acha," my mom said. "And are you girls 'hooking up'?"

"Mom!"

Strife couldn't stop laughing. "I love your mom," she said to me. "Um, no. Are you, Hecuba? No . . . no."

"None of you?" my mom said.

"Mom," I said.

"What does hooking up include?" my mom said. "What about oral sex?"

My face was in my hands. Now the other two were smiling guiltily. "Pecks on the cheek," Strife said. "Ainsley is where you send your kids to keep them *away* from boys."

"Acha, acha, but St. George's is right there."

"No," Hecuba said. "No way. I would never . . . No. I don't even . . . no."

"We hate them," Strife said. "They're the devil."

I looked up. "What? Nobody's said that to me."

"Well, yeah, you're friends with Liam," Strife said. "Obviously *he* likes them. But no, think about it, have you *ever* seen a girl in their cafeteria? It's totally allowed, but we never go into their part of the grounds."

My mom lingered on the stairs. "What is so wrong with them?"

"They're pigs," Strife said. "They're so sexist. They're so rude."

"Acha, but my girl," my mom said. "You don't include her in that."

Strife shook her head. "No, no way. They should drop bombs on that place."

"Interesting . . ." My mom asked more questions, including about Hecuba's boyfriend (he went to the international school up the street), until I forced her to go away.

But then I was frozen. My room was upstairs, next to my

246

parents' room, and I didn't want to bring them upstairs, didn't know where we would all sleep. And I remembered how, a few months ago, I'd thought me and Hannah and Whitney would be friends forever too.

"Hey," Felicity said. "What's wrong?"

"Just scared about tomorrow," I said.

"Yeah, you really should be," Strife said. "No offense, but you're being ridiculous. Angel's lying. So what? She's a liar. Didn't you know that?"

"It's fine if she thinks I'm not good enough," I said. "But she has people thinking I'm a sore loser. Or that I just cared about money. Or that I want to shove myself into a place where I'm not wanted. And that isn't true. It's not."

"Even if it was, who cares?" Strife said.

"But why would she lie?" I asked.

"Err . . . isn't it obvious?" Strife said.

Liam would laugh at me. Even Felicity would laugh at me, but I genuinely hadn't thought Angel was a transphobe. I just thought, you know, she was worried about the tax issue and about protecting herself from the government. But she hadn't mentioned even a *word* of that! Instead, she'd twisted the facts to make me look greedy and unqualified.

"She's a liar," I said. "And I'm gonna walk into that room and tell everyone the truth."

"Nobody is going to care," Strife said. "I know exactly how it feels. She could've told them the same thing she told us: she couldn't give you the award for tax reasons. And they would've bought it. But for no reason, she makes some big, dumb political point that makes her look like a champion of truth and justice. Because she gets off on it—she's arrogant, no offense, Antigone—and she just loves feeling like she's *right*. And if you call her out, it only feeds into that and makes her stronger."

"But she lied," I said.

"Oh my god," Strife said. "This is the whitest conversation I've ever had."

Hecuba was hunched forward. She took a deep breath. In all our discussion of what I was going to do and say when we got to the foyer of the mansion the next day, she'd barely said a word.

"Hey," I said. "You okay?"

"Yeah, just . . ." she said. "No, it's—"

"She's worried Princeton will revoke her acceptance."

Now Felicity glared. "Strife! Why are you making everything so much harder! Can't you just shut up for one second?"

"What? It's true. We don't want more trouble. We're willing to get into trouble if it's *for* something. But we won't do it just because Alecto's angry. That's not fair to us."

"I'm just so sick of you," Felicity said. "Have you ever done one thing to help the rest of us? All you do is give us shit. We accepted you after you basically ruined the club."

"Stop it," Strife said. "*You're* the outsider. I could do fine in the outside world. But you . . . ? Try to find three other girls who'd even put up with you."

Hecuba and I met each other's eyes. Now she did the same gesture as Strife, rolling her eyes a little. I got up from the table, and Hecuba got up too. She was in jeans and still wearing a sweater, even though it was warm in the house. She dusted crumbs off her jeans, and she came over by the door with me.

"Hey," she said.

"Can you believe the two of them are arguing about who's more unpopular?" I whispered. We were in the kitchen, in a corner between the stove and the refrigerator.

"Yeah, like . . . have you tried . . . both of you?" Hecuba said.

"Exactly!"

"I genuinely think each of them is like, *Wow, I'm this other person's only friend.*"

"No kidding."

"So, I hate to be the old person here, but you know high school isn't everything, right?" Hecuba said.

"That is a pretty old-person thing to say."

"If you lie low, nobody will remember this in a week."

"Yeah . . . that's a good point."

"And, okay . . . so . . . this is really insensitive, but I don't know why nobody else is saying this. If the Governor comes after you, Angel is exactly the person you'd want on your side."

"She won't protect me."

"Yeah, she would," Hecuba said. "She's exactly the person

who would. And pissing her off won't help. Hey . . . I heard something the other day about, like, a social worker coming to your house?"

Now my stomach churned. I'd texted Hannah when the social worker came, because her mom was a lawyer. But I hadn't thought she'd tell other people. For some reason I'd never even considered telling the Sibyls about it. Now I just tried to brush it off. "Yeah, I think it wasn't a real visit. Someone wanted to intimidate me."

"That is nuts," Hecuba said. "Why didn't you tell us?"

"I don't know." I blinked a few times. "What could you do?"

"Start a letter-writing campaign? Tell Angel? Do something! Come on, Liam is protesting about stuff that doesn't really matter. Like, here: just come live with me. My family lives in DC. I'll make them take you in. We're not super rich, but you'd be safer."

"My parents are still waiting for their green cards. The president and the Governor are the same party. We just can't risk them getting us in trouble with ICE," I said.

"I just . . . Do they have lawyers?"

"Sure," I said. "Hannah's mom is helping us."

Hecuba shook her head. "No. Is she good? Is this even her kind of law?"

"I don't know."

"And what's going on with getting you on the hormones?"

"Nothing. I don't know."

"Tara."

"I don't know," I said. "I don't know. Stop. I don't know!" I wasn't quite yelling, but everyone was looking at me.

Hecuba tried to hug me, but I stepped away.

"I don't need hugs," I said. "Just help me do this. Like, I don't care what happens to me. But she is *lying*. People can't just lie. That's not right. I'm not perfect, but I have *always* told the truth. Every single time, even when she's laughed at me for it."

"Tara," Hecuba said.

"No," Felicity said.

"I know you're mad," Hecuba said. "But this is a *bad* plan. Yeah, Angel is a liar. But she's not your enemy. Focus on yourself." Now she looked at the other two girls. "That goes for both of you. Focus on getting ahead. I love you guys so much. I would literally die for all of you. Just be calm and maybe we can all keep our scholarships."

"You're not a real Sibyl," Felicity said to her.

Hecuba took a breath through her nose.

"You're just like Angel," Felicity said. "You're a sellout. In twenty years, you'll be giving the same speeches."

"Hey," I said.

Hecuba shook her head. Then she went back to the table, and she started closing the pizza boxes. And in that minute, I really actually loved her—loved her more than any of the other girls. She *was* a real Sibyl. She was just like that tyrant in that story, showing with her actions what to do. Either of them would've gotten mad and left if they'd been called out like this. Instead, she was showing them she was still their friend.

"No, Hecuba's right. She's right."

"I am?" Hecuba said.

"All Angel cares about is herself. Fine, I can work with that. So I won't have a big, public callout. I'll do the opposite. I'll talk to her. I'll make her see how I can help her."

"Er . . . what?" Strife said.

"She took the same oath we did. She *is* like us. She's literally just lost her way. I get that she's upset, but she knows that she's lying, and I know she's ashamed of it on some level. So I'll just . . . talk to her."

"Yeah . . ." Antigone said.

"That's not a thing," Strife said. "What you're describing doesn't exist. People don't change their minds."

Hecuba put out a hand. "Hold on. Hold on a second." Normally we all seemed pretty much the same age, but right then Hec was looking much older—more like a sister, more than a friend—and I could see she was looking ahead to Princeton, to her life after us. And I saw Strife too, saw how her connection to Felicity was so frail, and if Strife abandoned us, it would snap. Like, I would still be friends with Strife no matter what, but Felicity wouldn't. Felicity was her absolute best friend. And losing that would kill Strife.

And I saw why girls didn't date their friends, which was something I'd thought was so dumb when I was a boy. Dating

Felicity would change things, push Strife out and make her sad. And without that, would Felicity be all right? Without Strife and Hecuba, with just me for a friend? By ourselves, Felicity and I would just be a lonely, angry-making pair.

"Okay," Hecuba said. "So you just want to *talk* to Angel. That makes more sense. That's what we'll help you do. Strife, we won't bring you along. You've got too much to lose."

"No, I—" Strife said.

"It's okay. Don't worry. We know you'd come if you could."

I sent Strife and Hecuba to my room—they hadn't brought anything to sleep in, and I heard laughing from upstairs where they'd gotten into my closet. They were texting us as they made fun of all my boy clothes.

Felicity's phone beeped, and she looked down at it and frowned.

"What's wrong? What is it?"

She shook her head, put her phone facedown. "Just Hec calling me out. Sorry. I was really hard on you. I'm sorry. Your idea isn't stupid. I . . . You should speak for yourself."

"Of course it's stupid," I said. "It's one of the dumbest things I've ever said. But her whole speech was basically about how I'm trying to get something I don't deserve. And you know what? She believes it."

"But she's wrong."

"Is she?" I said. "The thing is, Felicity. You're great and

everything, but you don't know me. Like, I asked you before why we were friends, and you said it was because I liked Latin. That's fine. But it's shallow. You only like me because I like you."

"That's not true."

I was on our love seat, and she was on the edge of the couch, and I saw instantly that we'd messed up. We should be next to each other. Instead, there were three full feet of carpet between us. I couldn't make myself get up and go to her—that would be way too embarrassing—so I rocked forward and back as I talked.

"No," I said. "What Liam doesn't get—and the whole reason I hate his protest so much, is that he's always like, *Oh, you should get this just because you're a trans girl.* But that's *not* what I want. I want to be a Sibyl because that's what I *am.* And ever since I got to Ainsley, Mrs. Gimbel and other people have been like, you're not special. You're not good enough. You have bad grades. You're a terrible debater. And other people have been like, *No, she's a trans girl, cut her some slack!* Except I don't want slack! All I want is to be good enough."

"You are though."

"I am, but I haven't shown you any of that goodness, not in the time we've known each other."

"Actually, you have," Felicity said. "You're obviously special. Whatever I said about you liking Latin was stupid, I see that now. As Strife may have told you, I don't have a lot of friends.

But of course you're special. You're the wisest person I know."

"What?"

"Yeah," Felicity said. "We talk about it all the time. How you're so wise. You're like the best things about all of us combined. That's why we laugh about your Sibyl name. Because you're not angry. You're so reasonable."

"Stop it," I said. "You don't say that."

"We do though," Felicity said. "I'm not joking. We love you. When we were talking about how much Whitney and Hannah sucked, and how much we wished you'd been picked, it was just so clear—we just sat around in a circle talking about all the funny, wonderful stuff you've said."

"Okay, now it's too much."

"You're not perfect, obviously," Felicity said. "You can be a little judgmental."

"What?" I said.

"God, the looks you give," Felicity said. "When we disappoint you it's like a puppy died. And you're shy."

"I'm not shy!"

"Umm, but you are," Felicity said. "You get such blushes! That's gonna be hard tomorrow. So many people looking at you! But I think you can do it."

I looked at Felicity, and my heart thumped. We were both leaning forward, almost falling off our seats. The lights were low, and I heard my parents snoring up in their bedroom. She was in jeans and a T-shirt, with her hair pulled into a ponytail, and I sat in front of her, feeling both big and small, afraid to move. I smiled helplessly at her, not even thinking, and as we sat there I thought, *There must be some way that we could kiss.* But it was completely impossible to cover the space between us. There was just no natural movement that could bring me to the sofa, and even if it did, I'd be awkwardly perched next to her, and I'd need to gather her up, make her face me.

"Hey," Felicity said. Her lashes were long and dark, and they moved very slowly as she smiled. "I really love you."

"Me too," I said.

"Like, a lot. You're like my best friend ever."

"Totally."

And we sat there looking at each other for a long time as I yelled at myself, *Just do it, just go over to her.* But eventually, somehow, the moment passed, and I heard myself saying, "Oh well, I guess we ought to sleep."

20

FELICITY AND I SLEPT ON opposite sides of my bed, while Hecuba and Strife took the floor. In the morning we got dressed without looking at each other. There was lots of scrambling. Felicity kept an extra uniform in her car, and Hecuba had one in her bag, but Strife didn't have any clothes, so we drove to her house and got them while I sat in the back, staring at my phone, trying to think of what to say. My basic tactic was to be like, *Ms. Beaumont, when have I ever called you out? When have I ever complained? Are you proud of the things you said about me? Why would you tell those lies?*

But in Angel's own book of speeches she said that you should always be totally prepared and never ask a question you didn't know the answer to. What would I say if Angel interrupted and just said, *I remember things the way I told them.*

Now can you please stop hectoring me? I'd have no response! And yet . . . I just . . . I couldn't believe that Angel—someone who loved the Sibyls *so* much—could be so blind to the fact that, out of all the girls who'd applied, I was the one who loved the school the most and represented the club the best.

My mom texted me, Good luck. We believe in you. Whatever happens, please call us and let us know you are safe.

Usually my mom texted me in a group thread that had me and my dad, but this time it was separate, and my dad texted me ten minutes later: We will call the hormones clinic today. It is time. You are a citizen and shouldn't be worrying about our visa issues. Worst comes to worst we will be fine in India, and we know you will be fine if you must stay here. You've made wonderful friends and done well for yourself. We believe in you so deeply, beti, and we are so proud that you discovered yourself at such a young age. I apologize for our intransigence, but not all people are so brave as you.

I wrote back, Stop it. I'm not brave. Wow, you're as bad as my friends. But thanks. I love you.

Felicity put on some dark, dire fast music that I'd heard before in movie soundtracks, but which I didn't know the name of. She said it was "Ride of the Valkyries," which made me smile. I thought of all of us in winged helmets, like creatures from Norse mythology, heading out to make sure everyone paid proper respect to the gods.

* * *

I'd expected some heaving mass of people: complete pandemonium, fireworks, burning buildings, shouts, news vans. Instead, the schools were peaceful. The guard collected all our school IDs, and he said, "Y'all are late! You're gonna get detentions!"

"Thanks, Daneel," Felicity said.

"Don't they cancel your ID when you get suspended?" I said as we pulled away.

"It's alumni day, so they're letting everyone back onto the grounds anyway," Felicity said.

The parking lot was completely full, and the teacher who was directing traffic told Felicity to drop us off and then go out into town to park. Hecuba and Strife and Felicity all looked at each other, doing their telepathic communication. The car was idling in the parking lot, and I was in the back, with Felicity, while Hecuba and Strife glanced at each other.

"What's happening?" I whispered.

"Fine," Strife said. "I'll stay and park it. I hate you guys."

"What happened? What was that?"

"You know Strife isn't really cynical, right?" Hecuba said.

"What!" Strife said. "Lies! I believe in nothing."

"No, of course not," I said. "Strife, I know you'd come with us, if I wanted you to."

"Yeah, she really wants to come," Hecuba said. "But she's in enough trouble as it is . . ."

Now we walked along the pathways, toward the playing fields, where big tents were set up. This was still a school day, but nobody was in class, and there were games and activities and food carts and tables. We saw lots of girls in uniforms, and a lot of younger kids, eighth and seventh graders I guessed, who must be visiting.

Spring had arrived, and the day was warm: the cherry blossoms were starting to bloom, so the grounds were covered in beautiful white petals. The three of us walked up the path, through the stalls, through the laughing girls sitting on tables and benches, through the alumni gathering around with name tags, smiling at each other. My heart went cold, and my mind was blank. I couldn't remember a single thing I had to say, but the line went through my head: *Can't I have my little pint full of womanhood?*

Then as we got up toward the mansion, I heard the crackle of a speaker, and then the chant: "NO MORE TERFS. NO MORE TERFS. NO MORE TERFS."

It was a crowd of girls and some boys too, and a few feet behind them, I saw teachers on their phones, talking hurriedly. Dozens of cars were parked on the driveway and along the veranda.

A teacher said, "Oh! Felicity, Andie, there you are. They've been waiting for you inside!"

"Thanks," Felicity said.

We walked through the chanting crowd: it was only maybe fifty kids, but we felt the energy, felt the kids crawling up the hill, felt the adults looking at them wondering what was happening, felt the phones out, recording.

Liam was on the steps, holding a megaphone, yelling into it. "END SEGREGATION NOW. END SEGREGATION NOW. END SEGREGATION NOW." Wow, so Liam was going there, comparing boys and girls schools to segregation.

Felicity went forward first, and Liam turned, said something to her that was caught in the noise. A hand reached out, brushed against me, and I jerked away.

"Tara?" It was Whitney, standing there with a sign that read, "I QUIT, SO CAN YOU." "Hey, Tara?"

"Oh, hi," I said.

"Glad you could come!"

She was still a few feet away. Suddenly there were girls around, asking how I was doing, thanking me for coming. I was taller than them, and I could see over them, see that Felicity was arguing with a guard at the door, holding out her key card.

"What's going on?" I asked.

"Dr. Pearson said if we don't leave, we're all expelled."

"That's dumb," I said. "She's not gonna expel fifty people. She should just expel Liam. And maybe you."

"What?" Whitney said. "Why me?"

"I don't know, to make an example?"

"Tara . . ." Her voice got both quieter and higher, so it cut through the noise like the tinkling of a bell. "Tara, I'm really sorry."

"For what?"

"Umm . . . I didn't support you."

"Oh. Okay . . ."

I looked around. Hecuba was next to me. She whispered in my ear, "Come on, I think we can get the door open, but we've got to move."

Then I was up by the door, and Felicity was waiting with us. The guard was gone. Dr. Pearson was gone. It was just us, with a couple of teachers at the end. Liam walked up to the door, and he battered against it. "Open these doors," he said. "Let us in."

"Liam," Felicity said. "Be a little calmer. This isn't Selma."

"Excuse me?"

"I said it's not Selma. It's just a school."

"Do you even know what people marched for in Selma?" Liam said.

"Umm . . ." Felicity looked at Hecuba, who shrugged. "Civil rights?"

"He's got you."

"You know how many people said to King it's just voting?" Liam said.

Now he slapped the door with his palm again, and then there were other hands near us, mostly boys, all of them banging. Drew Handy kicked the door a few times.

"Guys," I said. "This is going to look really bad on camera. A bunch of boys trying to break into an all-women meeting."

"Look," Liam said. "I know you still think they'll accept you, but they won't, Tara. Come on. Join us! This is your fight. We're your people, not them. What have they *ever* done for you?"

"Uh, are you serious?" I said.

The yelling was getting louder, and so was the banging. People yelled from the upper floors of the house that they were calling the police. We heard sirens in the distance, but people didn't stop or clear off. They didn't sound like police sirens either.

"Excuse me?" I said. "What did you say?"

But Liam was ignoring me. He was still hitting the door. The megaphone was in Whitney's hands, and she was trying to lead the chant.

I went to her. "Can I have that?"

She looked at Liam, then at me. More parents and alumni were walking up the path. A history teacher came toward us. He scratched his thinning hair and said something we couldn't understand.

I grabbed the megaphone, and Whitney gave it up without a struggle. I pointed it at Liam.

"Hey," I said. "What did you say to me?"

Then suddenly I had complete quiet. No shouting, no protests. Even the faces up on the balconies were silent. The parents coming up the hill stopped and backed off, as if I was dangerous.

"Hey, Liam," I said again. "What did you say to me?"

He came down, looking really sporty in his khakis and his blazer, with his wavy hair perfectly shaped and combed. He was wearing a tie with both ends hanging loose around his neck and the collar open on his shirt to show a hint of his tanned throat.

"Tara," he said. "Stop messing around."

"I am not a sellout," I said.

All my words were really loud, and Whitney covered her ears, so I turned the volume down.

"We only have a few minutes maybe before the cops get here," Liam said. "We've gotta get organized." His words sounded small and weak, compared to me. And I understood what power felt like. Nobody could hear him.

"Liam," I said. "You told me that the Sibyls had never done anything for me. But you know what? Antigone, Hecuba, and Strife, they came to me after the interviews. They came to my house. Have you ever visited me?" I went quiet for a second, but everyone just stared at me, open-mouthed. So I went on. And then I saw a pair of red lips looking out from an upper-floor window. It disappeared for a second, but I realized Angel was somewhere inside, and she was listening. So long as they thought I was speaking to him, they'd let me talk, and Angel would hear.

"Liam," I said. "A social worker came to my house the other day." My words were slow, even though my heart was beating, and I didn't have any stumbling or ums or ahs. "They asked about me being trans. Someone at the school had tipped them off. I live in Virginia, so it's basically not legal there. And they made a lot of insinuations and stuff, about how I wasn't a real trans girl because I'm not on hormones, and I tried to explain that my parents were afraid of getting in trouble, because they're waiting for their green cards, but the social worker didn't care. And I looked at the social worker, and I was like, *Oh, I get it, when you look at me, you don't even see a human being.*"

Liam looked at me, his eyes flaring, and he sighed. He could sense a trap.

"And you're the exact same way," I said. "And you too, Whitney. And, Hannah, I see you standing there. None of you care about me as a person. I'm just a trans girl. That's all I am. Everything I do or say is because I'm trans. Like, you want me to be a Sibyl because that's something only girls can do, and somehow it'll prove you think I'm a real girl, so it's a symbol of you not being transphobes. But you never thought, maybe I just *am* a Sibyl. You know, Persephone made the Sibyls because she hated the way kids at this school were taught not to think. How they got crammed full of facts and didn't get educated, didn't learn that the past is a living thing. She was a rebel. Her dad was the headmaster, and he hated the Sibyls. It was a secret society for a reason."

All the windows were open, and I saw a dozen women out on the balcony, but I kept my attention pointed at Liam.

"Our oath as a Sibyl," I said, "says never to forget our cruelty, our courage, our ambition. I *love* that line. Because it reminds me, I'm not looking for favors. I don't *need* any of this. Just ignore me. Just let me exist. That's what I want. Like, all of this here? This makes me a *target*. This makes my life harder. There are people who want to kill us, Liam. They want us to stop existing. And that is so scary. The government might take me away. But you don't want to deal with that. Nobody here does. I mention the Governor, and you ignore it. I mention wanting to be on hormones, and you change the subject. Instead, you focus on the Sibyls? That's so strange! The Sibyls are the best thing about this school, not the worst. If you destroyed the Sibyls, I'd leave this school. If you stopped it being all girls, I'd apologize for ever having wanted to come here. I love this school, and you know why? It's because of these girls, because they found me. They saw something in me. They're, like, genuinely good people. Genuinely good friends. They're like in the Bible, when God said he wouldn't destroy Sodom if he could find just ten righteous men in it. Antigone and Hecuba and Strife are those men."

I heard a burst of hooting and applause, but I cut through it. "Don't get me wrong, they can't stop the Governor either. They can't protect me either. Maybe nobody can. But at least they *care*. At least they're outraged. At least they sit with that anger. And you know why? I'll tell you why . . ." I licked my lips. "Because they treat me like a human being. Someone to *know*. Someone to make fun of. Someone whose advice they can ask about stuff. Someone to rely on and trust and complain to and about. And that's all I ever wanted. Seriously, that's all I wanted. Reject me from the Sibyls, fine. That makes sense to me, maybe I don't deserve it, but don't lie. Don't tell people I whined. Don't tell people I asked for something I didn't deserve. And don't tell people you didn't make the decision, when really you were the only one making it. And who knows, maybe I *should* have complained. Maybe I *should* have protested. And if people hate me for not protesting, then that's fine. All I want is for people to know me, and who I am. And Liam, when you protest them not accepting me, but you don't protest the lies, it hurts me. It really does, because it makes them seem true. Maybe I'm not smart, or a good speaker, maybe I don't deserve a scholarship or to get into Harvard. But I deserve to be respected, and I don't deserve to be lied about."

My blood was pumping, and I would've kept talking, but at that moment the door opened, and Felicity looked inside, then she said, "Come on, Tara, come on." And as I walked for the open door, the crowd cheered.

21

SIXTY FORMER SIBYLS WERE PACKED into the foyer of the mansion. They spilled down the wings and stood on the steps, most of them holding paper plates and plastic cups and chatting with each other. The applause had died down, and I made my way through the crowd of people leaning in, trying to get a word, congratulate me. I'd gotten ten business cards that I clutched tight in one hand—lawyers and political people who wanted me to intern with them or said they could help me. Because there were only two Sibyls a year, the age range was pretty even, with some girls who looked like they were in college and some women who looked really old and had short poufy hair and stood around in pink pantsuits.

Angel appeared at the top of the stairs, like Gatsby, and the eyes of the room diverted to her. Even in this room, she was a rock star, in her dress that was almost on the edge of being too short for business, so her long legs gleamed in the noontime sun. Her back was lit up by the floor to ceiling windows, and she leaned over the rail, smiling at me.

Tiny Dr. Pearson was next to the door, squinting up at me through her glasses. "Come now," she said. "That was quite a performance. Should we speak to Angel and see about getting you sorted?"

The crowd parted for Dr. Pearson, who walked with small but quick steps up the carpet. I walked behind her, feeling overdressed and immense and covered in a layer of sweat in my armpits and hair and back, like my boy smell was wafting through this whole room.

"Hello there," Angel said. "That was quite powerful. Was that planned out in advance?"

For the first time, I smiled. The crowd closed a bit around us, and we drifted toward the window.

"Yeah, I love speeches and stuff," I said. "I never told you, but when we first met, you said something about *growing old in the service of your country*. And I was like, George Washington!"

"Incredible," Angel said. "Yes, that line is a tic of mine."

We were in two chairs, sort of hidden from the rest of the crowd, looking over the playing fields, with all their tents and all their kids. Trees waved on the edges of the field, but the air inside our room was still stuffy and heavy with air-conditioning.

"So . . ." Angel said. "Let's talk man-to-man—"

I winced at that expression, but I didn't say anything.

"What are your ambitions?"

"Uh." The thought that popped into my head was *To kiss Felicity*, but I knew that wasn't the right answer. "I guess to call some of these numbers. To figure out my hormone stuff. Like, get on them. And figure out if I need surgery. On insurance, it's hard, and before eighteen—"

"Yes," Angel said. "I understand that. But I meant career-wise. Do you want to work in politics?"

"Uh," I said. "I don't know. That sounds good. Probably."

"Please," Angel said. "You must have *some* ambitions. What do they teach girls here? I'm offering to help you. You ought to have an answer prepared for this moment."

I couldn't look at her. Then someone came into view.

Felicity waved. "Hey, Auntie," she said. "Wasn't Alecto great?"

"She spoke very well," Angel said. But something in her voice made me shiver. It was cold and came from deep in her throat. She wasn't looking at me, and I didn't want to look at her, but I saw she was leaning forward in her chair, with her legs closed and tightly crossed. She'd turned back into the dark queen. She was like one of those people from a book of speeches: terrible and beautiful and otherworldly.

Felicity tapped my knee, and, knowing what to do, I bent my legs. She sat on them, just above the knees, driving my feet into the carpet. I oofed.

"We're in public, honey bear," Angel said. "Can you not be such a struggle-puss?"

I snorted. What a change in tone! I couldn't believe I'd never seen these two really talk before.

"Are you giving the ambition speech?" Felicity said. Her voice had gotten higher too, and she sounded younger, almost like a middle schooler. I wanted to wrap my arms around her, bring her back into the chair, but it would be wrong. Very wrong. This was a very serious place.

"Hey!" Hecuba said. "Oh, sorry, you know me, right?"

She sat on the air-conditioning unit, and I winced, thinking of the cold air blowing on her legs. Suddenly I heard the clinking of a glass, and I heard a throat clear.

"I'm sorry, I think we have to go . . ." Angel said. "Tara, can you—"

"Alecto is her name," Felicity said.

"Uh, yes," Angel said. "Can you come see me? Call my office. Felicity knows the number. Lovely talk today."

"You're not even going to make her a Sibyl, Auntie?" Felicity said.

"I'm Hecuba," Hecuba said. "My real name is Andie. I'm a Sibyl too. I was Calliope's year."

"Hmm."

The clinking started again, and Felicity called out, "Hold on, I think Angel is busy! Can we have a minute? She's congratulating Tara and offering her a spot!"

A smattering of applause broke out, and then Dr. Pearson's reedy voice. "Let's take ten minutes, then."

I was trapped in the chair, pinned there by Felicity's weight. She put out a hand, trailing it on my upper leg, across my skirt, and my eyes went wide. All the blood in my body went to, you know, another place. I grabbed her hand and put it firmly back onto her lap.

"Honey bear," Angel said. "I have to give a speech now."

"Auntie, what are you doing? This is just not right. Alecto saved you, and all she wants is to talk to you, but you're too busy? One thing is obvious to me and everyone else. You just don't like her because she's trans."

"That is *not* true."

We heard the scraping and sliding of a chair across the floor, and then Strife appeared.

"Hey," she said. "Oh, hey, I'm—"

Angel looked away from her. "Well, it's nice to see you are friends. Honey bear, you should bring—"

"She told you what she wants, Auntie," Felicity said. "She wants to feel safe."

"I . . ." Angel said. "My heart really goes out. These policies are just awful. Awful. But you have a lot of privilege. A lot of great friends, and now you have my number. Please call me any time."

"Ring," Felicity said. "Ring. She's calling now. Get her on hormones."

"I can't do that, honey bear," Angel said. "That isn't how the law works. You can't preemptively restrain the government. It's unfortunate, but in our system, you need to—"

"You stopped her from being a Sibyl, Auntie. You're the reason, and nobody else," Felicity said. "Why did you lie about her? You made her more unsafe."

"Let's talk in private, later," Angel said.

"You just hate trans people." Felicity's voice got louder. And there was something heavy and ugly in it. The voice was loaded up with rage. "I don't know why, but you hate them."

"Felicity." I rubbed her back. "This really isn't . . ."

"You can't stop the Governor, but you could've made Alecto's life a lot easier. But you looked at her and you saw a boy. Like when you look at Liam you see a girl. Just admit it. The first step is admitting it, and then you can—"

"You weren't in the room where she and I spoke," Angel hissed. "Ask her what she said, I went into that room thinking perhaps I'd give her a chance. But you've seen her, you've met her. For this person here, it's just about *appearances*. Not all trans girls are like that. But for her, here, it's about fun. It's about being *femme*." She said the word like it was an insult.

"I did kind of, err, objectify your aunt a little," I said. "She's right."

Felicity looked at me, her eyebrows getting sharp. "Don't be stupid, Tara," she said. Then she snapped her fingers. "What did you say? Come on. What did you say?"

"Just that your aunt, and, like, all the Sibyls, it was a woman's sort of power, that you were beautiful and well-dressed and your power came from that—"

"That's the biggest bullshit I've ever heard," Felicity said. "She said you're beautiful? You posed for *Vogue*, Auntie. What is wrong with you? That dress cost two thousand dollars. Nobody else here is dressed like you. Please."

"I do this because I have to," Angel said. "I have goals. Ambitions."

"People keep asking Tara about her *real* aims and *real* goals and ignoring the answer. She wants to be a Sibyl and an Ainsley girl. She just wants to be herself, that's all."

"Fine," Angel said. "But if all you want is to lie low and have an average Ainsley experience, then, with respect, I don't know if the Sibyls are for you."

I was going to speak, but Felicity put a hand on the arm of the chair, and she leaned forward, looking at her aunt. And Felicity's face lost that detachment I didn't even know it'd had—that sense of being slightly above and apart from everything around her.

"Maybe they should be," Felicity said. "Leaving aside how it makes no sense for you to describe anything about Tara as 'lying low' or 'average,' maybe we should be more normal. Maybe we have too many people who are trying to get ahead, and who're saying stuff they don't even believe. I mean, what about Cincinnatus? What about all the ancient Greeks and

Romans who got pressed into service against their will, because they were just that good and the people needed them? What about Socrates? What about people who just . . . love wisdom and love the truth. Maybe Alecto isn't ambitious because she knows that in her current body she can't even become a Sibyl, much less become president. Maybe she's ambitious just to talk to us, to change our minds, to show people what's right and what's wrong."

"Alecto is hardly the name of someone who loves truth," Angel said. "The Furies were mindless and obsessed with revenge. But enough. I've apologized. I was wrong. Can we move forward?"

"You haven't though," Strife said, leaning forward, so Angel whipped around. "You haven't apologized. And I think Alecto doesn't want an apology. I think she wants justice. And so do I, Angel. Your girl here knew about the money when she applied. So did every single legacy. But when I was honest about needing and wanting it, you punished me. You made me feel like a screwup, like I'd failed you. But I didn't. I was more of a Sibyl than you know how to be, and I can't afford to go through the next however many years until I graduate college, worried you'll take that money away."

Now Angel sensed herself cornered by four hungry girls. The party was dying down. She got up, stretched, looked at Strife. "I need to leave."

"No," Strife said. "You lied about Alecto. You lied."

"When did I lie?"

Now my voice was rusty, but I tapped Felicity on the side, and she hopped off me, and I got up. "You lied," I said, raising my voice. "You lied when you said you weren't involved in picking the Sibyl. You were."

"And you lied about Alecto switching to just get the scholarship."

"Her parents threatened litigation, I don't—"

"You're not afraid of her parents, Auntie," Felicity said. "You know Alecto is trans. You might think being trans is sick or wrong, but you know she didn't change genders just to get a scholarship. You know that."

"I . . ." Angel blinked.

Now she looked around. The other Sibyls were looking at us. And Dr. Pearson was in a corner, almost blocking off her escape. Nobody spoke, nobody moved. Angel's phone beeped— it'd somehow appeared in her right hand—and she looked at it.

"I have to go," she said. "It's really an urgent call."

She started to wend around us. Felicity was poised to say something, but I was already sitting back down. After a few minutes the rest of us sat down too. We didn't say anything, but our phones didn't come out either. More people came to speak to me, including a few who congratulated us for speaking out. I could feel that maybe some kind of reaction would start against her, but I wasn't sure. My phone was buzzing off the hook, and I was just incredibly tired.

Ambition. That's what I lacked. I hated *The Catcher in the Rye*, because it was horrifically boring, but I remember the part where Holden was like, *I just want to catch kids in a big field of rye before they fall off this cliff.*

And I thought, *You know people keep saying, "What do you want to be?" and I keep saying, "A girl." And they keep saying, "But what else?" And then I say, "A girl with friends who has sleepovers and gossips about stuff." And they say, "No, okay, but what about the serious stuff?" And I say, "A girl with friends and sleepovers who gossips about stuff and who can sometimes talk about old speeches with them."*

I laughed, then I remembered Persephone's letter. The oath she made us take: *To resist everything new. To ignore whatever they teach at school. To listen to my fellow oracles above all. To never forget my cruelty, my courage, my ambition. And to enjoy the freedom that our namesakes were denied.* That wasn't the oath of someone who wanted to be a senator. That was more of a *Catcher in the Rye* kind of oath.

"Why did you laugh?" Felicity said.

She got up from her chair, and she wedged herself in next to me, so that our bare knees touched, and for once I didn't jerk my knee away. I let it sit there, even though it made a painful shiver run through me.

"Thinking about the oath," I said. "I can't believe Angel swore that oath. *Resist everything new.*"

"That's what I've been telling you!" Felicity said. "Wow, I'd hit you on the shoulder if the angle was better. The Sibyls aren't about, you know, all of this stuff. And no, Strife, they're not about getting a scholarship and getting into Harvard either. They're about picking people who are just completely, totally, one hundred percent themselves."

"Wow," Strife said. "Profound."

"Shut up," Hecuba said. "I feel like Princeton is gonna email me any second to be like, *We're gonna have you arrested if you set foot here.*" But she smiled and rolled her eyes.

Then she and Strife exchanged a look, and between one second and the next they both got up. "Uh, we have to . . ." Hecuba looked at Strife.

"Go to the bathroom," Strife said.

"Okay . . ." Felicity said.

"Bye."

Then they were gone, and we were alone. Felicity put one leg over mine, and I had basically lost control of my body at this point. She turned, and her eyes were close to me, so I could count every one of her lashes. And a part of me knew: *We are about to kiss.* But the distance between my nose and her nose was too vast, and I imagined us being this far apart for the rest of our lives. And then a voice said: *You should really do it.* So I went ahead, and our lips touched, and our tongues came out, and it was wet and slimy and wonderful, and my mind was a blur.

And then Dr. Pearson grabbed our shoulders and said, "This is a disgrace!" and gave us detention. Her last words as she kicked us out were "In my day girls knew that's what the ladies' bathroom was for!"

Which made us go red and giggle and it took like twenty minutes to calm down enough to explain to Hecuba and Strife why we were laughing so hard.

22

THE SIBYLS GOT OFFICIALLY DISBANDED. We wouldn't have a special room. We wouldn't have any privileges. Instead, the faculty would select two sophomores every year, out of those who had above a 3.7 GPA, as the class's Ainsley Scholars. No concentration in ancient languages would be required. This year they picked Hannah and Whitney.

There was a lot of behind-the-scenes wrangling, but Hecuba and Strife and Calliope and Felicity kept their scholarships (I got nothing, of course).

Our special room was turned into a separate reading room. Angel didn't come back to the mansion. Felicity said she'd rented an apartment near Capitol Hill—Angel said the mansion was too big for one person, and anyway, a lot of people in her office were working remote.

People said the mansion was going to be turned into a

diversity center or something, but who knows.

Some of the old Sibyls were outraged, of course. They wrote letters. They wrote in newspapers. There was lots of talk. But some said, "Well in my day we weren't an official club at all, and we still survived. The girls will find a way. Or if they don't, maybe the Sibyls deserves to end." A lot of people reached out to say how brave I was, and one of them, a Democratic congresswoman from Virginia, said, "Trust me, I'll handle this." A week later Hannah's mom got a registered letter from the Virginia child protective services saying it had found no child abuse in my case and that my transition was medically allowed and even necessary.

The school had flipped its opinion around, and most of the girls were on my side. Lots of people said I should keep wearing my crown and blazer—that I was the *only* real Sibyl—and that nobody else should use our room, even though it had no door (they'd taken the door off its hinges). But I wouldn't go into it, and I persuaded Felicity and Strife and Hecuba not to go either.

Instead, we sat out in the main cafeteria, totally exposed to everyone. This was a bit awkward, since I didn't feel comfortable touching Felicity in public, and when I so much as looked at her, I blushed.

Other people came and sat with us—people Hecuba and Strife had known before they'd retreated into the room.

"Wow," I said to Felicity once, when Strife was deep in conversation with someone she'd known from middle school.

"You're the only person who doesn't have long-lost friends."

"That's because everyone hated her in middle school," Liam said.

He'd apologized to me one day, saying he'd gotten way too caught up in the Sibyl thing and should've been there for me, and I apologized to him saying, "Yeah, you were right, Angel really is a transphobe and was making my life a lot harder." We compared the weird messages we were getting from people online and argued about who had gotten it worse, and we sat together again.

"Hey," Strife said. "Too mean!"

"Liam," Felicity said. "*You* are my long-lost friend. I think that's obvious to everyone except you."

"Oh," Liam said. "Okay."

Whenever Felicity touched me, I felt awkward and vulnerable, but also complete, almost like my dysphoria had disappeared. I couldn't explain it. I'd asked Lailah and Madison about it, and they'd been like, *Er, no, that's not how being trans works. It has nothing to do with dating someone.* But somehow, just touching her made everything come together right—it shoved me into the "girl" category in my own head—maybe because Felicity never would've dated a boy, or at least not in the way she was dating me.

"Hey, Strife," I said. "Uhh, so, Antigone and I are dating."

"You're kidding, right?" Strife said.

"N-no." My eyes got wide. Maybe I'd forgotten some kind

of rule. Maybe Felicity and I weren't really official.

"I set you guys up!" Strife said. "I'm the one who told you to kiss. Remember? I was right there . . ."

"Oh." I remembered the voice. So that had been real, not just in my head.

Still, Strife sometimes seemed a bit uncomfortable when it was just the three of us, and she'd laugh or whatever but then she'd make an excuse to leave.

When I tried to explain it later to my mom, she asked, "But wasn't this the girl who encouraged you to see Felicity?" Hearing her say *Felicity* in an Indian accent made me giggle, and she tapped me on the shoulder, saying, "Tchup, it's your girlfriend who should be ashamed of her strange name—not me!"

"No," I said. "That's just how Strife is. She wants and doesn't want things at the same time. She's weird like that."

"So wise," she said. "My baby girl."

"You know, I *am* wise," I said. "I am widely known for my Solomonic wisdom."

"Well, if you've such Solomonic wisdom why are you sentenced to so many Saturday detentions?"

"Transmisogyny and racism!"

Shockingly, Mrs. Gimbel kept giving me demerits in class for every little thing. I pestered her to explain how that could possibly be fair, but she just refused to answer. I went and reported the demerits to the front office, and Dr. Pearson brought me into her room, and next thing I heard, Mrs. Gimbel was announcing she'd gotten a new job at a school in another state. I didn't get suspended for my demerits, but I still got detention on Saturdays.

My mom smiled at me, and she asked if I'd done my homework. My grades really were abysmal this year. But I'd bring them up. Or not. Whatever.

With the letter in hand from CPS and a bunch of other documentation that Hannah's mom got for us, we got an appointment at a gender clinic in DC.

They were really helpful and supportive and tried to ask me about my gender stuff and asked *how* I knew that I was trans and whether I *really* needed to be on hormones. And I suddenly got a flare of that same anger I'd gotten at Angel: *How dare you pretend this is about making sure* I'm sure *I need to be on hormones, when really it's about you being afraid of the Governor.*

But I heard my mom's voice saying something like, *Be careful, and don't sabotage yourself.* So I smiled and let them pat me on the back and tell me how proud they were of me for being double-dog sure before I went on my hormones. The idea made me burn with an unholy rage that I couldn't share with anyone, because if I did, they'd all want to know *What should I do? How can I make this better for you?* And there was no answer to give. The world was messed up. I saw girls in my online group all the time who were on hormones and weren't even out at their schools! But somehow I'd needed to go through a year of being socially transitioned, including a full-on government investigation, so people would know that I was totally sure.

And part of the reason I was angry was because I knew . . . if I'd just pushed my parents harder, I could've gotten on drugs earlier maybe. It was such a tangled knot, trying to figure out who was at fault for what. But when Liam and I argued about it, we both agreed that if transphobia didn't exist, all of this would be way easier.

I was nervous the day before going on the drugs, and my mom said, "You know you don't have to."

"Not helpful," I said.

So I took the pills, and within a month I was happier than I'd ever been in my life. My breasts were tingling, my skin was smoother, and I'd had a crying session or two, but what I hadn't expected was what would happen inside—the slow unknotting of something coiled up and tensed for as long as I'd known myself. I went around all day saying, "Wow, so I really am trans! Wow, it's real. I am trans. And it's real!" And people looked at me like, "Are you an idiot? Of course you're trans." But I was just so amazed. If I'd gone on this a year ago, or two, or three, I would've known just as quick that I really was the thing I'd always known I was: a girl.

And I remembered my mom, and Angel, and Mrs. Gimbel, and the social worker lady had all asked, at different times, in different ways, *Why do you want this? If you're really a girl, on the inside, why do you need a pill to make you a girl?*

And the answer was: *I don't know! I'm not a scientist! How am I supposed to get something that even doctors don't understand? What the hell is wrong with you? Why do you expect kids to understand this shit!? All I know is that if you'd let me get on this stuff back when I first asked, my life would've been ten times better than it was.*

Hecuba was off with her sometimes-boyfriend Nate, but Strife and Felicity and Liam and Whitney and Hannah and I still hung out a lot. Strife and Felicity were already bickering about whether the Sibyls were going to enroll new people next year, and this time do it in secret. Felicity was like, *Why not?* and Strife was like, *Just let it die.*

But the nights were warm, and we had a car, and the crickets chirped in the trees as we ate a late dinner at a diner by my house.

Liam had an arm around Whitney—they were dating—but I was still too shy to hold Felicity in public. And yet, with the hormones in me I genuinely felt, for the first time, like I was 100 percent girl. I was actually having that mythical moment when you don't even think about being trans—you just feel completely the same as any other girl in the world.

The waitress came out to take our orders, and I guess I must've been looking somewhere else because she said, "And what about your friend, what does he want?"

It took a second for the word to register.

"Uh, Tara," Felicity said. "Do you . . . uh . . ."

"She'll order in a second," Liam said.

"Oh gosh, oh no, oh, did I say the wrong thing, oh no, of course you're a girl, of course you are, gosh . . ." the waitress said.

I waved a hand, and I ordered a burger and a shake. The others tried to talk about it, but Liam put up a hand and said, "No."

Later on, when I was alone with Felicity, in her car, outside my house—my mom was trying to enforce her "no sleepovers with my girlfriend" policy—Felicity said, "Hey . . . are you okay?"

"I . . ." Slow tears were rolling down my cheeks. "I'm fine. Sorry . . . just makes you realize how far you've got to go."

"But you look great!"

"I know," I said. "I know . . . sorry . . . I know."

And if I'd told my parents, or Mrs. Gimbel, or that social worker, or Angel, they'd have said, *What do you expect? You're really a boy, and no matter how you change your appearance, you're only a girl if we let you be, and we'll only let you be if you stay quiet and cause no trouble.*

"I wanted to kill her," Felicity said.

"Who? The waitress?" I said. "She just said what she saw. She didn't mean any harm by it."

"You're too nice," Felicity said.

"No, I'm not."

287

But the moment stayed with me, and I kept thinking, *Do people really see a girl? Or are they just pretending to?*

And I kept thinking about how the three Sibyls faced down Angel for me. I hadn't spoken a word; they'd done it all for me. I had put those words into them. Over months of talking and scheming, I had convinced them I was right, filled them with my fire, and together we'd gone out and won.

Now that I was a semi-famous trans, I got emails all the time from other girls, all throughout the country, and they'd ask me: "What can I do? How can I be sure?" And I didn't know what to say. I wanted to be like, "Just go on hormones and you'll find out quick enough, at least if you're anything like me." But that wasn't completely right. There were lots of people who experienced their transness in lots of different ways, and I wasn't an expert. And I'm sure there were people who went on hormones and felt like it was a mistake.

But they were really asking me something else. What they were asking was, *How can I go even one step down this path, when the consequences might be so terrible? When maybe it means my parents hating me or other kids bullying me or girls not liking me or guys getting mad and killing me? Like, I'll do this if I have to, if there's no other way to live, but how can I be absolutely, 177 percent sure that this is the thing to do?*

And of course I gave them all kinds of information (essentially I was like, *I don't know who you are, but if you're the same as me, then transitioning is worth any cost, and it's basically the only way to live your life*), but a lot of times they wrote back with long messages about how their situation is different, and how for them it just was not time. And the thing is, a lot of them were right. A lot of them were in tough, dangerous situations. And all I could say is, "You know what? The effort other kids put into getting into the best college or winning some championship at sports? That's the effort we have to put in just to survive. And in the end, if you're really smart and really brave, the only reward you get is the chance to finally start being alive."

AUTHOR'S NOTE

The laws regarding trans kids and gender-affirming care are in flux—they've changed significantly even since the time I wrote the first draft of this note. As of this moment in April 2023, ten states have passed laws eliminating transgender care for teens. And one, Missouri, just a few days ago eliminated access to care for adults as well. Unlike in the world of this novel, Virginia is not one of those ten states. In 2020, Virginia elected its first Republican governor in years—a governor who won office in part based on a moral panic over trans kids in school bathrooms. He proposed several bills targeting trans kids, but as of now they've failed, and, unlike in this novel, there are no anti-trans laws in effect in Virginia.

The reality is that teens, in a number of states, face a dicey situation even if they socially transition (i.e., identify as a different gender in public). In some cases, laws are vague enough that they might even prohibit simply using different pronouns or going by a different name, and parents could face repercussions, up to and including charges of child abuse, if they encourage socially transitioning. Some say that these interpretations of the law would never be enforced, but their vagueness is precisely the point. This is a campaign of terrorism being waged against genderqueer kids and their parents. In a good number of these states, it's simply unclear how to follow the law and what the consequences of breaking it might be. Medically transitioning is even harder—in some states it is outright banned; in many states it is much harder, because doctors are terrified of the government.

I do not want you to take this novel as a guide to seeking or not seeking care. Initially I wanted to write an author's note where I would provide guidance for trans kids and their families on how to access that care. But I quickly realized that with the laws changing and with such huge variations across states, it would not be responsible for me to say anything specific. In some cases, accessing care is easy: you get a referral by your doctor to a clinic that treats trans teens, and they take it from there. In other cases, it's very hard: maybe your parents are against you seeking treatment, maybe the clinic is booked up far in advance, maybe your doctor or health insurance puts roadblocks in the way, or maybe the clinic tries to police your identity and whether you need a given treatment. It is hard to say what will happen. I know that if you're reading this and you do not have access to care, you probably either expect the best (you think it'll be no problem) or you expect the worst (you're so anxious that you're afraid to pursue care or even come out of the closet).

Moreover, I want to note early and up front that, with so much media out there about trans teens, it can often feel like *everyone* is transitioning and *everyone* is ahead of you. But the truth is, the number of teens receiving any form of gender-affirming medical care is very small. Although three hundred thousand teens identify as transgender in the United States, only five thousand began hormone treatment (including puberty blockers) in 2021.[1] Between 2017 and 2021, only fifteen thousand kids initiated care. That means the number of trans kids who are on hormones is minuscule compared to the number who identify as transgender. Although hormones can be life-changing, they're often quite difficult to get, both because of medical gatekeeping and insurance problems. Many clinics have long wait lists, and it's easy to feel despair over how slow the process is. But, as Tara sees, social transition can often do quite a bit to alleviate dysphoria, and even prior to hormone therapy it's possible to date and have friends and live a normal life within your real gender.

I don't note this because I think anyone needs to hold off on or delay hormone therapy, but merely because *some* amount

---

1 Robin Respaut and Chad Terhune, "Putting Numbers on the Rise in Children Seeking Gender Care," Reuters, October 6, 2022, https://www.reuters.com/investigates/special-report/usa-transyouth-data.

of delay is almost always unavoidable.

If you want more information, many communities have trans support groups, like the one described in chapter five of this book. A support group based in your community can be a great way to learn how people in your situation, in your town or city, begin to access care. But if you're looking for something more anonymous, I know lots of trans girls also use online support groups. If you are in a state that has criminalized teenage transition, it might be worth using a virtual private network when browsing the internet. Proton VPN is a good free option.

When you're googling advice there can often be a massive flood of info—some of it fallacious—but just take a breath, proceed methodically, google specific questions, and participate in communities (Reddit can be a surprisingly good source of information). Once you start actively asking and answering questions and interacting with other people, you often feel much more connected to the trans community and a lot more becomes clear—it's at least one way of breaking out of the *How do you know if you're trans?* Google spiral that can sometimes last for years or even decades.

Okay, so with the caveat that I'm just a novelist and not a doctor, let me give you some extremely broad and general remarks.

The trans community is divided on what to call trans girls, trans women, and transfeminine people who were assigned male at birth. To call us by the acronym AMAB (assigned male at birth) seems in some way to undermine the entire concept of being trans, which is that our birth gender was a mistake and didn't reflect our true gender at all. It marks us forever with the maleness we are often seeking to escape.

Nowadays on the internet, you'll see many transfeminine people calling themselves transmisogyny affected (TMA), which essentially means that we spark the part of society's collective mind that goes nuts when it sees people it sees as "boys" and "men" rejecting their gender (a union of transphobia and misogyny that we call transmisogyny). TMA's opposite is transmisogyny exempt (TME), which refers to trans people who, although they are often subject to transphobia and misogyny, aren't subject to the peculiar mixture of the two that affects trans girls, trans women, and transfeminine people.

Personally, I don't care about terminology. I am a trans woman. Nobody will ever be confused about whether I was assigned male at birth or whether I went through a male puberty—those facts are etched on my face and hairline, and they can be read easily in my height, hips, and shoulders.

In writing this author's note, I am torn between writing for two audiences: trans girls and everyone else.

First, let me address everyone else. Trans women and girls are overrepresented in the public's conception of transness, but we are a minority of the trans community. I've read that gender identity clinics see two trans boys for every trans girl, although

I have no idea whether this is due to biology or due to trans girls suffering more discrimination and being more discouraged from coming out.

When it comes to the medical side of transitioning, trans girls are in an odd position. Male puberty—triggered by the presence of testosterone above a certain level—has effects on the body that are far in excess of female puberty. The longer you have testosterone in your body, especially during youth, the more your bone structure and even your voice change in often irreversible ways.

Moreover, when an onlooker's brain assigns gender to a person, it tends to place a lot of value on visibly male traits. If a person has any male trait—the voice and facial hair being the most notable, but there are also certain marks of bone structure that are uniquely male—then they will often be gendered, to the casual observer, as a man.

This means that a trans boy or trans man who goes on testosterone at any age often experiences physical changes such that within a few years, they are gendered correctly. The moment those first beard hairs sprout, you're seen as a man.

This isn't true for trans girls and trans women. After a certain point, estrogen cannot reliably offset the effects of a male puberty. Many trans girls and women are lucky and they have body and facial structures that don't get in the way of their being gendered correctly, so after some time on estrogen, they start to be gendered correctly. Usually, most teens or people in their twenties fall into this category. But even these people usually require extensive retraining of their voice and laser treatments to remove their facial hair.

Others are less lucky, and they can only be gendered appropriately after facial surgery, hair transplants, and other interventions. I recently had surgery to correct the prominent frontal bossing (a protruding forehead) and distinctively male chin that make passing quite difficult, but I still have male-pattern baldness, and without a wig I am almost never gendered correctly.

(I'll leave out the issue of genital surgery in this author's note, since that's invisible to the casual observer.)

It's not the end of the world if a woman doesn't "pass" as a cisgender woman. Most people immediately clock me as trans, but I'm here, I'm still living, I'm married, I'm a mother, and I'm happy I transitioned. It's been immeasurably helpful in my life for the people who care about me to know my real gender. Going on hormones also reduced a lot of my dysphoria. I have no regrets about transitioning. Nor do I wish that I had done it earlier! Life as a non-passing trans woman is totally fine!

That being said, people who aren't trans girls and trans women don't understand how visible you are when you're a gender nonconforming person who reads to many as a "man" or "boy." The sight of your body arouses extreme reactions in people. Even the concept of you makes some people angry. People behave in intense, irrational ways. That's the essence of transmisogyny. There is something extremely threatening to society about deconstructing, dismantling, or rejecting masculinity.

One way to be safer is to read, at least in casual situations, as a cis girl. And if you start transitioning sooner, this becomes a more achievable goal. The key here is to delay or stop a testosterone-driven puberty. Once that's done, you can go on estrogen at any point—the main point is that the fewer number of years you spend with high testosterone levels, the easier it'll be later on to be read as a woman.

Also, even aside from the question of "passing," life for a trans girl or woman is simply better if she can meet certain feminine ideals. There is a reason all the trans girls on TV are slender and light-skinned and pretty. Being a trans girl often means plunging into the shark-infested waters of femininity and misogyny without any kind of guide and with terrible consequences if you fail. Being conventionally attractive can provide a lot of safety, and the less male you look, the more attractive you're going to read to the average person. Or at least that's how many trans girls and women think.

And that's why trans girls and trans women can be extremely anxious to get onto HRT as soon as humanly possible. If you read forums for trans women, you'll see hundreds of posts where girls as young as sixteen or eighteen worry whether it's "too late" for them to transition.

This ends the part of the author's note that is for "everyone else."

So let me speak to the transfems, trans girls, and trans women (the transmisogyny affected people) who are reading this. First of all, hey. Thanks for reading this book! I don't even care if you pirated it: I'm just happy it got into your hands.

Secondly, I don't know if you're out yet or not. If you're not out, if you haven't told a single person, that's totally fine—I'm extra happy you came across this book!

If you are recently out, you've probably noticed that the world is very confusing. People react to you in different ways than you might expect. You might've noticed people make assumptions about how you'll think and react to stuff. You might've noticed people say supportive things and then slowly stop being your friend. You might've noticed your parents—even if they are supportive of trans rights or are queer themselves—have trouble accepting who you are. You might've noticed that some of the people you like being around don't seem to get what it is to be trans. You might've noticed that other people *think* they get it, but when you explain your feelings to them, they become confused or angry and even insist that you're wrong.

The amount of weird stuff people do and say around transfem people is infinite. I've given up trying to understand what it is that we mean to other people, and I've given up trying to make our feelings palatable or understandable to them.

The fact is, being trans is different. Trying to explain gender dysphoria to someone who's never felt it is impossible, and sometimes you just have to resort to the cliche "I was born in the wrong body." But then they're like, *Except you never liked girly stuff when you were a boy*, and what're you supposed to do? Tell them, *Nothing about myself as a boy reflects who I really was?* Tell them, *I didn't have the ability to develop a self, so basically nobody knows me at all and I barely know myself?*

And maybe those things aren't even true for you! They're just examples! But the point is, cis people have a really difficult time understanding us.

It's possible you don't even know if you're a trans girl. That you're wondering about it, or even that you've read this book and said, "Nope, that's definitely not me." And that's fine. I wish that I could've gone more deeply into the earlier parts of Tara's journey, and maybe in a future book I can look at what it feels like to decide that you might potentially be trans.

There are so many things I've left out of this book! I am brutally aware that there aren't many books for a trans girl to read! So when I was thinking of what to put in this author's note, I thought, *Well, I cannot help people figure out if they're trans or not.* Ultimately, you have to figure that out for yourself. One thing is . . . if you just *want* to be a girl, that's a pretty good sign. If you dream about it, wish for it, and when you have sexual fantasies, imagine yourself as the girl, that's something right there.

Another thing is—sometimes you only know by doing it. The moment I went on hormones I was like: *Oh, okay, this is right. I am actually trans. Trans is real, and it is a thing, and I am that thing.* I was pretty positive even before then (like Tara, I socially transitioned for a year before going on hormones), but afterward I was dead certain. I almost immediately felt *right* in a way I hadn't before.

The problem is, adults in your life will want you to be sure even before you go on hormones. They see this as a very serious decision that you should only go into if you're 100 percent positive. And maybe they're right, I don't know. Meanwhile maybe you're sitting there being like, *If I am a girl, I need (for these biological reasons previously outlined) to figure this out right now!*

What's a person to do?

The thing is, I have absolutely no clue!

The world puts trans girls in a really difficult position. There are clear advantages to transitioning earlier rather than later (for one thing, you can just start *being* a girl and having a girlhood). But society also regards transitioning as the most serious choice a person can make. And it's true that, transitioning, at least for trans girls, has serious effects on your romantic and career prospects. I know tons of trans women who got fired from their jobs—even at supposedly very liberal companies—after coming out.

The adults in your life aren't wrong that this is a big deal!

At the same time, in most states you *need* the permission of your parents if you're going to have any kind of medical intervention. Nor are doctors and guidance counselors and teachers necessarily safe, even as confidantes—they often feel overwhelmed by these issues and run to your parents to tell them what's going on. In some states there is legislation intended to *force* these people to out you.

Even telling your parents you are or might be trans can have consequences. Many trans girls have ended up homeless after coming out to their parents. A huge number of trans girls have also experienced conversion attempts: therapists and medical professionals who tried to convince them they weren't really trans. Trans girls can quite easily find themselves in dangerous, abusive situations.

Nor can you sit tight and just wait until you are eighteen and then strike out on your own. Many trans girls remain on their parents' insurance until they are twenty-five or twenty-six, meaning if you get gender-affirming care, your parent will often see it under the list of charges to their medical care.

Moreover, in some cases trans kids have access to government resources (e.g., Medicaid, although whether it covers transitioning depends on your state) that they won't be eligible for after they turn eighteen. Which is to say, most trans kids find themselves in a bit of a quandary.

* * *

This puts trans girls in a very tough position. Life is *much* easier, infinitely easier, if your parents are on board with your transition. Like, you're just a kid—I'm sure you're smart and everything, but you probably don't know how to navigate insurance, find a doctor, pick up a prescription, etc. Your parents *should* be doing that stuff! You should have faith in them to help manage the medical side of your transition. And if you're in a state that criminalizes or bans teen transition, then its doubly important to have them on board so you can consider other options (e.g., moving or going to live with relatives in another state).

And yet, contrary to the depictions we see in the media of loving, gender-affirming parents, in real life there's almost always going to be a period of resistance. And during that time of resistance, it's going to be up to you to convince them that you really are trans and you really need this care. But oftentimes you're not sure yourself! And if you confess that unsureness to them, then they use it against you.

So right about now, you might be depressed (either that, or you're like, *Naomi, you are so old, you have no idea how easy and good it is for trans girls in my state these days*). And I am sorry for that. It is customary in these author's notes to be short and succinct: you say, "Hey, if you're struggling with gender stuff, then call this hotline."

I'm not gonna do that. You can look up hotlines on your

own, and anyway, these hotlines pop into and out of business so quickly. I remember when I was depressed, I would call suicide hotlines and get a busy signal and just feel even more alone. It is cruel to kids to let them think just calling a number will solve all their problems.

A lot of times you'll be alone on this journey. And the scary thing is you can't just wait. You often can't practice in secret. You can't emerge fully formed as a beautiful young woman. Instead, you have to go through an initial period of transition where you are intensely visible and ill at ease.

The trans girls and women I know are unbelievably cunning and intelligent when it comes to getting the care they need. You have to develop a sixth sense when it comes to whom to trust. You need to develop people skills to learn how to persuade and compromise with people. You need to learn how to figure out yourself in ways that don't hurt your relationships later on with people you need to be on your side. And you need to learn when to be difficult and uncompromising, even if it makes doctors and authority figures angry, because sometimes the only solution is to turn yourself into a problem they're forced to deal with.

I don't know what that smartness will look like for you. For some people, it'll mean saying, "My Bible-thumping parents are not gonna handle this well, so I won't tell them." For others it'll mean saying, "My Bible-thumping parents really love me, so they might misgender and doubt me for a while, but maybe they'll also help me get puberty blockers."

Being a trans girl or woman entails a lot of careful calculations. And it also means making a lot of mistakes and opening yourself up to a lot of risk. It means putting on makeup for the first time and not knowing if you look ridiculous. It means shopping for girls' clothes for the first time and feeling like a pervert. Sometimes it means calling out your parents, shouting at them and fighting with them, and sometimes it means the opposite: making some kind of compromise with them, telling yourself you're overlooking the anti-trans stuff they said at first or overlooking them misgendering you or overlooking that they make you hide your gender when around extended family.

For some of you, particularly in states where transitioning is criminal or all-but-impossible, it might mean DIY transition—buying estrogen and spironolactone illegally and taking it at whatever dosage you hear is the right one—the path Lailah advocates—but I cannot recommend doing this! Not just for the sake of legality, but also for practical reasons. When I started estrogen, I developed a blood clot in my leg, and if my wife (a doctor) hadn't caught it, I would have died. I was later diagnosed with Factor V Leiden, a condition that predisposes a person to blood clots. I am now on transdermal estrogen (patches), which is much less risky. People *do* die from DIY transition, and although you might not care about those risks, they are very real and could cut short a long life. Please exhaust every possible alternative before even considering DIY. It's not something to do just because you're afraid of an awkward conversation.

If you are unable to legally access puberty blockers or estrogen, *please* do not despair. I know you are worried that you will never be able to pass, but believe me, it is *not* too late. You haven't been on testosterone that long. You'll probably be fine. Most trans women and girls are *not* like the skinny CW girls. We start on estrogen much later than eighteen, and we find that it radically improves our lives. The fact is, you only have one life to live, and oftentimes worrying about how you're going to look is just a waste of time. Nobody knows what estrogen will do to a particular body. For some people the effects are massive, for others, less. And remember that most cisgender women fall far short of society's physical ideals.

But what is true is that if you're a trans woman, the mental effects are often life-changingly good, even if the physical effects are marginal. I know this is hard to believe when you're mired in dysphoria or can't afford to identify as a girl, but believe me, you owe it to yourself to stick it out and try to turn your life around. And if you can't think of yourself, then think of every other trans girl or woman who'll come after you. I can only write this book because of the actions of millions of trans people who refused to be silenced, refused to be told they were sick. They suffered and often died in order to be themselves, and it's only because they made themselves unignorable that

that we got to the point where a major publisher is even willing to put out a book like mine.

Once you turn eighteen you can try to access care through your insurance, if you have any, or see if your city has a free clinic for trans people, or go to Planned Parenthood or other sources of gender-affirming care and pay out of pocket. Estrogen and spironolactone are not the world's most expensive drugs (although obviously for some people even fifty dollars a month is too much). It is difficult to access care without insurance and without supportive parents, but it *is* doable.

The thing I want to emphasize is that if you are trans, the rewards are worth it. I think it's hard for a trans girl to be happy or lead a good life, in the long run, without coming to terms with her true gender. People have literally given up their families, their countries, their careers, their health, just to live as their real gender. And when you finally start being treated like who you really are, the world changes completely.

For example, after I transitioned, I literally got smarter. Suddenly I could read dense books that hadn't made sense to me before. My work got easier. My depression abated. And although I have lower energy levels (I sleep an hour or two more per day), I get much more done. Transitioning doesn't necessarily solve all your problems, but, at least if you're trans, it reduces the terrible drag of dysphoria, which, without you realizing it, has potentially weighed on every decision you've ever made.

* * *

Finally, I want to close this by saying, it's not the end of the world to think you're trans for a while and then be like . . . *No, I'm not!*

After all, I was a gay man for a while, and then I was like, *No, just kidding, I am a bisexual man*, and when I married a woman everyone was like, *Oh, they just had a gay phase and are now a straight man*. Was it embarrassing to do my learning in public? Totally. But you survive. In practice, despite all the horror stories from detransitioners, society rarely punishes you overmuch for confirming the status quo. If you're like, *Oh, I thought I was a girl, but now I realize I'm really a guy*, people might make fun of you (and there might be some physical consequences, including sterility, if you were on estrogen), but you'll probably be better off economically and socially than if you'd continued to identify as trans.

Nor is it the end of the world if you put off transitioning until later, until after you've had life experience, and you circle around to it at age thirty or (gasp!) forty and say, *No, this is what I want, this is who I am.*

Yes, your life will be different than it would've been if you'd transitioned earlier, but there can be advantages too. I transitioned at thirty-four, and I may never be easily gendered as a woman, but because I published novels as a man, it was much, much easier for me to get the opportunity to write and publish this book, which is one of the very few books on the shelves that is by and about a transfeminine person.

307

* * *

So with that, can I recommend one thing? If you've never ever in your entire life told anyone that you think you might be a girl, then pick one person—a friend or relative is best—and tell them. Not an online person—someone you actually know in real life, so that the knowledge is attached to you in person. Obviously don't do this if it'll put you in danger, but at least consider it!

The moment the secret is out, often everything becomes much clearer and more manageable. And that is how, whether you're really a trans girl or not, you'll find that you have to proceed—you'll walk with small steps, trying and failing, being willing to accept risk and embarrassment—and after a year or two you'll realize you've gotten to a place you could not have imagined.

Also, the temptation right now might be to shoot me an email or a direct message! You can definitely do that. If I have the time, I'll answer, but authors often get a lot of mail, so I can't promise I'll be helpful. But if I don't answer, please don't let that put you off the idea of asking for help! People will frequently disappoint you, but they'll also surprise you as well.

And with that, I leave you. Thank you again for reading this book.

ACKNOWLEDGMENTS

The biggest acknowledgment *must* go to my editor, Steph Guerdan. They bought this on proposal even when there were strong reasons not to, and they've been unfailingly courageous and understanding throughout this process. They're one of the good ones!

My agent, Christopher Schelling, is also one of the funniest, most capable, and most ethical people I've met in publishing. I'm happy to count him as a friend.

The production editor, Mikayla Lawrence, and copy editor, Erica Ferguson, also did an amazing job: they treated the book with a light, but deft, touch.

Then I've also gotta thank all the writers who helped me and commiserated with me throughout this process: Jill Diamond, Julia Foster, Kelly Loy Gilbert, Chris Holt, Dustin Katz, Peng Shepherd, Taymour Soomro, and Zoe Young.

Courtney Sender, of course, who I've probably texted every day for a good ten years now.

Bradley Heinz and Sasha Novis, my loves.

My in-laws, Thomas Rutishauser, Karen Sim, and Merilyn Neher, for all the childcare help and emotional support they gave during this process. My parents, Sonalde Desai and Hemant Kanakia, for being really good parents who taught me to love books. My alma mater, St. Anselm's Abbey School for boys in Washington, DC, for giving me a great education and not being an acutely awful place to spend my youth. And in particular Father Peter, Henry Achilles, Jeffrey Harwood, Herbert Wood, Claudette Colvin, and all the other wonderful teachers who I really wasn't mature enough to appreciate at the time.

My wife, Rachel, is the smartest and most caring person I've ever met. It's really true, what they say: the absolute most important decision you'll make in life is who to marry. Sometimes I think my real job in life is just being her wife. Oh yes, and my daughter, Leni, didn't really help me write this in any way, but she's pretty cool, and she pronounces "things" as "ztings," which makes me laugh.